About the Author

This is my first attempt at writing a novel, so strap yourself
in, and I hope you enjoy the ride…

Save Me

Mark Bishop

Save Me

Olympia Publishers
London

A CIP catalogue record for this title is
available from the British Library.

ISBN: 978-1-80074-252-9

This is a work of fiction.
Names, characters, places and incidents originate from the writer's
imagination. Any resemblance to actual persons, living or dead, is
purely coincidental.

First Published in 2022

Olympia Publishers
Tallis House
2 Tallis Street
London
EC4Y 0AB
Printed in Great Britain

Dedication

To my amazing, strong, brave and rock-solid wife, and in her words 'Cancer picked on the wrong bitch' and to our little boy, everything we do is for you…

Prologue 1

August 2007

My name is Archie Parker, I am a born and bred Londoner, north of the river, who loves nothing more than a good old naughty sesh with my crew. One of my big problems is, I fucking love drugs. Now by drugs, I don't mean smack or crack, I am no junkie. But I do love my good time drugs. Speed, pills, Charlie and the odd joint now and then, well, the latter every weekend, and sometimes during the week. I am a hardcore raver, raving it what I do, and with raving comes drugs, party drugs of course. Going to a club without drugs would be like eating toast without butter, fucking pointless. So yeah, I guess I am a junkie of sorts, a weekend junkie! My Holly on the other hand, she can take it or leave it, and she has warned me many times that my love of narcotics would one day be my downfall.

Sure, I had made some stupid decisions in my life, like popping that one extra pill or ticking that one extra gram, when really, I should've gone home, which more often than not would result in me turning up for work on a Monday morning, still gurning my face off, if I turned up at all that was, they were always stupid decisions.

This one time, I must have been around fifteen years old, I was seeing this bird, and rather than go round her house one night for a quick fondle, I made up some bullshit about going to see my gran or something, but instead I chose to stay and get stoned with the lads down the park, only thing was, this park was next to her house, and she clocked me from her bedroom window, needless to say, that was the end of that, another stupid decision. But the decision I made three weeks ago on Haad Rin beach was by far the most stupid and regretful decision of my life.

The last three weeks have been awful, utter chaos, the worst three weeks of my life without a doubt, and as I found myself sitting here, alone, shitting myself as to what might happen next, surrounded by a bunch a fucking psychos', my only thought was, how the fuck did I end up here?

It was breaking my heart what I am doing to my family back home, and one of my life's biggest regrets is the relationship with the old man. As much as I was jack; the lad, the party starter, the life and soul of the night out, I was a bit of an arse to my dad, for no other reason, than he was my dad. I was always the black sheep of the family, I got myself into a bit of bother here and there, nothing to serious but enough to give the olds a few sleepless nights, I'm sure. But never ever did I think I would end up in a Thai prison, 'thousands of miles away from home, well done Archie, you proper fucked this one up, mate!

Prologue 2

2013

The first time I set eyes on this particular new inmate, I was intrigued; I hadn't seen many westerners since Ferizio. There was a Russian Guy here for a while, a hardened drug dealer, who seemed to have some influence on the guards and other inmates, he was nice, but I wanted to keep away from any temptation of drugs in here, it was hard enough as it was let along with a drug problem to deal with too, popping pills in a dirty nightclub is one thing, but chasing the dragon in a Thai prison, no thanks. There were of course the German body builders, but they pretty much keep themselves to themselves, there was also a Spanish guy here at one point, but he was so far lost in the abyss and depression of this place that I avoided him too. But this new guy was the first Yank I'd seen and, I dunno, he just looked out of place. I couldn't quite work out how old he was through his smashed-up face, but I guessed he was in his early 20s. What had such a young man done to end up in this place?

Word soon started to spread what this animal had done, and I took an instant dislike to him. He was a young American geezer who had travelled to Thailand, met a local bird, apparently fell in love with her, but then one night, in what is rumoured, he snapped in a jealous rage when his new found missus was flirting with another American chap, apparently one of his friends too, and went on to rape and brutally murder her in their beach hut on the island of Koh Samui. The more people spoke, the more the details got depressingly violent and disturbing. Fucking little cunt, I thought, another one to stay well away from, I've never had time bullies and that certainly wouldn't change in here.

This was big, big news in Thailand though, a young American had taken the ultimate liberty with one of their own, if there is one thing the 'Thai's really frown upon, it is rape, so it was no surprise he'd had the shit kicked out of him by the guards or the blueboys, or maybe both, and probably the locals too, for good measure. He suddenly fitted into this place like the furniture with all the other rapist and murdering pigs, I wanted nothing to do with a man capable of such barbaric behaviour, His name was Mason Stone, and as far as I was concerned, they could feed him to the fucking Cockroaches, fuck him, fuck them all, and fuck this fucking place!

Part 1

Chapter 1
March, 2007

Brighton beach at 7a.m on a Saturday morning in March is a pretty cold place, but this is where we found ourselves. We had left the sweaty hot clubbed hours ago, all it took was for one of us to say, 'Let's get the fuck outa here', and we were now full on into the messy after party. Most people would go home after the club, but not us, the weekend was yet young. The girls stayed in the room to chat about whatever girls chat about around a line of Charlie, they sent us on a cigarette and alcohol mission as it was too cold for them, fair enough we thought, so me and Ronny were happy to accept the mission. We always thought we had enough supplies, but we were running low on fags, and this was a cardinal sin in the life of the after party, the four main ingredients were, Drugs, Alcohol, cigarettes and of course close mates, not the fuckers you had met in the club all those hours ago, who you would declare to, 'I love you man' during an embrace on the dance floor, no, this shit was too weird for those lot, I am sure they were having their own weird after party tucked up at one of their houses, curtains closed, but they were certainly not welcome at ours.

It was day light by the time we found an open shop down by the beach front, and a nice little spot on the edge of the cobbles for a quick pit stop to put a little one skinner together and a scoop of Charlie, we had a hotel room for fucks suck, but in this moment, this place felt like the right place to be.

The summer months were on the horizon, and it was around this time of year we would normally book our annual pilgrimage to Ibiza. Ten years in a row (I think) we have now been descending to the white isle, and the place just seemed to get better year after year, but as me and Ron got chatting, we pondered on the idea of going somewhere else this year. Josh and Lens were travelling around the world somewhere, and they would be in Thailand in July, shall we go see them for a few weeks? I miss those cunts!

We'd heard stories of the legendary full moon party on one of the islands, surely this was on the bucket list of any respectable raver?

'But, what about Ibiza,' said Ron?

It was a perfectly reasonable question...

'We could always sneak over for a closing party or two in late September, early October,' I said,

We both pondered on this for a few moments...

'Let's call them, I ain't got much credit, but fuck it. I think they are still in Australia.'

'OI FUCKING OI' we screamed down the phone when Josh picked up,

'What you fuckers doing up? Ain't it morning time over there?' He laughed

'Yeah, but its Saturday morning, we've been out in Brighton with the birds, and us two are now on the beach talking to you dicks, where's Lens at?'

'Ha ha that fucking prick is pissed out his head asleep next to me, LENS, wake up Archie and Ronny are on the phone... Nah nothing, he is out cold'

'Listen, Josh, we're thinking of coming over to Thailand in the summer, when you going to be there again?' I said.

'Your fucking joking,' Josh said, LENS, WAKE THE FUCK UP THEY ARE COMING OVER TO SEE US'

Still nothing from Lens, he was proper out of it, eyes rolling away in his own little world, legend.

'Get it booked chaps, we will be there from end of June time, meet us in Koh Samui then we can travel the islands together and rock the full moon party, you bringing the birds?'

'Yeah, of course, we'll tell them when we get back to the hotel'

'Ron is trying to skin up, but he keeps forgetting what he's doing,' I laughed

'Ha ha ha,' Josh laughed,

'Fuck off you knobs,' gurned Ronny,

'Dam I miss you lot,' said Josh,

'Don't worry man, they will be plenty of sessions when you get back, and anyway this is costing me a fortune, so we're going to go, but will let you know when it's all booked'

'Yeah, cool bruv, have a good one down in Brighton, I am going the pour some water on Lens' head, and get his sorry ass up,

'LATERZ,' they all shouted together and that was that, Thailand in July it was, we best check the birds are up for it.

Josh and Lens were very much like me and Ron, thick as two short planks, and it's a wonder how they get through life, let alone travelling around the world together, surely this would end in disaster, someone along the lines? They had also been best mates since an early age, like me and Ron. We knew of each other from the local scene, but we first properly met them at an after party at a mutual friend's house; one morning when Josh turned up with a big juicy bag of Mitsubishis, that was it, we bonded straight away, and our beautiful journey

17

began. We were gutted when they told us they were fucking off for a year or so, and of course we were tempted to go with them, but we had birds and they didn't, so we agreed to let them go...

Me and Ronny Thomson had been brothers since the age of eleven, when we first during a conker fight in the school playground, well, it started as a conker fight, then it quickly escalated to a full blown tear up between the two of us, which was stopped as quickly as it started by the teachers before we were frogged marched to the head mister's office and sentenced to a week-long lunch time detention, a week fucking long I thought, that was a bit tough, but as it turns out, this is where mine and Ronny's friendship blossomed, and from that moment on the teachers wished we'd never met, and we were forever grateful they punished us into a brotherhood that would last a life time.

For the remaining five years of school, we got into all sorts of bother together, nothing serious, or nothing ever serious enough to get his kicked out, we always seemed to get away with the big stuff, and always got caught doing little things like making darts out of rolled up paper and using an elastic band to fire said darts at unsuspecting victims across the classroom, and flicking ink out of fountain pens on people's backs when they weren't looking, cowardly I know, but fuck we laughed. The odd lunch and after school detention never really bothered us too much, this was where we plotted most of our petty crimes anyway.

The bottom of the school field was where most of the action took place. One lunch time in year eight I think it was, me and Ron shared our first proper kiss with a girl, the same girl in fact, Becky Wilson, and in later years we would both share private encounters with the infamous Becky Wilson in a much more private and secluded situation, but that's another story.

We also smoked our first cigarette together down the bottom of the field, that one was in year nine, Ron's older cousin bullied us into it, well, it didn't take much persuading that's for sure, and on that very field we also smoked our first joint together in year ten, how we got away with it I will never know, I am sure some of the teachers turned a blind eye, either that or they were stupid fucks, either way we didn't give a shit.

At the age of seventeen, we participated in our first clubbing experience together, some dingy little night club in town where everyone knew everyone, and you could get away with anything. This was where you would now find us every Friday night for a year or so before we headed to bigger and better things, this was also where we took our first pill together, and that night changed everything, and I mean EVERYTHING!

Ronny Thomson was my oldest and very dearest mate, we had been through so much together that we could have wrote a book about it. We had laughed, cried, worked and raved together through the years, proper fucking geezer my Ronny, my brother!

Of course, the girls were up for it. Holly had been in the UK for two years now, and she loved clubbing, she had never been back in the US and we opened her eyes to it. She had never even heard of Ibiza, and she was blown away when I took her out there for the first time a few years back. I will always remember the look on her face when she walked down the back stairs into Privilege for the first time, she had never seen anything like it, the mass of people rocking the dance floor, a cross between what she was witnessing in front of her very eyes and the bass from the Funktion. One speaker up above literally took her breath away, Boom, another Ibiza baby! So of course, she and Maggie were up for it, they were up for anything.

Maggie, AKA — Mags, is Ron's missus, and she is an all singing, all dancing cockney. She was originally from south the river, but moved north after meeting Ron at the Cross in Kings Cross one Friday night, they instantly fell in love and were a perfect match for each other, she was the most loyal and trustworthy person I know. She took Holly in with open arms when I introduced her to the crew, they became sisters, they were so different in so many ways, but they became the very best of friends. Proper good girl, that one!

The next couple of months the crew was saving as much as they could for their trip of a lifetime, whilst still keeping up appearances on the clubbing circuit. The countdown was on, Thailand here we come.

Chapter 2

Me and Holly had been together for around two years at this point. I was twenty-eight and she was twenty-six. She was a good girl who wanted nothing more than to start her own little family one day. We had spoken many times about the idea of getting married and having a couple of kids, this was something we were both extremely excited for. If truth be told, she would have stopped it all today and started her family, but she knew I wasn't quite ready, I still had too much partying to do. Holly also loved a good party, and for that reason she was happy for us to carry on living the crazy life for a while longer.

We were happy, we were in love, and one day we will settle down and start our own little family, but for now it was time to arrange a trip to Thailand with our closest friends and perhaps have the biggest rave of all time at the full moon party, maybe this would be my last one, maybe this was the one I needed to get out of my system before I put a ring on it?

Holly is the perfect girlfriend for me. She loves a rave and a chill just as much as each other, if she didn't fancy it one night, she was more than happy for me to fuck off out with the lads which would often last all weekend, and I knew that she would be there to help me pick up the pieces on a Sunday before getting back in my box for another week. For the first time in my life, I was in love, madly in love actually, and for some crazy reason she seemed to worship the ground I walked on. Happy days, Archie!

Holly Jax landed on English shores two years ago after making the toughest decision of her life to leave her loving family for the very first time and chase her own dreams.

She grew up in the Printer's Row area of Chicago, Illinois, just south of the downtown area. After she left the South Loop School, she started working in the family run hair dressers called Jax Designs, and although life was good, and she dearly loved her family, she also longed to work over in the UK, and one day open up her own salon in London.

We met by chance really, as most people do, I guess? It didn't take her long to land a job in London, she was a skilled hairdresser, she was polite and loved meeting new people, and she was also a beautiful blond American bird who would fit into the London lifestyle perfectly! Her first job in London was in the trendy part of Camden Town, and the end of her first week, a couple of the girls from the salon were heading up to Peach at Camden Palace and asked her if she wanted to come along to get a taste of a real night out in London, she jumped at the chance and guess who else happened to be heading there the same night? Yep, little ol' me.

I have no idea what the time of the night it was, as I had recently double dropped and was coming up like a trooper on the dance floor and decided I would go on a little mission around the deep, dark and long meandering corridors that weave through this classic old venue, and I found myself sitting at the bottom of a small flight of stairs, just chilling and chatting shit to whoever wanted to listen, when suddenly out of the corner of my blurred eyes a body come crashing past me and landing in a heap, literally at my feet, scared the fuck outa me,

'Fuck, you all right there darling,' I said as I helped her

up,

'The fucking step was wet, I lost my footing,' this foreign accent replied,

'WOW' I think I said out loud, after a few seconds as my eyes adjusted, and my mind tried to replay what had just happened, when I saw for the first time the sheer beauty of what was in front of me. Sure, I had my raving goggles on, but she was fit-as-fuck!

'An angel fell from the sky, shit, did I really just say that?' I said to her,

'I am not sure about an angel, more like a lost, drunken fool,' she laughed as she pulled herself together and sat next to me on the step,

'American?' I asked her.

'Yes, and this is my first week in London, in the UK actually, and what the heck is this place? I have never seen anything like it?'

'Welcome to London,' I said with my chest puffed out in a proud cockney accent, whilst offering a polite hand shake, does the falling angel have a name?'

'Holly, Holly Jax, from Chicago.'

'Archie Parker, from London, nice to meet you Holly, Holly Jax from Chicago. What you have here is one of London's finest establishments, where 'thousands of people gather every weekend for a night of drug and alcohol self-abuse and to forget about the worries that exist outside of those doors, I come here regally and I fucking love it', Nice little speech Archie, I thought to myself,

'Well, Archie Parker, from London, nice to meet you and thank you for the honest review, this place is nuts, but I kind love it. I have lost my friends, and from what I can work out, the beer is dam expensive, but if this is London Life, I guess I should get used to it.'

'It wouldn't be a good night, if you don't lose your friends and meet a random guy at the bottom of some dirty stairs in a sweaty, stinky club like this now, would it?'

'Well, I guess not, Archie Parker' She laughed.

We sat at the bottom of those dirty stairs for what seemed like an eternity, we chatted about this and that, and I promised to show her the rest of the best of London nightlife if she enjoyed this one. At one point we headed down to the dance floor and right at the front sure enough I found Ronny and Maggie and Josh and Lens having it right of and introduced her to the gang.

At the end of the night, we all left together, and I safely got Holly into a cab for the short journey back to the hotel where she was staying, and I managed to grab her number just before she left. I am sure she thought I was full of shit when I said I would text her, whilst gurning my face off, but she gave her me her number anyway.

"She was nice Archie,' Mags said to me as we headed back to the underground arm in arm to try and navigate our way home.

"Mags, I know I am off my tits, I'm proper buzzing, no fucking doubt about that, but I think I am in love, I miss her already, fuck it I'm going to text her now' Mags laughed and egged me on.

And that was it, we were hooked on each other almost instantly, I had honestly never met anyone as warm and passionate and down to earth as Holly Jax, and we hit it off straight away.

Holly took to raving like a duck to water, and as promised,

I introduced her to some of London's finest establishments over the course of the next few months.

I remember the very moment I fell in love with her. It was in the box at Ministry on one our first proper clubbing trips out together.

She was in it, the music had a hold of had her, her blond ponytail weaved in slow motion through the strobes, the front of her hair was dripping down her face, she was sweating uncontrollably, she was a mess but she didn't give a fuck, no one gave a fuck, everyone was a beautiful mess, she was biting down on her bottom lip with her top teeth, her head was bouncing side to side in time with the kick drum, she was in the groove, she was lost in music, and I was fucking smitten!

Over the next six months, we saw each other regally. From clubbing nights with the crew to date nights in nice restaurants out West to chill nights together cuddled up in front of the TV.

It was the summer of 2005, and I was certainly staying alive. As my late Grandad Ted would say to the family, whilst sipping on his first pint down the boozer on a Sunday lunch time, 'Happy Days', Happy fucking days indeed!

Chapter 3

The day finally arrive for Archie and Holly and Ronny and Mags to begin their travels half way across the world to meet up with Josh and Lens for two weeks of Travelling around the beautiful Thailand Islands Koh Samui, Koh Phangan and Koh Tao.

This was the first long haul flight I had been on since I travelled to South Africa with my Mum, Dad and Sister as an eleven-year-old boy to visit my dad's family, and I was pretty nervous about it, I was nervous as I don't do sitting still too well, especially not for that long. I am pretty sure I pissed of the poor guy sitting behind me with my fidgeting, this was confirmed by some short sharp kicks to the back of my seat half way through the flight, as if to tell me to keep the fuck still, or I will throw you the fuck off this plane!

We boarded out flight with Qatar Airways bound for Bangkok via a stopover in Qatar at 9 a.m. UK time, we touched down in Qatar six hours later for a two hour stop over and change of plane. I had never been to Qatar, so I was not prepared for what happened, we stumbled off the plane in our hoodies after leaving the pissing rain in the UK, and the heat smacked us in the face with the full force of the desert sun, Proper hot!

Anyway, a quick stop then we were back on our way again and destined for Bangkok airport in Thailand, a night stopover in the city before heading south to the island of Koh Samui.

Krung Thep, as the locals call it, or Bangkok as us westerners, is a beast of a city, it seems to be alive 24/7, it was chaos, the tuk-tuks weaved in and out of each other in a rush to get their passengers from A to B. It was hot and humid and full of exotic smells that you certainly didn't smell walking down the high street back home. If I am honest, I didn't really like my first impressions of Thailand, and if I have known at that point what was around the corner, I would have turned around and got on the first plane out of there.

We were all pretty tired from the long journey, so we just decided to have a wonder around Sampeng Market then back to the hotel for a few drinks and try and get kip.

I couldn't wait to see Josh and Lens, I hadn't seen those freaks for six long months, I was sure, in fact I knew, we were in for a wicked couple of weeks, travelling and partying around some pretty special places with some pretty special people. Next stop, the paradise Island of Koh Samui.

Chapter 4

As we had planned to slum it in beach huts with Josh and Lens for the two weeks, we thought we'd treat ourselves to a night in a plush hotel for the first night in Koh Samui. The hotel we chose was The Centera Grand Beach Resort Hotel.

Tonight, was meant to be a chilled night at a plush hotel with our birds before the madness, but little did we know, Josh and Lens had blagged to us by saying they were arriving on Koh Samui the next day, but really, they were at the hotel waiting for us when we arrived, well, that changed everything!

It was around eight p.m. when we walked into the hotel lobby to check in, and suddenly round the corner out jumped Josh and lens,

"SURPRISE MOTHERFUCKERS,' they both shouted and scared the fuck out of us,

'Fucking hall chaps, screamed Maggie,

'OI FUCKING OI' screamed the rest of us

The next couple of minutes we spent hugging and kissing, finally we were all back together after six long months, our crew, together again, happy days!

'Well,' I said when things calmed down a little,' we were planning on a chilled one, but I guess that's gone tits up?'

Everyone laughed out loud, as we all knew that a quite night was the very last thing that was going to happen now.

We gathered our belongings and checked in and for a quick wash and a change and arranged to get back down in the bar in about 45 minutes.

'Drinks for the room, Holls?' I asked,

'Yes babe, get some beers in, and I'll see you up there.

'Will do, love you,' I said as she gave me a kiss and whispered to me,

'I love you Archie Parker, you know that, right?'

'Of course, darling, I love you too, now go do yourself up'

I wasn't one for hanging around too long when getting ready, quick shower, find some new clothes then I'm outta there.

'I'm ready love, see you down the bar, don't be too long,' I said as leaving the room,

'Be 5 mins Arch, get us a Mai Tai in,' she said.

"Sure, see you down there,' I said as I rushed out the of door.

I found Josh and Lens at the bar, Ronny was literally straight behind me, whilst waiting for the girls we got stuck into some serious beer and catching up,

'Look! how fucking brown you cunts are,' Joked Ron, 'all right for some ain't it, travelling around getting smashed and sunbathing, whilst us fuckers are back home in the pissing rain working our fingers to the bone.'

"Not Jealous, hey Ron?' Laugh Josh.

'Anyway' I interrupted, where we off to tonight? What delights does Koh Samui have to offer for a bunch of retards like us?'

'Ahh mate this place is buzzing at night down,' said Lens, 'We stopped here for a couple of nights before we went down the west coast, I can't remember much about it, but I'm sure we had a good night?' Laughed Lens,

'Nothing changes Lens, you fucking tosser,' laughed

Ronny

We all laughed out loud as Josh gave us a more accurate account of the bars, and what else was down there.

The girls tuned up about 10 minutes later, looking smoking as always, we necked the Cocktails and were ready for the off. These were the best nights, the unplanned and impromtu ones where you thought you were staying in, then, next thing you're on your way out, and God only knows what was going to happen.

We all jumped into the back of this old pick-up transit thing which was open at the back with two parallel wooden benches running along each side. The old truck weaved down the long winding road from the hotel to the main street at the bottom of the hill and onwards towards our night's location.

As we got closer to what looked like neon lights and action, we drove past a group of lady boys passing us in the other direction, and let me tell you, you only knew they were boys when they opened their lips and said,

'HI BOYS,' in a deep man's voice, oh we chuckled, I'd heard of lady boys but didn't realise there would be so many out here, 'get use to that,' laughed Josh, 'I'm pretty sure Lens has been with a few of them so far.' Ha, ha, we all laughed at that one.

We soon arrived at our destination, it was a large courtyard horse shoe shape place full of bars, the place was buzzing with tourists from all corners of the world, all out to have a good time, and to get absolutely smashed and not remember a thing in the morning, and that included us. There was different music pumping out of every sound system of every bar you went past, it reminded me a little bit of the West End in Ibiza, a place we avoided like the plague, but out here, it seemed OK, and we were going make full use of its services for as long as we could stand.

We settled on some tables in the middle of the courtyard, we could hear each other talk, but the music still bounced away nicely in the background. There is nothing quite like sitting outside drinking till your heart's content in a hot foreign country with your most favourite people in the world. This is our night. We had so much catching-up to do and so many a story to share, both of new adventures and old memories that will never be forgotten. It was one of those nights where we didn't even get up and dance, we just drank, chatted and smoked a thousand Bensons and got pretty fucking smashed, those buckets were evil!

I don't really remember much past a certain point, in fact, the last proper memory I was standing up near the entrance talking to Josh about some shit or other, and then I fell backwards down a couple of steps, I hazily remember see Josh cracking up laughing and then my memory stops for a while…

The next thing I can kind of remember, and it wasn't a full memory, more a photographic one as if looking though a scrap book of pictures from a night out gone wrong, but I kind of remember coming around in thick undergrowth and trying to crawl through big sharp forn bushes, on the other side of the bushes seemed to be a bar, or at least some people sitting on chairs and drinking, but they either didn't see me or they just turned a blind eye to another wasted tourist crawling through the undergrowth.

Memory stops again…

The next thing I knew, I came around on a beach, face down in wet sand, I could hear the waves braking gently in the distance, groups of voices talking and laughing, not too far away but not close enough to be laughing at me, I think. I tried to stand and gather my thoughts, where the fuck am I? I can't be that far from the hotel, the van ride was only 2 minutes away, again, I think! As I walked along the beach front, I check my pockets. Still got my wallet, result! Still got my phone, result! No credit, bollocks! No Money, shit! No room key, fuck! As I was searching through my pockets for any clues to where I had been and how I got here, I realised that I was literally covered in sand and was soaking wet, how long had I been laying on the beach for? Had I been in the sea? Had I pissed myself? It was difficult to tell at this stage.

Back at the hotel Holly was growing increasingly worried about Archie,

'Where the fuck is he, Ron?' She cried,

I don't know Holls, but he's a big boy he can look after himself,' said Ronny,

'He'll be fine, he's probably just at a strip bar or something.' Laughed Lens

'Not helpful Lens,' moaned Holly,

'The last time I saw him, he was stumbling around near the entrance, I laughed and thought he'd be all right,' said Josh "I have seen him do it a million times, and he's always fine'

Archie had been missing for around three hours, and Holly was getting increasingly worried, she was about to go down to reception and have them start calling the hospitals and police stations to see if he had been hurt, or arrested, when there was a knock at the door…

My next memory after coming round on the beach and heading in a direction was coming up to the back of a hotel which I thought looked familiar, I am not sure what I was basing this on as we had been here less than twenty-four hours, and it was pitch black, but It felt right so I followed my drunken head and headed for the hotel grounds.

As I entered the grounds and saw the insides of the hotel, I could not believe my luck, it was only our hotel, Archie you jammy fucker, you made it. Fuck, I must be in trouble for this one, how long had I been gone? I somehow made my way up the couple of flights of stairs towards what I thought was our room and knocked on the door...

'ARCH, where the fuck have you been we've all been so worried,' cried Holly.

Archie stood in the door way, covered head to toe in sand, literally all you can see was his hair and the whites of his eyes between blinking the sand away.

'Fuck knows babe, but I need a drink, you got any water,' he said as he stumbled into the room, leaving trail of sand everywhere behind him,

"See, told you he'd be all right,' laughed Ron 'See you in the morning, you fucking knob head,' he laughed again as he said good night and went off to bed with Maggie.

Chapter 5

I am not sure what time I woke up the following morning, or indeed what time I went to bed, I did manage to somehow have a shower though before going to bed to wash all the sand off, or so I'm told. There was a trail of sand all over the room, and my clothes were in a wet messy heap on the bathroom floor,

'What the fuck happened last night babe?' I apologetically ask Holly,

'You scared the fuck out of me, Arch, that's what happened, we literally had no idea where you were, we were about to send out a search party,' Holly exclaimed.

'Yeah, so sorry about that, I think I got a bit over excited seeing Josh and Lens again, you know how it is, right babe?'

'I guess so, I'm just glad you got back OK, you fucking idiot'

'Guess I should lay off the buckets for a few days,' I said,

'Good idea, babe, now get your lazy ass up, I'm hungry and were missing out on the sun outside.'

We made our way downstairs where the others were already eating lunch.

'Oi, oi, how you feeling bruv?' said Ronny, with a cheeky little grin on his face 'I knew you'd be OK, I told Holly, didn't I babe,' he said to Mags as if seeking a pat on the back,

'Not feeling too bad, considering how much memory loss I have from last night, it's all a bit blurry', I said.

'Nice chilled day round the pool recovering for everyone

today,' Maggie said, 'I'm not feeling too great myself.'

'Where's Josh?' I asked, as he was the last person I remember seeing last night, before it all went wrong,

'Last time I saw him he was talking to some lads over at the bar,' said Lens from behind his sunnies, trying to hide his hangover.

Then on cue a very excited Josh appeared from round the corner,

'Ladies and Gentleman, have I got something to show you,' He said, 'oh hello Arch, you're alive then,' he changed the subject slightly to my misfortunes last night, 'What the fuck happened to you?'

'No idea bruv,' I sighed…

'Ha, ha! Anyway, I got chatting to some lads over at the bar, and they told me about a pool party tomorrow night up in the hills in some villa and the only way of getting there is by showing the taxi drivers a special flier, and guess what Joshy has in his back pocket? YES, YOU FUCKING DANCER' he cried with excitement.

'Nice one, Josh,' I said, 'But right now the thought of drinking again is making me feel a bit queasy, but I'm sure I will be all right by tomorrow, let's eat I'm fucking starving!'

'Good work, Josh,' Ron and the others all offered,

'Best think about what we're going to wear for the this one,' Holly said over to Mags, who was in and out of consciousness, whilst floating about on her Lilo,

'On it, babe, something nice n chilled as its proper hot up in the hills, I've got just the thing, will show you later,' She said as she drifted back to sleep and slowly floated off down the pool,

"She all right?' Holly asked Ronny,

'Oh yeah, she'll be right as rain once she is fed and slept again, don't you worry about her, Holls,' he said.

The rest of the day was spent mostly chilling round the pool. They had already checked out of their posh rooms, as this was the last day in the hotel before they headed down the beach to the next stop in the beach huts, where the real 'traveling' part would begin.

Chapter 6

We had two days left on Koh Samui before taking the boat over to Koh Phangan, the second of the islands we would be visiting, and the home of the infamous Full Moon Party on Haad Rin beach. Today was a day of chilling in the sun on the beach then off to the pool party tonight, might stay off the buckets for this one, I thought.

"So, Josh, where exactly is this pool party tonight?' I asked,

'No idea mate, somewhere up in the hills, the chaps I met just said jump in any taxi, show them the flier and they would take you there,' he replied

'They could be taking us anywhere,' replied Holly and Mags at the same time,

'Jinx' they both laughed,

'That's the beauty of it Holls, my love,' laughed Josh, 'who knows where the fuck we will end up, who cares either, as long as I am with all you wankers, we will have a great time, that I know for sure, Just someone keep an eye on Arch,' He winked.

I watched for Holly's and Maggie's reaction to Josh's words of wisdom, and they seemed to except what he was telling them with a look at each other and a little nod.

'Honestly though, those chaps I met seemed to think these parties go right off, there are no rules up there, just half naked people dancing around a pool off their heads, proper little naughty night they said,' explained a rather excited Josh. Both him and Lens were single and loved nothing more than ogling over half-naked woman dancing to some shit hot music under the stars, and possibly jumping in the pool, or jumping down their throats, either way, I am the two of them will be in the elements up there. I for one am intrigued to see what a pool party in the hills of Koh Samui had to offer, I didn't think It would beat Ibiza, but I was going into it with an open mind, and maybe a cheeky bucket, just the one…

I have to say, at this point, apart from my little disappearing act the other night, this was turning out to be a pretty special holiday. As much as I love getting bang on it, I also love chilling on a beach with all my crew whilst chatting the day away, and that is how today went, I didn't even have a beer until we went back to the room to get ready, perhaps my subconscious was warning me to take it easy after the other night, either way, I was happy and today was good day!

The plan was to meet at the bar across the street when we were all ready, have a little wonder down the road to grab a bite to eat then jump in a taxi to the mysterious pool party, somewhere.

We arrived at the entrance to a villa around 20 minutes after jumping in a taxi and presenting the driver with our ticket to the Promised Land. The driver dropped us at the bottom of a steep dark long driveway, which was lined both sides by tall mysterious trees. As I stepped out of the car, I could hear the rumble of the bass up ahead. We climbed the hill and the beers began to kick in, strobe lights from up ahead pieced through the rustling trees overhead in the breeze.

The first stand we saw was decorated with all the floru glowing gear, you would expect to see in Thailand, the young

English girl manning the stand ask if we wanted to buy some neon wrist and head bands along with some other cool looking bits, we liked the look of it and went in without hesitation as the young English girl dressed us all in our new lights and took the money off us and promised us a crazy night!

Unlike any pool parties I have previously been to, the pool may as well not of been there as no one ever go in the fucking thing, but not this one, up in the hills of Koh Samui, I remember Josh saying earlier…

"There are no rules up there.'

And he was right, this place was going right off, there were people having it in every direction and that included in the pool, sweet, this looks all right, let's get the get on it.

The night went off without any major incidents, well, Lens was out of it straight away, but he seemed to survive, just about, oh and Poor Mags fell through a loose floor board next to the pool, and she now has a bruise the size of a football on her leg, but she was a proper trooper and carried on the party none the less, I am sure she would feel that in the morning though.

We all had a great time, jumping in the pool and dancing to whatever the DJ was playing, I lost some money, and then found some on the side of the pool, it was more than I'd lost, so happy days to that, and we all managed to walk back down to the taxi rank, well, Lens needed a bit of help, but we got there in the end.

The morning after the pool party we were all feeling remarkably fresh, so we hit the beach for one more day in Koh Samui, tomorrow we would leave to Koh Phangan, we were all proper buzzing for the next leg of our magical tour, but little did we know at this stage what laid ahead.

Chapter 7

The trip from Koh Samui to Koh Phangan was an interesting one.

The day started off as another beautifully sunny hot day in paradise, we started our journey to the second of the three islands we had planned to visit, this was the big one, well, in my eyes anyway, this was Koh Phangan, the home of the full moon party, was this to be one of the greatest raves of all time? I truly hoped so.

We bordered the ferry on Thong Sala Pier via some very unsafe looking sheets of what can only be described as corrugated metal, and we were off to Koh Phangan.

The start of the journey was nice n' chilled, we were all on top deck soaking in the gulf of Thailand sunshine, the six of us sailing across the bay, laying on our rucksacks, the girls discussing what they were going to wear to the full moon party, the lads just messing about as lads do.

All of a sudden, and what seemed to be out of nowhere the storm clouds gathered up above as if someone had just opened a door in the sky, and they came rushing in. Christ, I thought, as the boat started tilting this way and that, the heavens opened with a force and velocity that I had not witnessed before. People were running for cover, but there was very little of it on top deck, and there was no way on earth I was going to try and stand and make my way downstairs, I would have been thrown overboard for sure, no thanks.

I grabbed what I could, and that was my rucksack and Holly's arm and held them both as tight as I could,

'What the fuck Arch,' Cried Holly,

'Just hold on to me and that rail next to you, and do not let go,' I screamed back at her.

The sound of the rain smashing against the plastic deck with the wind and waves crashing against the boat was deafening, we could hardly hear each talking. In the carnage around us I could see Ronny and Mags, but Josh and Lens were nowhere to be seen,

'HAS ANYONE SEEN JOSH AND LENS,' I tried to shout over the horrendous noise,

'Just before the storm came, they went looking for the bog, so my guess is they are downstairs in the dry laughing at us, or they went overboard, either way right now I couldn't give a shit ha, ha,' Ron nervously laughed.

That's my boy Ron, we are on the verge on capsizing in the middle of fuck knows where, and he still manages a laugh.

But his laugh soon turned to worry when the boats engine cut out, it just couldn't cope with the force of the storm which was coming straight downwind at us.

'I'm scared Arch,' Holly lip-read to me,

'Just hold on tight babe, the storm will pass soon, I'm sure of it, I said reassuringly as if I was now a fucking weather expect!'

For the next 5 minutes or so, but seemed like an eternity, the boats engines fired up and cut out repeatedly, and I was starting to get worried now, holding on to both Holls and my rucksack with my arm round a bar on the boat was getting harder and harder by the second,

'Archie?' Shouted Holly

'Just hold on tight babe, I've got you,'

'No, but Archie,'

'Seriously, it's not the time for chat Holls, just hold on'

'Archie, the rucksacks are undone at the top, what about the passports?'

'FUUUUUUUCK THE PASSPORTS…!

All of a sudden, as if the big door in the sky was closed, the rain stopped and the clouds cleared and the boat settled down to a more gentle crossing, fuck me that was some scary shit.

'Is everyone OK, and where the fuck are Josh and Lens?'

Just as I said that they came stumbling up the stairs next to where we were sitting,

'Fucking hell that was insane,' Shouted Lens,

'You couple of tits, we all nearly went overboard up here,' Ronny Shouted,

'Ahhh, mate, there were people puking up and all sorted down there, Josh was in the bog getting thrown about all over the shop.'

We all laughed at the thought of Josh in the tiny little room getting covered in piss, and God knows what else.

As the clouds cleared the coastline of Koh Phangan appeared, we had made it to island number two, we had made it to the promised land, just about anyway.

Chapter 8

We were buzzing for the full moon party, I think we all even stayed in last night for an early one ahead of it, well, I'm not sure about Josh and Lens, but I'm sure they will be fine and up for it no matter what they got up to last night.

The day was mainly spent chilling round the pool, munching out and washing it all down with a few shandies in preparation for the party of the year tonight.

'Ron, what we going to do about supplies for tonight, we just sticking to the buckets and shrooms?' I said out of ear shot of the girls.

We'd had long discussions about whether to try and score down at the full moon party, it was proper risky, we had been told by many people, and read, not to trust the dealers, some of them wouldn't even be dealers, but would be undercover Thai old bill who love nothing more than nicking a westerner for drugs. We had decided it would be too risky so let's just stick to what we can get over here, most of which would still be illegal back home, but let's go with it. We had promised the girls that we would stay away from temptation, which trust me was going to be hard, but we couldn't let the girls down.

'I dunno, Arch, what you thinking mate?' He replied after pondering for a short while.

'We promised the girls, right? Plus, I don't fancy getting nicked and end up in some shit whole in the middle of fuck knows where,' we both agreed, we would see how it goes but probably best we go with the intention of not getting anything.

I have known Ronny my whole life, since we were little cunts getting up to all sorts of mischief in school all those years ago. From the first illegal high we shared on that first joint down the bottom of the school field way back, we had pretty much been high ever since, especially at parties, clubs etc. It was just who we were and what we loved doing. I knew what he was thinking, and he knew full well what I was thinking! But I just kept telling myself, Arch, it's not worth it mate, just have a good time and enjoy yourself and don't do anything stupid.

It was after lunch the others finally appeared down the pool,

'OI, oi, what the fuck you lot been up to?' Mags cried in her authentic cockney accent,

'Oh, don't babe,' Josh mumbled 'I have no idea what time we got in last night/this morning, and more to the point where the fuck we ended up last night?'

'Fuck me, we ended up at some naughty pool party somewhere with some bird we had met in OZ a few months ago, proper random! I think it was in some geezers' villa,' slurred Lens,

"Surprised you remember anything Lens, you were asleep on a bed next to the pool most of the night,' Josh explained

'Fuck off, was I?' Lens shouted back.

Everyone laughed out loud as this news was nothing anyone didn't expect from Lens, total fucking legend this guy, and he never lets you down.

'You guys going to be OK for tonight?' Holly asked from behind her ray-bans whilst bronzing herself on the Lilo in the pool,'

'Course we will Holls, don't you worry about us, bit of grub and a couple of shandies, and we'll be well up for it,' Josh said in his excited little voice he uses when he's up for something

'Good lads, I think this is going to be one to remember,' Mags pipped in with another notch of excitement

'Right, I'll get the drinks in, we've still got a couple of hours before we need to get ready, beers for everyone?' I asked.

The excitement was growing nicely, the butterflies were building, I should eat something but my tummy was flipping with nervous energy, I'm not sure I could physically do it, what was going to happen tonight? This could be the craziest night of our life's, shit the bed… I couldn't fucking wait for this one.

Chapter 9

As per usual, the chaps were ready first and were drinking down at the bar, whilst waiting for the girls to finish mastering themselves, which the lads always found funny, especially with these two mash heads, as 10 minutes in the night they looked like they had been dragged through a bush backwards, but that's why we loved them, as soon as they were on it, they didn't get a fuck what they looked like!

The girls finally found their way down to the bar, and they looked amazing, as always. Holly had a plain white vest on with some little denim shorts which showed her perfect figure, and little white trainers on. She had written down both of her arms in Fluro paint FULL MOON PARTY 2007, her blond hair was tied back with some glow in the dark cotton ribbons of some sort, Fuck I love this girl!

Maggie rocked up with her brown, tight, curly hair looking mean and sharp and ready for action in a pair of three-quarter length, desert camouflage trousers, a plain black vest and down her arms she had FUCK LIFE, THAILAND ROCKS, in big bold Fluro paint, these bitches mean business.

'Let's fucking have it boys' cried Maggie.

'Who wants glowing up?' Asked Holly.

'YES,' we all said in unison.

So for the next 20 minutes or so whilst necking shots and beers and chain smoking fags, we got glowed up with a mixture of obscene words, just because we can, and with whatever crazy patterns the girls could come up with.

We were buzzing for it.

But, deep down, something was missing.

We started the short walk from the Resort to Haad Rin beach for what promised to be the party of the year, the streets were a joy of activity, all kinds of people from all walks of life and all corners of the world were descending to the beach, all covered in different glow paint, some head to toe and some a bit more refrained to a few simple patterns on the face, but all with one thing in mind, to get absolutely fucking smashed at the full moon party.

But something was missing.

The distant rumble of the bass got louder and louder with each step they took, a sound they were all very familiar with and it was always a welcome feeling, that feeling when you get when you hit the queue for a club, as the jaw starts to chatter and the feeling grows as the bass gets louder. There was a no better place to experience this in the world than entering Passion at the Emporium back home. Deep in the middle of winter, freezing your balls off and queueing down the road in the pissing rain, as the bass gets louder the narcotic energy starts to flow through your bloodstream and warms you from up the inside, the bouncers turn a blind eye, get your coat peg number, don't lose it this week for fucks sake, walk down the long dark corridor, bass starting to vibrate your core, Melodies can now be heard, the hairs on the back of your head stand to attention, life almost seems to be going in slow motion with the flicker of the strobes up ahead, you are now full into the first come up of the night, people are rushing around, smiling and gurning as one, I'm nearly in the coliseum, just a few more steps, then BOOOOOOM I'm in, I'm straight in, fuck the bar that can wait, I'm heading for the front line, listen to what JFK has just dropped…

The streets also got busier, and the excitement was growing as we wonder though the neon lights and dancing glow sticks, and before we reached the beach my mind wondered… 'Are all these people first timers like us or have they all been here before? Either way they all looked proper up for it,' my mind often wondered in time like this, usually when I was coming up, all sorts or random shit would go through my head from little made up conversations with complete strangers to full on putting the world to rights with these same strangers. Actually, the strangers could wait, they would get their turn with me later on that's for sure, but for now it's all about the six of us, and I honestly wouldn't want to be walking down this street with anyone else in the world, we were united in our mission, our mission to rock the full moon party like it was the last night of our lives.

Still though, something was missing…

We paid out 100 Baht to enter the beach, and it was a sight to behold, as far as we could see in both directions was a-wash with neon lights and Fluro painted skin and decorations, a different sound seemed to come from every direction, from House to Techno to Reggae to Pop, it was all here, whatever your taste, you ears would be spoiled! There were two places we were heading, first to the nearest bar, then off to the nearest House stage to get our groove on, let's do this, motherfuckers!

The drink of choice at the full moon party is of course, the infamous 'bucket' which is literally a little plastic bucket you had at the beach as child but, instead of being full of innocent sand it is full of M150, a Thai version of Red Bull which is heavy on the ephedrine, a 300ML bottle of vodka and a can of soda, a couple of these shared between you and your well on your way!

Archie and his crew had partied at some top places over the years, from Gatecrasher to Ministry Of Sound in the UK, from Space to Privilege in Ibiza and all over Europe, but this, this was something different. Sure, they had danced on beaches before, many an after party at Bora Bora, but the atmosphere down here at the full moon party was something very new and very welcoming, but there was something missing...

It didn't take long for the buckets to kick in.

We soon found ourselves having right off in-front of one of the stages banging out some pretty decent house music. I have always been a bit of a music snob when it came to clubbing and nights out. Sure, we went for the drugs and camaraderie of the night, but me and Ronny were definitely there for the music too, most of the crew couldn't tell the difference between tunes, but these very tunes were the reason me and Ron were there, we'd be like...

'Ahhh lads, do you remember so and so track coming on last weekend?' and the normal reply would be something along the lines of...

'Nah mate, I was off me nut, I can't remember shit, fucking good night though bruv.'

We just couldn't understand how they didn't remember such moments, these were the moments we lived for, clubbers moments, lost in music, well fuck em, that's their loss.

All six of us were together, it was a beautiful sight, it had been so long since we'd all been together like this, back in Ibiza last summer, I think it was. The heavy kick drum was leading the charge, the sub bass shaking our insides to the very core and the melodic breakdowns talking us away to the land we longed for, where we belonged, where we felt at one with the world. The full moon up above surrounded by a million dancing little stars just added to the atmosphere. Josh clocked me and came over,

'Fucking hell bruv, what you think? Crazy shit, right?'

'Mate, it's fucking insane, I'm so happy we're here.'

'You see that little hill up over there?' Josh pointed to a hill just beyond one of the stages with a sign saying 'Mellow Mountain.'

'Oh yeah I see it, what's up there then?' I asked

'Magic mushroom milkshakes, my friend,' He smiled with an almost sinister look on his face,

'Let's go, round up the crew,' he said.

Up we went, in single file to the promised land of Mellow Mountain. Looking back across the bay, and there were people as far as the eye could see with so many bright colours; it was a real treat for your senses. I've had magic mushrooms before, but never in a milkshake, but hey ho, I'm always up for something new.

We were greeted at the end of a short queue by a small, overweight and moody looking Thai lady, I am sure she had served a thousand or more tourists from all walks of life and she looked pretty fed up if truth be told, then again, so would I in her situation.

'Sawasdee Krab,' I said, in a very poor attempt to use the only Thai word I knew,

'Six shakes, please love.'

After trying, and failing miserably, to make conversation with miss moody pants, we gathered our new beverage's and headed back down to the beach,

'Get this down ya boys and girls,' Josh cried excitedly.

We proceeded to down our drinks, it took some longer than others but we got there in the end,

'Mate, that is fucking rank,' screamed Lens, who never hung around too long when trying sometime new, the guinea pig we sometimes called him.

Nothing was really said for the next minute or so as we tried to digest our shrooms. I don't like mushrooms, so there is no way on earth I will ever enjoy the taste of their magic cousins. I was, however, very interested to see where this trip would take us,

'Let's check out the trance stage just down the beach there,' I said.

Off we went again to look for a new spot to dance whilst waiting for the shrooms to kick in. We found a little area to the side of the trance stage, this was perfect, the DJ at the helm was banging out some trance classics, this was it, this was perfect, I was dancing on a beach, at midnight, at the full moon party in Thailand, with my crew, my absolute favourite people in the world.

I don't know if it was the setting, the company, or what, but hold on, I am sure something is happening. I feel warm, not the warmth you feel from the sun or a radiator, no, this is a different type of warmth, a warmth that comes from within, from deep within, somewhere deep in your bones, I think, although I'm not really sure, I feel mellow, of course, mellow mountain, I get it now! Things look wavy, and tripy, and beautiful, just like my Holly, she is proper fit, look at her dance in her little shorts and vest, but why is she dancing in slow motion? Ha, ha, look at Josh, what the fuck is he doing with his head in that speaker? I can't really work out where the speaker ends and where he starts, well weird. Lens is down, someone help him up, I can't, no fucking way. Why is Ron's face merging with the side of the stage? I wonder if Judge Jules ever plays out here, surely, he would, I mean what better place to DJ than here I thought, Actually, what the fuck am I thinking? Ahhh who fucking cares, listen to the tunes!

Chapter 10

For the next couple of hours at the Full Moon Party, Archie Parker and his crew done what they do best, they raved, they danced on that beach in that very spot and got proper lost in the music, even Lens was back up on his feet.

Archie and his crew, especially the lads, were proper hardcore ravers, and soon enough the shrooms started wearing off, and they naturally started thinking they needed something else, something to accompany the strong arse red bull to take to them to the next level.

They had promised each other they wouldn't buy anything from the locals, but Archie, in his drunken state thought he could pull it off as surprise for the lads, fuck he'd be a hero.

Archie, the seasoned raver, had one eye looking out for dealers and people buying most of the night, how was it done over here? He wondered. Look at the state of some of these people, there must be class A's knocking about. Did people sort it out before they came? Or were they managing to score of the locals? Earlier on I saw what appeared to be a westerner buying something from a Thai man down near the sea front, I watched how they done it, and it inspired me.

'Fuck it, he who dares my son, he who dares,' Archie thought as he took himself off to the toilet and on a little mission, he had a plan, he would find a dealer he like the look of (his reasoning was if he liked the look of him, he could trust him) and tell him to leave twenty pills in a bag in the sand then walk away, when he picked up his goods he would then leave the money for the dealer to grab in a moment or two, whilst he got the fuck out of there.

As he bustled his way to the toilet, he was approached by a few locals,

'Yo boy, you English? Speed, pills, weed, what you after?' they all offered.

This excited Archie but it was so risky, he kept walking for now and just politely declined all the offers and carried on to the toilet, so he could think very carefully about his next move.

Whilst in the toilet he decided that he did like the look of one of the Thai's, he seemed younger than the rest, surely too young to be old bill? With the M150 still running riot through his body, he decided the young Thai would be the one,

'You can pull this off Archie,' he whispered to himself, whilst washing his hands in the toilet, 'You'll be a fucking Legend,' he thought!

As soon as I left the toilet, I saw my soon to be new, but short acquaintance, I approached him and placed my order.

'Sawasdee Krab' I said, whilst trying to be polite. A trait that my parents had installed in me from an early age.

'Be nice to people, and they will be nice back' My old man would often say to me,

'Simple manners my boy, you will go a long way in life with simple manners,' he also preached to us.

Surely, if I am polite to this geezer, he will sort me out and disappear into the night, the one and only time we would ever see each other, a nice little business deal done and dusted in under 60 seconds, it all sounds too perfect!

I said as quickly and politely as I could,

"twenty pills please, put them in the sand just over there, walk away, and I will put the money in the same spot'

I had seen it in action earlier on, was this the way it works over here?

The deal was on…!

The deal done…!

I'd pulled it off, I'm a fucking hero…!

Archie went to the toilet a good half an hour ago and he hadn't come back yet.

'Ron, have you seen Archie?' Ask Holly 'Please tell me it hasn't happened again, what state was he in when you last saw him?'

'Oh, he was fine Holls, he went off to the toilet, and he was fine, he wasn't wasted at all,' replied Ronny.

'Can you go see if he is all right Ron'? she asked.

'Of course babe, wait here with the rest,' Ronny went off to look for Archie.

He returned about 10 minutes later but was by himself,

'Where is he Ron?' Holly asked with a slight panic in her voice,

'Not sure Babe, he can't be too far away, he probably found another stage and is having right off with some randoms, you know what he is like,' he said,

Josh saw the panic on Holly's face and jumped in,

'What's up' he asked, 'Where's Archie?'

'We don't know, Josh, he went to the toilet a while back and he hasn't returned,' Holly was getting upset now, 'Can you come with me to look for him?'

'Of course,' said Josh, 'Ron, you go down the beach, me and Holls will go check the bars, and you lot stay here in case he comes back,' Josh said in his organized and willing to help a friend out voice.

Off they went in opposite directions,

'Josh, you don't think he has done anything stupid you do?'

'Like what babe?'

'Tried to get some pills or something, he promised he wouldn't,' she said

'Then I'm sure if he promised he wouldn't then he wouldn't,

'It's just…'

'What Holls, what makes you think he has?'

'I dunno, it's just, Ronny looked a bit suspicious when I said Archie hadn't come back from the toilet, and I saw them talking closely before he went off.'

Josh didn't really answer, he didn't know what to say if he was honest 'oh Archie, please don't of done something stupid,' Josh thought as he sped up his walk through the crowds.

They stopped at every toilet, every bar and every stage they went past in the hope of finding Archie somewhere, they hoped he had found some new friends as he often did back home. He would disappear for hours and come back with this new friend and that new friend at various points in the night. They always had an area in the club or festival which would be base for the night, and there was always a couple of them hanging around in base camp, but out here was different, they were a world away from the chill out room in Passion or the box at Ministry where they knew people, knew the layout and knew what they were doing. They were a thousand miles away from home, and there are different rules out here, it's a totally different world, and Josh was now starting to get worried.

'Right' said Josh, 'Can you remember your way back to the other guys?'

'Yeah sure,' she replied

'Get yourself back there, I bet he is already back with the others, but I'm going to run back to the beach huts and see if he disappeared off that way, you know he can't really handle his drink these days, and he may have just wondered off not really knowing what he was doing, you got your key on you?'

"Yeah, sure,' said Holly as she handed Josh the key, 'Find him Josh, find that wanker.'

'Will do, Holls,' he said as he disappeared off the beach in search for her Arch.

Josh was still tripping his nut off on the shrooms so walking in a straight line, whilst trying to think rationally was proving to be a little difficult, he just needed to keep reminding himself what he was doing and carry on with his mission.

He walked slowly up the busy streets, whilst trying to look in shops and bars as he walked by, he couldn't quite sort his vision out and everyone he went past looked like Archie, fuck Josh, pull yourself together man. He poured his bottle of water over his face, this'll sorted him out a bit.

After a short walk he made it back to the beach huts, Archie and Holly were in number 15 which was pretty easy to find, he let himself in and called out for his friend, expecting to see him lift his drunken head off the floor and say the words he had heard him say so many times over the years.

'What's going on, mate?'

But there was nothing, no lights on, no movement, no nothing, he checked the bathroom, the bedroom, but there was no one here. He checked the grounds outside in case he had fallen over and sparked out, still nothing. He checked the huts the others were staying in, but still nothing, there was no sign of Archie anywhere. Josh was starting to sober up and see straighter now and headed back to the beach, surely, he was there, he would defo be back there by now.

Before Holly had got back to the meeting point at the side of the trance stage, Ron had come back alone, without Archie,

'Babe,' he said to Maggie, 'come over here before Holls gets back.'

'What's up Ron, do you know something?'

'Well?'

'Well fucking what babe, now is the time to say something, where the fuck is Archie?'

'Look, I dunno, he went off to the toilets and whispered to me before he went that he was on a mission, you know what I mean?'

'Oh fuck, Ron, what are you saying?'

'I dunno, but I'm worried about him, I asked if he wanted me to go with him, but he just laughed, winked and said,

'Nah, I'm just going to the toilet mate'

'Fuck, I should have gone with him'

'What? And both of you end up in trouble somewhere, no thanks,' she snapped back at Ron.

'Listen, please, please, please do NOT tell Holls, not just yet,' he begged Maggie,

'Ronny, man, you're asking me to lie to my best mate?'

'Just for now, let me go on another search, chances are he will show up any minute, and I don't want her to panic any more than she has to, promise me, babe?'

'OK, OK, go find him I will keep Holly occupied,' she said as Ron disappeared again.

At first, it seemed to worked, I quickly swapped the pills for the money and got the fuck out of there. I got 20 yards away, 50 yards away, 100 yards away, a big smile started to appear on my face, I had pulled it off, they would fucking love me for this, I had just turned a top night into an unbelievable fucking night. Then, I felt a hand on my shoulder, I turned around to see a big scruffy fat fuck of a Thai man and in his broken English he seemed to be saying

'I give you shakedown, I give you shakedown'

'Nah mate, fuck off, I replied.

He grabbed me hard,

'I give you shakedown,' He screamed again, I tried to pull away but I was flanked by another man, he was bigger and stronger than the first one, he grabbed me hard and at that moment, I knew I was in deep ship, and everything seemed to start moving in slow motion, the lights flickering, the bass pumping all around me, the day glow tripping out in the neon lights, ohhhh, FUCK, what have I done!

Ronny knew full well what Archie had been up to when he went on his "mission', he just wished he had gone with him, was his friend OK?

'Think, think' Ron,' he said to himself whilst trying to work out where Archie would have gone to score, he knew he was heading for the toilets so he would check there first. He also knew his friend was pretty clever at knowing the difference between a dealer and undercover cop, or at least Archie thought he could spot the different, so he took a gamble and waited to be approached by the local dealers and would make an educated guess if they were genuine or not.

The first couple he wasn't so sure about, they looked a bit

too old to be dealers, he couldn't tell for sure, but he trusted his judgment on this one. The third one to approach him between the back of one of the stages and the toilets, which is where he thought Archie headed, intrigued him, but he went to the toilet first to think about what he would say.

'It's ok Ronny, you're not buying anything, just enquiring about someone,' he reassured himself whilst in the toilet.

I was quickly ushered off the beach and down some dark alley, at this stage I wasn't hundred percent sure if I was being arrested or mugged?? I actually hoped for the later. At the end of the alley was a beaten-up old van which I was thrown in the back of, we had now been joined another two Thai men, four of them all together, one driving, one passenger in the front and the two big fucks in the back with me. They kept shouting and screaming at me 'KhunKhay Ya', KhunKhay Ya,' they searched my pockets and sure enough they found the twenty pills I had just brought from that 'friendly little Thai kid' little cuuuuuuunt, I thought!

I protested they were not my drugs, but they either didn't understand me, or they didn't give a fuck.

'You fucked now white boy' they kept shouting, 'KhunKhay Ya' I had no idea what that meant at this stage, but I knew it wasn't good. You pay money, or you fucked, they kept shouting.

The old van started up and off we went. Oh no, my Holly, did she see what happened? I promised her I wouldn't do anything stupid. I hope she didn't see me getting nicked, oh fuck, my parents, what am I going to tell them if this spirals out of control? My mind raced off in a million different directions. Pull yourself together Archie, surely this can be fixed, twenty pills, it's hardly dealing, is it? I had no idea where I was going, I was proper scared now, literally 3 minutes ago I was walking towards my friends on Haad Rin beach with a smug smile on my face and a bag of pills, and now I was, well, God knows where I was going.

'Excuse me,' Ron said to the young Thai man,
'You want pills, coke, weed?' replied the Thai,
'No, no, sorry, I am looking for my friend, I know he came though this way' Ronny said apologetically.

Ron took his phone out of his pocket and searched for a recent picture of Archie, a good fresh picture, surely if the Thai had seen him, he would recognize him?

The young Thai man took the phone of Ron, for second he thought he was going to run off with it and was ready to give chase, but then a rye little smile slowly appeared on boys face, and he looked up from the phone and said to Ron,
'Your friend fucked, your friend sell drugs on beach, you friend fucked,' he said with a sadistic laugh getting louder and louder every time he said 'Your Friend Fucked', and in that moment, Ronny's heart sunk as knew exactly what had happened!

'He pay money, he might get away' the young Thai whispered in Ron's ear,
'How much, how fucking much you little cunt, and where he is?'

'He at police station, you turn up with 10,000 Baht in two hours, they let go, he taken an hour, you running out of time white boy'

'FUCK' he shouted out loud, 'think, think Ron,' he said to himself, he couldn't go back to the beach and tell the others yet, especially Holly, if there was a chance he could get his friend back, he was going to do everything he could.

The road was bumpy, it was fucking horrible, I was being thrown about in the back of this dirty old van, my two co passengers were sniggering and laughing and poking me in the ribs me.

The journey seemed to last a lifetime, I was so desperate to get out of this van and make it all right, but then on the other hand, I was petrified of what laid ahead when we got to our destination.

The van finally screeched to a halt, and I was quickly ushered out of the back door, and through what looked like the back entrance to a building. I couldn't tell for sure as there was very little light, but I assumed it was a police station?

I was taken in to a caged area down a few corridors, it was damp and dirty, and dark, horrible rotten place, my new friends followed me into the room.

'If your friends show up in two hours and pay money you go.'

'But they have no idea where I am, and they probably don't even know I am missing yet,' Archie explained,

"Shut the fuck up,' one of them shouted as he stabbed his baton into Archie's chest.

Archie screamed out in pain, and he was sure he felt a rib break, he soon realized these guys were not fucking about and decided he didn't want any more broken ones, he would sit here in silence and pray that Ronny would figure it out and come help him.

They stripped me down, they searched me, they took all of my belongings then left me in a heap on the floor, and as they left the room the boss man looked back and said,

'You wait here white boy, you friends show up with money or you fucked,' the others looked back and laughed as the door of the cage slammed shut, it was literally a cage in the middle of a dirty room, a bared cage with no walls just solid steel bars, the men left the room with an almighty bang of the door.

Where the fuck am I? This can't be real? I sunk to the floor with my back against the cold damp bars. I wanted to cry, scream and shout all in one, but I was too in shock to do anything but sit here and try to gather my thoughts, but my thoughts quickly realized, that the life I have been living has suddenly spiralled totally and utterly out of control, but still no tears, just shock, pure shock!

10 minutes later the boss and his three sidekicks marched back in,

'Why you sell drugs on my beach?' the boss said calmly to me,

I took a deep breath and tried to explain that I wasn't selling drugs, that they were just for me. I tried to tell him I have never sold drugs in my life,

'You sell drugs on my beach, you English fuck,' he kept repeating.

I begged him to believe me, but he wasn't having any of it, he then calmly said to me again,

'You sell drugs on my beach, you either pay or you go to prison, for very long time'

I had let Holls down so much, she was going to hate me, I promised her I wouldn't do anything stupid. Perhaps, Ron would figure it out and come looking for me alone to get me out of this fucking mess, so she would never know. I hated lying to her, but on this one occasion I would allow my conscience deal with it.

They had plenty of money in the safe back at the hut. Ronny scrambled off the beach and ran as fast as he could back to where they were staying, luckily, he had the key in his pocket otherwise he would have smashed the door in. It was a shorty journey and he managed to get into the hut sharpish, picked up a load of cash from the safe, he didn't have time to count it, but he thought it was around 10,000 baht, that makes 13,000, that should be enough. He had no idea where the police station was, he assumed there would be one on this side of the Island as this is the tourist part, and where there are Brits on the piss, there are normally preying old bill rubbing their hands together waiting for one of them to fuck up, and fuck up they did!

There was a taxi rank down near the pier; he had seen it when they arrived a few days back. There was a small queue of people, but he pushed his way to the front claiming he had an emergency, which he did, and the others in the queue seemed to except this and moved to one side,

'Police station, please,' he said quickly as he jumped in the back of the cab. 'Can you tell me how far it is please?'

''Twenty-five minutes,' the driver said back,

He worked out that it must have been around 20 minutes since he left the beach; that gives him roughly 40 minutes to find the police station, and pay for his friend's release.

The roads were narrow and slow and bumpy,

'How far is it?' he asked the driver again.

''Twenty-five minutes,' he repeated, 'I drive as quick as I can.'

'Can you go any faster sir, please?' Ron asked as politely

as possible, 'I will pay you double if you put your foot down man,' he was proper on the edge now, what the fuck will he tell Holly if he doesn't get there in time?

Roughly an hour had passed, had they noticed me missing yet? I wondered. I could hear the guards, excited by something in the next room, the door opened, and I heard a phone ringing, that's my phone, I knew it was my phone as it was my ring tone, I shouted out,

'Please, please, sir, answer my phone, or let me answer it, give me a chance here, please I beg you,' I shouted out, but they just laughed and the phone stopped ringing. It rang again, then again, then again, surely this was a good sign, they had noticed me missing, Ron would figure out what to do, I am sure he would.

Over the course of the next half hour or so the phone kept ringing, I shouted and begged for their help on every ring, but nothing, the door was opened every time, then quickly shut again, the fuckers were teasing me, I could hear them laughing, followed by another slam of the door! I was alone again, in the dark damp holding cell with only my thoughts, are they coming for me, or not?

Josh arrived back at the meeting point on the beach, alone,

'So sorry babe, but he wasn't there' he said to Holly, 'I looked everywhere, in bushes on the way, in all the shops up the road, but I couldn't see him.'

On this news Holly broke down, she had been confident her Archie had just stumbled back to the hut, collapsed and was fast asleep on the bathroom floor, which is where she had found him numerous times over the years. She sunk to the floor whilst holding Maggie's arm,

'Fuuuuuuuck,' she whispered to herself,

'Have you all tried his phone?' Josh said,

'Yep, said Lens, but it keeps ringing out, and now Ron's gone off to look for him and his phone keep ringing out too.'

'Has anyone searched the medic areas yet?' Ask Josh.

'I don't know,' answered Holly, she couldn't think straight, and it was breaking Josh's heart, he could see her falling apart in front of his very eyes.

They had searched every square inch of the beach, they checked the toilets, every stage, the medic areas, down at the water front, Mellow Mountain, every nook and cranky he may have fallen into, but Archie Parker was not at the Full Moon Party any more. They all met back up at the meeting point and decided to head back to the beach huts; surely they would find him up there somewhere.

A short while later the door rushed open and the police stormed in mod handed,

'What's happening, are my friends here?' I asked, my heart started racing at the thought of seeing Ron in the corridor, handing over some money, I would forever be in his debt, my friend, my dear best friend was coming to save me.

'You fucked, you friend not come with money, you go to Bangkok now,' One of them screamed at me whilst marching me out of the cage. I was so scared, I literally couldn't get any words out, I was frog marched out of the cell faster than my legs for carry me. I was slipping and falling whilst receiving some short sharp stabs in the chest and stomach from their batons, wankers. They threw me in the back of a waiting car outside, and we sped off down the drive towards the main road,

I glanced at the time on the car clock, it was 2.10am, I had been gone around two hours. We left the compound and turned right onto the main road, I had no idea where I was going. Did he just say Bangkok? Surely not, but fuck knows. It was the middle of the night and the streets were pretty empty out here, where the fuck are they taking me?

Shit the bed! We nearly hit a taxi head on, which was screaming in the other direction, perhaps having a car crash wouldn't be so bad, I might have a chance to escape, and I was pretty sure I could disappear in the forest and somehow make my way back to my friends.

The rest of the drive was horrible, the roads were horrible, why such a rush at this time of night?

The taxi swerved an oncoming vehicle travelling at a fast speed before turning left into the grounds of the police station and screeching to a halt. Ron paid the driver his double fair as promised and scrambled to the entrance. He pulled on the first door he came to, 1 time, 2 times, 3 times, it was locked, 'FUCK,' he shouted, there must be another way in. He went round the back of the building, over a locked gate and found another door, locked again 'FUCK,' he shouted again, he continued following the building perimeter and got back round towards the left side of the building, when suddenly another door opened, which he hadn't seen upon arrival,

'Oh, excuse me sir,' Ron said to a scruffy old looking Thai man, he didn't look like a cop, but then again he hadn't seen any Thai cops, 'I am looking for my friend, I believe he may have come here, is there an English man inside the police station? Please, is he in there, I have money?'

The scruffy looking man look at Ron, standing there looking desperate, he said his very broken English whilst laughing,

'English man gone to mainland, he fucked, you no pay in time,' said the man,

'FUUUUUUCK NOOOOOO!' Ronny screamed whilst the man just casually walked off laughing to himself,

'Hold on hold on, has he left the island?' Josh begged the scruffy man,

'He go to boat,' was all he said,

Ronny has just come from the pier, that must be where Archie is heading, fuck it!

Around 20 minutes later we took a right turn, and I recognized where we were, we were back at the pier. Fucking hell! My beach hut was a stone's throw from here. I had one chance to escape, but I was outnumbered four to one, the car stopped, this was your chance Archie, when they get you out just fucking leg it, and don't look back until you are far away, they don't know my name, or where I am staying, I could do this, it was risky but I had no other choice, it was now or never.

The door slowly opened, I could hear what sounded like the engine of a boat nearby, I could smell the two-stroke, fucking hell, is that boat for me?

There was a long driveway which took a left turn, and Ron could see across the scruffy football pitch in-front of the building that the taxi was still there. It was pulling away slowly towards to main road on which they turned off to enter the grounds of the police station, he legged it as fast as he could across the field, he played a bit of football back home, so he was fairly fit, for a mash head, and he caught up with the taxi just before he pulled off into the night. If he had missed this, he would have been fucked, he was God knows where in the middle of Koh Phangan, it was 2 a.m. and the dark night time roads were dead!

'Wait, wait,' he yelled as he opened the taxi door,

'You crazy what the fuck you doing?' Shouted the driver,

'I need to go back to the Pier mate, please take me back there as quick as you can, I will pay you double again!' he begged him.

Within seconds they were back on the main road and heading south towards to the coast. They drove through little villages and shops, some were open some were shut, the taxi driver drove as fast as he could but the roads were awful, they were full of pot holes, and every time he got a bit of speed going, they braked sharply, Ron was getting increasingly pissed off with the situation, pissed off that his best mate was in deep shit, and he couldn't help him, pissed off that Holly was going to be beside herself when she found out, but most of all he was pissed off with himself for letting Archie go off to score, or at least go off on his own in this foreign land!

Ronny Thomson was far from religious, he had sinned for most of his adult life in one way or another, but he found himself having a little word with the Almighty, in the back of a cab 'thousands of miles from home in the middle of the night, he asked God, 'Please man, if you are up there, if you are real, can you please on this one occasion in my life help me the fuck out?' I will never EVER bother for your help again, I promise,' he even said a little 'amen' as he finished, but was it all too late to save his friend?

'Out, get the fuck out,' one of police me shouted at me,

'FUUUUUUUUCK YOOOOOU,' I shouted as my feet hit the gravel, all four of them were standing in my way. This was my one chance; I tried to run through them like a bowling ball. I put all my power into it. I was nearly through, when one of them tripped my legs from under me, I was sent tumbling through the dusty road, and they were on me quick sharp, I was outnumbered and outpowered by the four of them. A small crowd was gathering, and the police men started beating the fuck out of me, a couple of the onlookers tried to intervene.

"Leave him alone,' Leave him alone,' some of the crowd shouted, clearly seeing I was in distress, but the police just pushed them back whilst screaming God knows what in Thai.

More people stopped and tried to help, the old bill didn't even have uniform on, so it looked like I was being attacked or kidnapped, were any of the people my friends? I tried to look at the crowd, but didn't recognize anyone, fuck fuck fuck!

I was pulled up of the ground and carried by my all four's toward the pier and the waiting boat, I screamed out for help,

'CAN ANYONE PAY TO GET ME OUT, MY FRIENDS HAVE MONEY,' I shouted in my last-ditch attempt for help, but it was too late, they were pissed off now, and they wanted to fuck me over good and proper. I was launched onto the deck of the boat, and they set about giving me the kick-in of my life as the boats throttle kicked and pulled away from the pier. I remember looking back at Koh Phangan, my freedom, my freedom was disappearing into the night, my Holly, my Friends, my everything. I saw a taxi pull up and someone run down the pier, I tried to lift my head to say that my friends were there with the money, but a wicked blow hit me right between the eyes, and that was the last thing I remember!

Ronny started to recognize few of the shops and bars as they approached the pier, the streets were busier down here, all the party goers hanging around, the taxi driver knowing that I was in a rush, although he must have had no idea what this crazy westerner was doing, honked his horn to move all the people out of the road. We turned left and headed straight to the pier where the taxi skidded to a halt next to the speed boat for rent signs and sending a cloud of dust in to the night sky, there was crowd of people standing around as if waiting or watching something. Ron jumped out and ran down the pier, but it was too late, the boat was about 100 yards out at sea, he shouted after the boat to stop and turn around, but it was no hope, the engines roared and over powered his shout, it's all over he thought, he sank to the ground and lent on the railings with his head in his hands, he had failed his friend in his hour of need. Between the two of them, Ronny and Archie, they had royally fucked this one up.

He sat there, numb, he couldn't move, he just couldn't comprehend what had just happened to Archie, surely this was all a joke, and he would appear out of the night any minute, or he was having a nightmare which he'd wake up from, but both of those were just fantasy, he knew what had happened, and all he could do was pray that Archie hadn't been caught with too much gear.

'Ron?' he heard a familiar voice coming from up the pier, a female voice he knew very well, an American voice with a hint of cockney in it…

'Ronny?' this sweet little voice said again, 'where's Archie?'

At first, he didn't look up, he wished it would all go away,

'Ron, please mate, talk to me?'

He looked up and saw Holly standing there, looking all vulnerable like a little girl who was lost form her family,

'Where is my Archie, Ronny?'

'Oh, Holls, we fucked up, I am so, so, sorry, I done all I could, but I kept just missing him'

With that Holly collapsed to the floor, she knew what had happened. The others appeared behind, Maggie tried to comfort her, but at this stage there was no words in the world that could have helped. Holly sobbed uncontrollably, lying in Maggie's arms while they embraced on the floor, not one of them could find any words to say, for a few moments the whole gang sat on their own with their thoughts. What was going to happen to their Archie? The crew was broken, broken hearted!

Part 2

Chapter 11

The next 24 hours were a bit of a blur. I think I must have had concussion from the nasty kick-in I took to on the boat. I kept falling in and out of consciousness, every time I came round, I seemed to be somewhere different, was I dreaming? I wondered. I'm sure at one point I was on a plane. It was like one of those bad dreams where you are trying to wake yourself up, like you are scared or being chased, but every time I came round, if only for a brief moment, it seemed more and more real.

When I finally came around and tried to gather my thoughts I was in other cell, the cell was bigger than the one in Koh Phangan. It was dark and as my eyes slowly adjusted to the light, or little of it, I realized I was not alone, this startled me as I was not expecting to see other faces, I thought I would be on my own, but I was far from it. I managed to pull myself up slightly, but soon realized the room was packed with people and floor space was at a premium. Some people looked at me, some didn't bat an eyelid, but one thing I could see in the badly lit room was lots of heads, and all, or at least the ones I could focus on, were locals. I must be in a local Thai prison somewhere, but where the fuck was I?

I tried to look around the room for any westerns that could help me out, but there was none, not that I could see. The room was pretty quiet apart from the odd moan and groan, Jesus, I thought, am I in some kind of mental asylum? I whispered to the guy sitting next to me,

'Excuse me, sir, sorry but do you know where we are?' nothing, I asked the other side,

'Excuse me, where are we?' this went on for a while, I was getting louder and louder and more desperate to find out where I was, either the locals didn't understand me or didn't give a fuck, so they just ignore me,

'Help me, anyone, can anyone speak English?' I begged,

Finally, an angry guard appeared at the bars,

'What all fucking noise, English boy?' He shouted,

'I am so sorry, I just want to know where I am?'

'You in Chonburi, now shut fuck up!

I had no idea where Chonburi was, so I was none the wiser, but I didn't fancy another beating so I done as I was told and tried to think of what to do next.

I had no idea what the time was, but it was clearly night as the only view of the outside world was though a little window. It was dark outside, it was dark inside, my whole life had become a very dark place, and that first night in Chonburi was a pretty desperate time for me, I tried to get as comfortable as I could with very little space and settled in to try and get some rest.

The next morning, after very little sleep, if any, I was taken out of the cell to meet the lawyer who had been assigned to me. It became clear in day light of the desperate living conditions in the cell where I had spent my first night. I hoped at this stage that it was just a holding cell, and I would soon be moved to better conditions, or even better someone would come and get me out of this terrible mess and take me home, back to Holls, how naive was I?

I was taken through to what looked like an interview

room, by that I mean there was a small wooden table with two wooden chairs either side, there was no sign of any tape-recording devices you would expect to see in the UK at this stage.

I sat there alone for a while before I was eventually joined by a smartly dressed but very young-looking Thai man, he introduced himself as my lawyer, Chati, and he went on to explain what had happened to me, where I was and what to expect from life for the foreseeable future.

I don't remember everything he said as to be honest, some of it I could not believe what he was saying, but this is what I remember.

CHARGED WITH SELLING CLASS A DRUGS AND ASSULT OF FOUR POLICE OFFICERS.

He told me that after my arrest I was taken by a specially arranged speed boat from Koh Phangan to Koh Samui, funnily enough he hadn't mentioned the beating I had taken at the hands of the police, where I was then taken to a Koh Samui police station and thrown in a cell for a couple of hours to wait for the first flight to Bangkok in the morning. I was then carried from the cell and taken on the plane for the short flight to the mainland where when we landed. I was taken from the plane on the runway and transported to Chonburi police station. He tried to tell me I was so wasted from the full moon party that I had slept for the majority of the journey, but I knew that was bollocks, I was stone cold sober when I hit the deck of that boat, it was more like I had been so badly beaten that I was in and out of conciseness for the last 24 hours, but I didn't protest, I just figured it best to keep my mouth shut at this stage, fuck my head hurt.

'So, what is going to happen to me now, how can I get out

of here? You are my lawyer, please help me,' I begged, but what he proceeded to tell me broke me in half.

'You not in good position,' he said in his broken English

Chati, who at this stage was my only hope of going home, went on to tell me that I had been caught dealing category A drugs at the full moon party in Koh Phangan, and I had assaulted four police officers, and I could now be looking at 10 plus years in a Thai prison. He told me I am currently in Chonburi police station, but casually added that I would probably end up in Bang Kwang prison, I had never heard of either of these places, but I certainly didn't want to spent the next 10 years of my life in either of them!

"Ten fucking years?' I screamed, I had been trying to keep calm as I was sure this mess could all be sorted, I would get a slap on the wrist and probably made to pay some corrupt Thai official a large number of Baht, but I lost it there and then in that little room,

'Assaulting four police officers, are you fucking sure, mate, look at the state of my face, them fuckers attacked me,' I screamed. I went into shock, my head could not compute was this little fuck was telling me, my mind raced in a million different directions, I was left speechless and numb to my core.

'Possession, yes' I finally said after trying to calm myself down 'But dealing, no way, and certainly not assault,' I went on, 10 fucking years for being caught with a couple of pills is madness!

After seeing the pure horror on my face, Chati showed his first side of compassion by coming round to my side of the table and telling me to keep my head down, stay out of trouble, and he would see what he could do.

As I returned to the cell with my twenty or so fellow bad

boys, the reality of what was happening began to sink in, how could I have been so stupid? I was so angry with myself, I really should have known better, I have let every single person I know down, and I just prayed the judge would be lenient on me, but seeing as I was a foreigner taking the piss on their turf, I very much doubt that would happen, and the fact that I was being done for dealing and not just possession really didn't look good, and on top of that the fuckers who kicked the shit out of me back in Koh Phangan are claiming that I attacked them, if they call me trying to get past them attacking them, then they are bent as fuck. I knew what I was and wasn't guilty of, so I would stick to my guns and fight the case all the way.

Chapter 12

The first visitor I had was by the far the hardest thing I had ever had to deal with in my life. Holly, Ronny and Maggie had traced my journey by asking the right people, the right questions. The Koh Phangan Police lead them to the Koh Samui police station which lead them to Bangkok and on to Chonburi, it had taken them three days to get answers to what happened to me and where I was, but they got there in the end and now they were waiting to see me.

I was told I had a visitor, I assumed it was Holly, I didn't even know if my family knew what had happened yet.

I walked through to the visiting area, at this stage I had no idea what the procedure was, I had only been here for three days! I was told to sit on a long wooden bench and wait. Was my visitor going to join me on the bench? There was a wire fence in-front of me, then a 2 metre or so walk way, then another wire fencing. After a few moments a door behind the opposite fencing opened and there she was, my Holls in all of her beautiful Glory, when I saw her, I just broke down into a million pieces,

'Oh Archie,' she said through the tears, 'Hold up babe, it will all be ok,' she whispered across the way. I know she was only trying to make me feel better, but something inside me said that this was not all going to be OK, and I could see it in her eyes too.

'Holls,' I said, 'I fucked up big time, I am so sorry, I don't even know what else to say.'

'You know, over the years we have been together I have never seen you cry, pull yourself together, you wanker,' she said with her little smile and her American cross cockney accent, which I loved so much, and she had the only smile in the world that could make me feel somewhat hopeful in this dire situation.

'Your parents, Archie, have you spoke to them?' I haven't yet as I wanted to see you first, do you want me to speak to them?'

'No, no, no, oh fuck what am I going to say to them?' I said,

'Your parents love you no matter what, you know that, right?' she said,

'But this babe, I am not so sure, this could break them. I don't want them to come here, OK? I need money to buy a phone though.'

'Sure babe, we can sort that for you, whatever you need, we can help,' she said whilst holding tightly onto the fence as if holding my hands,

'I need you to go home,' I said abruptly,

'Oh, fuck off, Arch, I ain't going anywhere,' she snapped back, 'and don't even try to make me.'

'What about the others, I don't want to see anyone else, just you babe, fucking promise me?'

'OK, OK, I promise, Ronny and Mags are outside,

'No way, it's too hard babe, not at least till I know what's happening.'

Holly agreed and they carried on talking for the next 10 minutes until time was called on visiting. They said their goodbyes across the way, they were so desperate for contact, but in a way, this was maybe better, if he did get hold of her, he would, have never let go.

'I will be back Arch, let me figure out what to do about getting you supplies and money, OK Babe?'

On that I broke down again and just walked away, I couldn't say goodbye to her, it was too hard, it felt too final, and I was just not ready for that curtain call, and I couldn't bring myself to tell her that I was told yesterday that I could be here for 10 years.

Chapter 13

For the next 2 weeks I had regular visits from Holly, she brought me supplies and gave me money to buy slightly better food than what was on offer.

My lawyer, the useless prick, had not come back to see me, so I still had no idea what was going on, but I was trying to keep as positive as possible as I couldn't help but think this nightmare would be over soon, someone would come and save me, right? Maybe I was still in shock and wasn't thinking straight, maybe I was just being naive in thinking that this shit could not be happening to me, whatever, but I was desperately clinging on to something, not only for me but for Holly and my family.

With the money that Holly had been giving me, I managed to get hold of a mobile phone. I had to ring my parents and that was without a doubt the hardest phone call of my life. My parents told me that they would be on the next flight to Bangkok, but I asked them not to, please do not come and see me in here, I am not sure I could handle it and you do not deserve it but, a few days later they turned up. It turns out they had already spoken to Holly and made arrangements to come and help out with anything they could do.

It was in the first two weeks that I met an Italian chap called Ferizio, who had been caught smuggling 2 Kilos of smack out of Bangkok Airport, his charges were certainly more severe than mine, but meeting him just may well of saved my life and taught me a valuable lesson of life inside a Thai prison.

He warned me not to accept anything from any of the Thai prisoners, as soon as you did you would be under their command, and that was the worst thing that could happen to you in a place like this. The guards can be nasty bastards, but the locals, most of them with very little to lose, despise westerners, and they would be more than happy to make you their bitch if you showed any sign of weakness.

One night in my second week whilst I was still learning the ropes, I was washing down before lights out when I heard a voice from behind me say,

'You want a smoke, boy?'

'No thanks mate, I'm all good cheers,' I hurriedly replied,

'You look nice, you need looking after, you need friend in here?' one of them said,

'I'm all good thanks chaps, I can look after myself.'

With that one of them grabbed me by the throat whilst shouting in some messed up language I had never heard, I started to panic, but there was no way I was going to become a Thai man's bitch, so I pulled my knee up with a full force and kneed him straight in the bollocks, he winced over in pain and the other one came at me, I ducked out of his way and landed a full on blow to the bridge of his nose, this seemed to scrambled his senses, and out of the blue Ferizio appeared and landed another wicked blow in the same spot right on his nose. He grabbed me by the hand and pulled me away and back to our cage before the guards had chance to turn up see what was happening, this all lasted less than sixty seconds I guessed.

Ferizio explained to me that the two Thais who tried to

attack me called themselves the 'sisters of mercy', and what we had done was the exact right thing to do otherwise your life would become hell in here very, very, quickly. After that the sisters never bothered me and Ferizio again. We became good friends during our time together in Chonburi before he was finally sentenced to life in prison and taken Mia Chai where I never saw or heard from him again, I hoped he was OK as he really did save my life in those early days.

The moment I saw my family across the walk way behind the wire fencing was without a doubt the most ashamed I had ever felt in my life. Dealing with Holly was emotional, but she knew what I was like and she knew how to handle me, my family on the other hand, my Mum, Dad and Sister, they were a different beast to deal with. I saw the look of pure horror on my poor mother's face when she saw me across the walk way in my dirty old stained overalls like a proper convict, her precious little son locked up in a dirty prison in a foreign land, and there was absolutely nothing she could do about it, she couldn't even give me a reassuring cuddle to tell me everything would be OK like any mother would do for her son is such desperate times. My sister was proper emotional too at seeing her little brother locked up like an animal, this is why I desperately did not want to see them, but my dad was the real hero here, he was the chilled one of the family, and he held it together for the sake of all of our sanities. My Mum and Sister both sobbed uncontrollably but my dad kept it real,

'Listen son, it doesn't matter what you have done, we are your family, and we will always be here for you,' my father said to me,

'Oh guys, I am so sorry for bringing this on you.'

'All that doesn't matter right now, Archie, what matters is staying strong, you have a rocky road ahead of you, and we will be here every step of the way.'

'I love you guys so much,' I said whilst holding back the tears,

'I have brought shame to the family name, and for that I will never forgive myself, you have to believe that.'

'We believe you, Archie,' my dad said in his calm voice.

We carried on chatting for the next 20 minutes or so, my mum and sister didn't really talk much, I guess they just couldn't find the words to say, but at the end I asked them to look after Holly for me, she is a tough cookie, but this may break her if it goes horribly wrong, at the end of their first visit my father said the words that will always stick with me.

'Just keep your head down son, don't get in any bother, and do as you are told, the way we brought you up, remember the way we brought you up? Remember your manners at all times, if you ever need to be nice, this is the time', and with that we said an emotional goodbye across the path, and I disappeared quickly out of sight so they couldn't see how much this was killing me.

Chapter 14
13 Months later

Whilst waiting to be sentenced in Chonburi, I became aware that if it was not for the assault charge on the police officers back in Koh Phangan the night I was nicked, that I probably could have bribed my way out of this shit situation I was in, but because of the four arresting cops' testimony of me apparently attacking them, which was utter bollocks, along with no witnesses coming forward, that any chance of bribing my way it of this mess was out of the question. So instead of being done for possession, I was being charged with dealing and GBH on four Thai police officials, something it looks like they were not willing to forgive me on, which I guess didn't help my case as there was no way on earth, I was going to say I was guilty of these charges, when the only crime I was guilty of, was wanting to sort my mates out and have it right off at the full moon party.

Waiting to be sentenced was a nightmare, me and few others had multiple trips to the courthouse just to be told nothing would happen, and I was to come back, on another date. The whole ordeal was derogatory, we were handcuffed and thrown into an open top old van and paraded through the streets, so the locals could get a really good look at us, any pride we had left was taken away from us on these visits to the courthouse, any bit of dignity was gone. Some of the guys I shared these soul-destroying trips with were rapists and murderers, and then there was little old me, a raver from North London who made one silly little mistake, as I was now paying the ultimate price for it.

For over a year now they had been dragging me off to the court house to be immediately taken back with no action or sentencing taking place, I was beginning to think this was all part of the process to break us, but there was no way I was going down like this, at least not yet. When the day finally came for sentencing, I was nervous as fuck, but on the other hand I was relieved that I would finally know my destiny, this was a very strange mix of emotions, but the way I looked at it, was that every emotion breaths life, and whilst I am still breathing I still had fight in me, but that fight wouldn't last long.

Waiting to be sentenced was killing me, I had always confessed to carrying the pills, but had always denied dealing, and I certainly didn't batter the four old bill, which was the truth, but in their eyes, I was carrying twenty ecstasy pills, a grade A drug in Thailand, and they were trialing me for dealing, an offence which can actually be punishable by death or life in prison and with the GBH charge on top it wasn't looking good for me.

I had begged Holly not to let my family come to the sentencing, but when I walked in to the courthouse that hot and sticky afternoon in September 2008, the first face I saw was my mother, she looked tired and worn out, she had lost her smile, her sparkle, her soul, she looked broken and as if she had aged twenty years in the last year or so. Either side of her was my father and sister and then Holls was next to the old man. I smiled across the room at them all and whispered 'it's all ok, I love you all', before taking my seat next to my lawyer to wait for the judge to arrive.

After reviewing all the evidence, and by reviewing, I mean quickly flicking through some papers on his desk, he looked up and said in his broken English a few words that will live in my memory for as long as I live.

'For assault and attack of four police officers and possession of twenty Grade A ecstasy tablets at the full Moon party in Koh Phangan last July, you will do ten years in Bang Kwang Prison.'

"Ten years.'

"Ten fucking years?' I screamed out.

I looked up at my parents, my mum didn't move or so a word, Holly and my sister embraced together, and the old man who is normally cool as ice lost it and started screaming at the judge, I can't really remember what he was saying as I could just hear shouting and crying, but I couldn't handle it, I shouted across the courtroom,

'I'M SORRY, I LOVE YOU ALL SO SO MUCH,' and with that I asked my lawyer to get my fuck out of there as it was killing me, I couldn't look at them any more, I couldn't be in the room any more. The shame and anger and guilt were too much to handle, I wanted to it all to go away and leave me the fuck alone, I honestly wanted to die in that moment, that moment of madness when the judge said the words "ten years' I was done!'

Upon exiting the courtroom, the police, or guards, or whoever the fuck they were informed that I was to be transferred to Bang Kwang prison, AKA The Big Tiger. I had heard some horror stories on Bang Kwang whilst waiting for sentencing in Chonburi. Needless to say, I was not looking forward to what may lay ahead, but I needed to be prepared for the worse, and the very worse was heading straight in my direction.

Chapter 15

Bang Kwang is everything you would expect in a Thai prison and a whole lot more. An absolute despicable place on earth, barbaric and archaic are two words that only come close to describing it. It is also home to the most insane and low forms of humanity known to man, and I don't just mean the inmates.

It is the end of the line for most of the shackled prisoners who enter its big gates, but I swore I would not go down in this place, I was still pretty strong when I entered the big tiger, both mentally and physically, that of course would all change in due time.

The approach to Bang Kwang for the very first time was truly terrifying. We drove through the busy local streets inside a cage on the back of a truck like an animals, the cage was full of desperate looking men, we drove under dangerously low hanging power cables which seemed to be everywhere, just above head height in some places, the locals looking at us as new scum being delivered to their town, it was hard to imagine what life was going to be like in the coming minutes, days, or even years, that was all I could think of whilst pulling into the gates, it almost sucked you in, you could feel the misery from beyond the walls before we had even entered. Did all of these local people we were passing have any idea of what went on their very own door step? Did they even care?

As we passed through the beautifully kept grass and flowers on the way in, the first gate slammed shut behind me with a ferocity that I can still feel today, it shook my whole body with fear, as we passed through more gates, more doors, each slamming with more meaning and ferocity than the previous, as if stating each level of hell you are going to go through, before life as you once knew it would return. We were led off the back on the van, or pushed to be more specific, a few of the men tripped over in the commotion and were set upon by the guards, they made us all stop and watch as they beat a couple of the new Thai prisoners senseless with their bamboo sticks, literally ripping flesh away from bone, proper fucking rank, I felt sick,

'You do as you told or this happen to each and everyone one of you,' the head guard screamed in his broken English, followed by what I presume was the same in Thai so the locals would understand him.

The men were left in a bloody heap on the floor whilst the rest of us were made to strip down and prepare to be searched. When the search was completed the guards, along with the help of the blueboys, made the three Thais stand up and take each other's cloths of to searching each other, and by that, I mean they were made to check inside the other inmates for any hidden drugs or sharpened objects in a final soul-destroying show of power, and the mini-Hitler in charge of this shameful show of human power kept repeating,

'We in charge, you do as you told or you die,' and after witnessing what I had just seen minutes after entering Bang Kwang, I believed every word the little horrible cunt said!

The first night was probably one of the longest nights of my life, we were sent to a holding cell, the twenty or so of us new guests, which was no bigger than your average living room and already held yesterday's new prisoners, so imagine forty, odd grown men in such a confined place, each battling for a small spot where they could sit and gather their thoughts, if that was possible. It stunk like shit. The only spare space in the room was a corner, which I thought strange at first as it had two walls to lean against, If I was to get any rest surely that's the place to be, so I pitched up and tried to settle in as this would be my home for the next thirty days until I was categorized into either a good inmate or a bad inmate.

It was shortly after taking my place that I realized why no one has sat here, there was a hole in the floor where some of the most disgusting creatures known to man used as an entrance to their night time feeding ground, the holding cell.

Cockroaches — the size of your thumb were soon descending into the cell, bringing the most awful smell with them, foraging around for whatever they could get hold of, nibbling at your bare feet, there was nowhere to go, it was hell, you just had to keep flicking them off and trying to ignore them, it got worse.

When night time approached, and the Florissant light above my head flickered on, the local flying squad came to life, buzzing around my head and looking for their daily feed. I felt like a wild animal in the African plains you see off the TV with the flies hanging around on them, is that what I was now, a wild animal?

I had no pillow or cover so the only thing for it was to just pull my top up over my head to project my face and eyes from the flies and mosquitoes, nothing I could do about the cockroaches, in a way I almost which they would just gobble me up, so I could escape.

In the morning we were given our new cloths, by new I mean dirty filthy overalls that looked like they hadn't been washed since the day they were first worn, and stunk of God knows what! We were informed of how daily life would work around here. We would be awake by 6 a.m. for wash, breakfast and wash teeth before being allowed in the yard for the day with very little to do, then back to your cell in the late afternoon, this would by my life for the foreseeable future.

I wanted to try keep fit to stay sharp both mentally and physically, but there was very little room to do so, I would soon learn how to improvise though.

Eating food, apart from when I was of me head back in the UK, was one of my favourite past times, as is most people's, but when it came to feeding time in Bang Kwang, there really was not much to look forward to, especially in the beginning before I knew how the system worked.

The food they served us can only be described as slop, slop with maggots and other terrible crawly things that you wouldn't even feed to an animal, but we had to eat, somehow, we had to eat.

I soon leant that anything you need, anything you want, you needed to pay for, if you had the money, you could get hold of almost anything. I guess in some ways I was one of the lucky ones as my family regally sent me money, which would go straight into my prison bank account, yep, we all had our own prison bank accounts, what the fuck has my life come too!

The violence in Bank Kwang was like nothing I had ever seen. There was unimaginable suffering and Doctor Death was at the centre of most of it. I had seen fights before, some brutal ones at that, I did grow up in North London after all, but the violence I saw in here, I mean real nasty Violence, shocked me to my core, and it wasn't a prisoner attacking another prisoner as you might expect, it was a guard attacking a prisoner. Only pure hatred can pour through a man's veins to commit such harm on another human being, a normal stable person could not do this, no way! It looked right from the off that this place was rife, even thrived on, violence, and if I needed to survive, I would need to grow thick skin.

One day, a Thai prisoner was led out into the yard in-front of everyone, I had no idea what he had done, probably very little, but he was forced to strip down and to stand against a tall wooden stake concreted in the floor, I later found out this was called 'karThrman' the torture Stand. Doctor death was at the front of a preying queue of blueboys, he started off the brutality with a thunderous blow to the prisoner as hard as he could across the cheek, opening him up and blood splattered everywhere, the blueboys then took turns, one blow at time before joining the back of the queue to come around again, and again, and this seemed to go on for an eternity, he was forced to pick himself up and stand for every blow until he was so badly injured he couldn't stand any more, he was then lead away, and I never saw him again, I prayed I never found out what happened to him after that beating, but I am pretty sure I knew.

Just another two days later, I witnessed more barbaric behaviour right out of days gone by at the hands of doctor death. I am not sure what this poor chap had done either, but I was pretty sure he didn't deserve what he got. I was walking past the kitchen area trying to mind my own business, when suddenly a commotion started inside the kitchen. I could hear shouting but it was all in Thai so I had no idea what was happening to start with, until the guards marched this man out of the kitchen and into the yard, so everyone could see what was going to happen to him.

They made him kneel down on the ground whilst another guard delivered a big lump of wood, the type you would see a lumberjack cutting their firewood up on with an axe. He was forced to kneel down and place his hands out flat, palms down on the block of wood whilst Doctor death started sending ferocious blows down on the man's fingers and hands with what looked like a wooden chair leg. Calculated, precision blows, the man screamed out in pain, but no one came to his rescue, I wanted to dive and stop this behavior, but a little voice in my head said, 'Archie, don't be silly, this is not your fight, stay the fuck out,' so I decided not to.

This punishment went on for a few minutes, his fingers and hands were mangled, I am sure every bone in his hand was broken; it must have been, he would be lucky to keep his hand. The blows finally stopped, and the man simply crumbled to the floor, I think he passed out as he didn't move for a while. Doctor death simply wiped down his baton and calmly walked away, this pure brutality unnerved me incredibly.

I later found out the man was on bread making duties when he was spotted peeling off the corner of a loaf to eat, the poor bastard was starving but that was it, that was all it took to lose a hand, fuck!

Rumours have it that Doctor death used to be an actual doctor, it's impossible to believe that this horrible bastard of a man once wanted to help people. Doctor death hated everything about prisoners, the absolute scum of the earth in his eyes, especially westerners who came to his country and abused the laws.

One of his weapons of choice was his precious knuckle duster, he would walk around with his hands in his pockets, but you knew that any second, and often without warning or reason, he would whip his hand out and with furious power would deliver one of his infamous blows to a prisoner, his favourite spot was the bridge of the nose, a full-on punch right on the money would disorientate the unlucky receiver, and he could not defend himself from the vicious beating that was coming his way.

No one knew why he was the way he was, some of the 'Thais truly believed he was the devil, or at least sent from the devil to do his dirty work. He really was the most despicable excuse for a human being that I had ever had the unfortunate luck to meet.

The thing that shocked me most was that he came to life when beating somebody, he got off on it, it seemed to turn him on, pure and absolute rage oozed from his every pour of this terrible little man.

If you thought the guards were nasty fuckers, the blueboys were in many ways much worse. They were a group of prisoners who won themselves extra privileges through pretty much grassing up other prisoners and generally ass kissing the guards. They were given blue overalls so you knew exactly who they were, they walked about with their batons like they owned the place, what they didn't realize though was they were there to do the guards jobs when they didn't want do themselves, I am sure most of them actually reveled in the power they were given as most of them were murderers and violent criminals, they could now act out violence and not get punished for it, happy days for them.

There was one or two of them that weren't that bad, they just saw an opportunity for any easier life on the inside and who could blame them, a few of them I know for sure turned a blind eye to drug use, which was everywhere by the way, and the same few Blueboys even helped smuggle drugs inside behind the guards' backs, but that was only a few of them, the rest were nasty cunts!

It wasn't just raw violence that was rife in Bang Kwang prison. Also neglect, neglect for human life.

One day, a very young-looking Thai boy turned up, I honestly thought he was the son of one of the guards to start with, as he looked way too young to be in here but, on second look I could see a deeply trouble young man. I learnt his name was Bobbi, which I thought funny for a Thai man, but there was nothing funny about his story.

At this time, I couldn't speak any Thai, and although I tried to communicate with Bobbi he couldn't speak a word of English, or a word of any language by the sounds of things, but I slowly learnt the young man's journey. At the age of thirteen his father had pimped him out as a prostitute, I am told in some circles of the rich in Thailand they like boys, young boys, and I guess his father wanted some of the cash rewards for such an atrocious thing. Anyway, he was a full-blown heroin addict and also had AIDS all the by time he was eighteen years old. He had been caught selling a couple of grams of heroin and banged up for it. He would walk, or even cruel, around the prison begging people for help, he was clearly in a world of physical and mental pain but no one would help him, he used to beg the doctors for something to take the pain away so he could sleep, but they just brushed him aside, he would fall to the floor and people simply stepped over him and carried on with their day. I felt so helpless, but there was literally nothing I could do. The next time I saw Bobbi, he was being carried out in a body bag, probably with no-one to take his body away and bury him the way every man deserves to go. Like I said, total neglect for human life.

Welcome to hell, welcome to Bang Kwang!

Chapter 16

The first couple of weeks in Bang Kwang were proper tough, I just couldn't get my head around what had happened to me the last year or so. It was a really tough pill to swallow, and it took me a while to except the position I was now in. Holly had gone home as her visa had run out. I was all alone thousands of miles away from home, but there was no way I was going to let this defeat me. I tried my hardest to pull myself together and it took a while, but I slowly learnt to deal with my punishment, at the end of the day I had taken a liberty in a foreign country with different laws to back home, so I needed to hold my hands up, and just get on with it.

In the early days after my sentencing, sleep was very hard for me, and therefore dreaming of time and land far away was near on impossible, so instead I mastered the art of day dreaming, something I had always been pretty good at to be fair. One morning, I found myself sitting alone in the yard, it was an unusual quiet day, there didn't seem to be any shit going on, just people going about their daily mundane life inside these walls, and I found myself reminiscing.

There was this one day a few years back. Me and Holly were by now a full-on couple, proper in love and in the honeymoon period. It was summertime, my favourite time of the year by far. Josh's parents were away on holiday, the sun was shining, it was a Saturday afternoon so there was only one thing to do, pile round to Josh's house for a BBQ, his parents owned a successful printing firm and were pretty loaded, they had a big gaff and a massive garden which was made for a day like today.

This one time, we had nowhere to go after the pub kicked us out, it was pissing it down so Josh snuck into his house trying not wake his parents and took the factory keys,

'Perfect,' he said as he came running out of the house and jumping into the waiting taxi, we then got dropped off at the factory and 'broke in'. Obviously, Josh knew the alarm code and there was no CCTV, so we had somewhere to hang for a few hours. Shortly after 'breaking in' to the factory Lens had disappeared, I just assume he had fallen asleep under one of the machines or something when suddenly one of the folk lift trucks fired into action, and who came flying through the factory with the biggest grin on his face. Yes, it was Lens,

"What the fuck are you doing?' Screamed Josh,

'How do you even know how to drive that thing?' I shouted.

That was one of the funniest things I have ever seen, Lens driving a forklift truck through the middle of Josh's dad factory at two in the morning whilst off his head, what a legend!

Anyway, we all got Josh's place around midday, this was going to be a good one, I could feel it in my bones. Me, Holls, Ronny and Maggie spilled out of the taxi with our crates of Fosters, forty Bensons each and some food, we could smell the BBQ had already been fired up, that unmistakable smell of summer, the great British summer BBQ, followed by a cheeky sesh, Love it!

As the day progressed more and more people turned up,

Josh knew how to put a party on so he invited everyone we knew, every single one of them was on top form and wearing their very best summer outfits, the lads with their shorts and the gals with their short skirts on. The food kept coming, the beers were flowing, Dre Dre's 'Keep Their Heads Ringing' belting out of the speakers that we had now placed strategically in the garden. The decks would be out later, that's for sure. This was, as Ice Cube once said 'A Good Day.'

I soon snapped out of my day dream and returned to reality. Even when I get out of this place, I know that my life would never ever be the same, long gone were the carefree days!

If truth be told, prison life for me, at this stage, wasn't too bad. I was much luckier than some of the other prisoners. I had a loving and supportive family on the outside, and we were in constant touch through letters and telephone calls. I also had money, which many men did not have. My family kept my prison bank account topped up, so I could get hold of anything I needed, within reason of course, but some people didn't even have a tooth brush. Don't get me wrong, there was unimaginable human suffering in this place, but I kept my head down and got on with my jobs without ever causing a fuss.

March 2009.

For the six months after my sentencing, it took me a while to adapt but I kept busy, I was given a job in the kitchen, which was great as this was a full-time job from early in the morning till late at night, as far as jobs went inside prison, I had hit the jackpot. I also tried to keep fit, this wasn't particularly easy as there wasn't equipment in the yard. There was a group of

German guys who had made a makeshift gym by using what they could salvage which consisted of some metal bars put together like a small scaffolding for chin ups and pull ups, and some straw bags they had found from somewhere which they stuffed tightly with mud, sand and anything else they could gather that would fit in the bag without splitting it, which they used to good effect for weight lifting, They were hardened international drug dealers, but they could speak good English, and they didn't seem to mind me using their gear, as long as they weren't using at the time. The Thais didn't seem that interested in keeping fit, to be honest most of them were junkies with a life sentence, so all they were interested in was getting high and avoiding another beating from Doctor Death and his merry men.

Although I was not here to make friends, I figured that if I could speak Thai, even just a little, my time might a little bit easier, so I set about trying to learn as much as I could.

The first friendship I built up in Bang Kwang was with a Thai man called Paavo. He was an ex, Thai marine who had travelled the world in his earlier years and could also speak very good English. We worked in the kitchen together, so we had plenty of time to talk. Paavo was in for murder, he had come home one day to find his wife in bed with another man, he stabbed him thirty times and after numerous threats of the death sentence, he was finally sentence to the rest of his living days in prison, that was twenty-five years ago, he was now fifty-six years old and in pretty good shape, so I figured he has many more years left in him before he dies. He had been here since I was in infant school, I mean fuck me, think of all that I have done in those years whilst Paavo had been going about his daily life in Bang Kwang, all that has changed in the world in that time, this blew my mind. I asked him one day if he regretted his actions and his reply shocked me a little,

'No, Archie, I not regret a thing, man deserve to die for what he done, this my life now,' he said. I just couldn't get my head around what he said, this was now his life, in amongst all the human depression and death and God knows what else, but he seemed happy so who was I to disagree with him.

Anyway, I became friends with Paavo in the first few months on the inside, he taught me basic Thai every day and before I knew it I could speak the language pretty good, I even took it one step further and started to teach some of the locals English, it even turned into a little business, I had a make shift class room out in the yard for one hour every morning before work, and over the next six months I worked with around fifty Thai men of all ages, some got it, some didn't, but I think they were just grateful for something to do, Paavo was my assistant and we even had a couple of the guards joined in to learn basic English, all but Doctor death, but one day it suddenly came to a stop and my relative easy life in Bang Kwang became anything but easy.

Maybe he was having a bad day, maybe he was in a bad mood, maybe he thought I'd had it too easy under his watch, or maybe it was just because he was a cunt, but Doctor Death one day decided he did not like the little classroom I had set up in the yard and brought an abrupt end to it! He came crashing through our little circle we had formed, me at the front like a teacher and six of my regular students in semi-circle in-front of me, with three or four of his favourite Blueboys, they steamed in with their canes, randomly swinging and attacking each of us like a pack of wild dogs whilst screaming at us to stop what we are doing immediately.

The attack stopped as quickly as it started and two of them picked me up, so I was eye level with Doctor Death. This was my first proper encounter with him, I had avoided him pretty well so far, perhaps he was sussing me out before he decided to make my life hell. I was bricking it, I had seen what he was capable of, and I didn't fancy any of that, he calmly looked me in the eyes and said in his shite English,

'You not teach horrible language any more, you go to Hot Box for two weeks you fucking pig,' and with that, me and my six students were frogged march away and thrown in the box, my first visit to the dreaded hot box, I had not been looking forward to this, my relatively easy prison life had just nosedived right of the edge of a cliff.

Chapter 17

On the 22nd January 2013, a young American chap called Mason Stone arrived in Bang Kwang prison. He looked like a proper arrogant fucker, he looked like he thought he was well above everyone else in here, like he was too good to be here, and this was not meant for him. He didn't talk to anyone, he didn't make any attempt to meet and befriend people, and if I am being honest, he looked like one of those nutter kids from the states you would see on the news, who shot up his whole class room for no other reason than he was bored.

Doctor death took an instant dislike to Mason for the terrible crime he committed, and he pledged to him from day one that he would make his life hell in this place, right up to his execution.

Chapter 18

Where I come from, the term Hot Box means something entirely different. In here, the hot box is the ultra-punishment block. It was deep underground, like a war time bunker, the only way in and out was through a large concrete slab at ground level which was pulled back and forth by the guards with massive chains. A big concrete room full of sweet, shit, piss, insects and some pretty fucking nasty people!

No one on the outside knew about the box, it was extreme punishment which the Thai officials would not allow against human rights, if the prison had any visitors lined up, the box would be locked and the entrance door hidden out of view by any means necessary. Sometimes with people still inside.

The hot box, or just the box as it was called, was situated in the middle of a grassy knoll in the yard; you couldn't see it until you were literally standing on it.

I first heard of the box shortly after my arrival, but I wasn't too sure if it was real, and if so where the fuck it was. The first time I was frog marched to the box, I thought this was it, they were going to put me on the wall and shoot me there and then just for teaching English to some locals, when suddenly a door appeared in the ground, and down I went, into the bowls of hell.

Dehydration was the biggest problem in the box, it was so bad that your tongue would swell and become compressed in your mouth and indented by the teeth, which makes talking and eating very difficult, not that there was much of either of these two activities going on but the pain was excruciating.

As extra punishment, sometimes in the heat of the day the guards would open the entrance door, and let the searing heat pierce away at the skin of the poor inmates in the box. This would do two things...

1. Almost blind you from the white light suddenly piercing the darkened room,

2. Sunburn 'your already sensitive and damaged skin.

It was a free for all to try getting the little bit of shade which would often end in terrible violent between the unlucky tenants, I am sure this was part of the reason the guards would open the door, for a bit of entertainment.

On the flip side to opening the door in the scorching heat, they would also open it up in torrential rain and then there really was nowhere to hide, you would be soaked through within seconds, and coming out of the box with pneumonia was pretty common. You never knew when the door would be opened, I swear they would sometimes wait for the inmates to fall asleep then pop it open, absolute human barbaric behaviour from the very people who were supposed to be looking after you, fucking dogs!

Most of the punishment the guards and blueboys inflicted on the men were far more violent than the crimes the inmates had committed on the outside. I did often wonder who are the real criminals in the Thailand justice system?

Every man has his breaking point, and one night a young Thai prisoner called Kimi met his. Kimi landed in Bang Kwang shortly after me. He was a bubbly bouncy young Thai man who simply looked and acted out of place in here. He accidentally ran someone over and killed him on his motorbike in Bangkok when he skidded off the wet road, he never tried to get away with it, he accepted all charges thrown at him, and in his own words,

'No punishment will bring that man back, so I will accept and honor anything that comes my way,' which I took my hat off to him for. He was on a manslaughter charge, but for some reason the guards took a instant dislike to him, they goaded him day and night to try and break him, they threw him in the box for absolutely no reason at all other than for their own amusement, so it was no surprise that his health, both mental and physical, slowly went downhill.

I had been in the box with Kimi for nearly two weeks, when one night I was woken by the fucking guards opening the door to introduce us to the monsoon which had just landed, there goes our good night's sleep, I thought.

Kimi was right at the bottom of steps as he had nowhere else to go. After a couple of hours there was no letup in the rain, and I could see Kimi was on the edge, he was whispering to himself and shaking, I tried to calm him down.

'Kimi, listen man, chill out,' I whispered to him through the driving rain,

'Kimi, can you hear me?', he finally looked up, looked deep into my eyes and I swear on my fucking life, deep in all of his agony a little smile appeared on his face, he picked himself up and launched up the stairs with a deranged scream that only a man who has lost his mind can muster and started swinging,

'Kimi, Nooooooo, stop!'I shouted as I ran after him, I managed to get to the top of the stairs, and to be fair I saw him get some good hard blows on the guards, but it didn't last long as he was out number 10 to 1, they all steamed in the fucking cowards whilst one of them pushed me back down and slammed to big concrete door shut!

I hoped he hurt some of those fuckers, I really did! It wasn't until afterwards that I replayed his final moments in my head that I realized, he wanted to die that night, he just couldn't take it any more, physically and mentally they had finally broken him. My lasting memory of Kimi was that little smile he gave me before he ran to his death, the same cheeky smile I had seen when he arrived here, he was now at peace. RIP Kimi.

Chapter 19

I was finally released from the box a couple of weeks after poor Kimi had met his maker, and it was then that I learnt of the pure horror of what happened to the once smiley Thai man I had known for a brief period.

After the guards had beaten him to within an inch of his life, they left him out in the open in the monsoon until Doctor Death clocked on the following morning for another shift in his miserable life, by which time the rain had stopped and was replaced by searing heat which was melting away at his torn skin and doing untold damage to the poor kid. They had beat him with their bamboo sticks, not the hardest and most blunt of weapons, but a tool that would cause unimaginable pain whilst literally ripping the skin away from your bones. The evil doctor, when hearing of Kimi's actions, wanted to make an example, once again to show everyone that he was in charge and that no one fucked with him, and if you did you would meet the same end. They dragged his limp body, barely alive by now, over to the grassy area at the back of the yard where they tied him to the floor so he couldn't move, not that he could anyway, but they left him there for a whole week, day and night and he literally got eaten alive by the giant green ants that lived there and other insects that crossed his path, I was told that the smell of his decomposing body was enough to make even the hardened guards sick, especially the ones that were given the unfortunate job of clearing up and disposing of his rotting caucus, no one on earth deserves to go in such a way, pure fucking rank mate!

In the first year or so I really struggled to deal with the violence I witnessed. I had never been a violent man and that wouldn't change simply because I was now in prison, but I did need to grow a thick skin as violence and neglect was part of everyday life in Bang Kwang. On the outside I had no idea that such atrocities happened like this in this day and age, but I had to keep reminding myself that I was a world away from home, and it truly was a different world, even planet, over here.

I never wanted to see the inside of the box again and tried to avoid Doctor Death at all costs, which was pretty hard, and now he knew I was terrified of him, I was sure that it wouldn't be too much longer until out paths crossed again, he was a typical bully who prayed on the weak and loved it. I mean he really loved it, fucking sick bastard, and as sure as I was it didn't take too much longer until he was up to his old tricks.

It was during this time that I would often use my skill of letting my mind wonder off to times gone by, good times, good memories, and on this particular time my mind wondered back to Ibiza…

The year was 2001, proper 'back in the day', we were in our clubbing prime, and it was before we'd all found decent birds to keep us under control, it was also our first visit to the white isle, it was nearly our last time due to the damage we done to our bodies in that two-week period, which in years later we would often laugh about, last year indeed, ha, ha!

Anyway, we had been hard at it for a couple of days now, beach to pre-party, pre-party to club, it all just kinda rolled into one big mess, but we were in the thick of it right where we belonged. We found ourselves at the legendary Manumission in the biggest club venue in the world, Privilege. It was all inspiring, the place was bigger and wilder than our imagination had dared to dream. Although we were hardened ravers, by the time we reached Manumission on that second or third night we were all feeling a little ropey, and we found ourselves chilling in one of the little garden areas away from the main club room, but as the vodka and red bulls slowly energised our bodies again we soon found our way down to the main arena, and as if the DJ at the helm behind the swimming pool like a god delivering to his loyal followers, John Kelly, had been waiting for us to enter the arena, he dropped the absolute classic Ibiza track 'Cafe Del Mar' and BOOOOM we were off again, the main room at Privilege came alive, 'ten thousand or so like-minded people came together for an unforgettable moment, a moment that will live on in our memories for ever, even here in prison thinking about it brought a little smile to my face. In every direction you turned there were smiley faces, 'thousands of hands and arms in the air, the strobes flickering and weaved through the raised hands to the uplifting sounds that was oozing from speakers up above us, the smoke machines and lasers worked together to form a slow-motion affect that can only happen with the ingredients in this room. At one point I just stopped dancing and stood still with my hands on the back on my head and tried to take it all in. I was here, I had made it to the promised land and I wasn't going anyway for a very fucking long time!

We danced in that main room in that very spot until the morning sunlight filled the room to the left and before we knew it, it was 8 a.m, and we were just about ready to board the looney bus, and off to the infamous Manumission carry on party at Space, back in the days in all its glory before the terrace roof was put on, dam they were the days. But every time I came around from my day dream and reality hit me in the face, I would realize that those days were long gone, just a distant dream that for whatever would happen to me going forward, my days will never ever be the same again.

Chapter 20
A couple of years later

Over the course of the next few years, I settled down to life on the inside. I took the old man's advice and kept my head down as much as I could. Sometimes it was impossible to avoid conflict and confrontation, which would often end up with a short stint in the box for one, or both parties, involved in whatever beef was going around at that time.

I had been in Bang Kwang for around five years now, half way though, but it still seemed like an eternity until I could go home. Luckily enough, I had only been sent to the box three times in four years. The first was for the teaching incident with Paavo. The second was for having a fight with a local chap over a piece of fucking bread, this is all it took sometimes for some pretty nasty shit to kick off, and the third time I was literally in the wrong place and the wrong time, when a rival group of Thais broke out in a mini riot, and guess who was caught in the middle of it all? Yep, me! There was no point trying to protest your innocence in such situations, this could result in even more severe punishment and beatings, not thanks mate, I'd rather do the time, but one thing is for sure, on any given day the box is a living and breathing beast and is always willing and waiting for new guests, it was like an evil pit of despair that sucked you in, and didn't always spit you back out. But, three trips in four years, wasn't too bad considering I saw some guys go down there and not return for months on end, some never returned!

Over the course of my time in prison so far, my family made as many trips as they could to come and see me. I didn't really want them to see me in here, but they insisted and if truth be told, I fucking missed them and seeing them gave me something to look forward to, and it also gave me a massive boost once they had been.

Holly on the other hand, she made even more regular trips, she was the one that kept me grounded and on the straight and narrow. She stuck around through thick and thin, when she could have bailed and gone back home to the states at any given time but, she stuck by her man and one day when I get out of here, I will give her the lifelong dream of having a family and getting married, this was all that kept me going, the thought of getting home and sorting my life out with my amazing Holly Jax, top, top bird.

One of the toughest visits I had to deal with through was when Ronny and Mags rocked up one day. I had been writing to everyone back home, and Ronny had begged to come see me, but I just didn't want him to see me in here. We had been through so much together over the years since we were spotty teenagers to best of best friends and full-time clubbing brothers, we'd had so much fun over the years that I just didn't want him see me in such a dire situation. But one day out the blue when I was told I had some visitors, Ronny and Mags appeared across the walk way, and for the first time in a while I felt like crying.

Seeing Mags was proper hard too. She was one hell of a trooper, and I'm sure she had kept Ronny together through all of this shit. But they had made the long journey, so I would honor their commitment and not run off back into the prison like I really wanted to.

'Geezer, how's it going?' This was a simple question that Archie and Ronny had said to each other hundreds of times over the years, but never had it ever been in such a shit situation.

'Well, you know Arch, still going mate,' replied Ron,

'How you holding up, Archie?' Asked Mags,

'Ahh, you know babe, not too bad if I'm honest, you looking after this prick for me?' Archie said whilst winking at his best mate. This seemed to lighten the mood for a few brief moments as they all shared a laugh. That was until Ronny interrupted the laughing with,

'I'm so fucking sorry bruv, I tried everything to catch you man, but I literally kept missing you.'

'Listen, Ron, you didn't make me go try and get some gear, did you? That was on me, this is all my fault, there is no one else to blame.'

'But…' Tried Ronny,

'No fucking buts man, we promised the birds we wouldn't do it and you stuck to your promise, I didn't, simple as that, end of,'

'But I was so close Arch, back at the port on Koh Phangan, I was so fucking close brother,' and with that Ronny broke down and wept in his arms, Mags tried to conform him but he was gone.

'I tell him, Arch, I have been telling him for five years that's it's not his fault,' said Mags,

'Daft brush ain't he?' Archie tried to lighten the mood again with a joke,

'I think coming here and seeing you will help him, Arch. I know you didn't want to see us and I get it, but Ron has not forgiven himself for not being there for you, he misses his brother so much, we all do, babe,' offered Mags,

'Actually, it's been real nice seeing you both, I just wish I could come round there for a hug, that would be nice, but they won't let me,' said Archie.

'Ronny, pull yourself together you prick, you ain't come all this way to cry like a little girl, talk to me man, how's the scene back home?'

This was what Ronny needed, he needed to see his brother in arms was doing OK, it would now be slightly easier to deal with knowing that his Arch was doing OK. He perked up a little and for the rest of the visit time, they had a good old catch up about things back home and about this and about that. It was nice. Ronny and Mags were going to be in Thailand for two weeks so they arranged to come back as much as they could. Ronny even came back a few times by himself, just to chill and talk shit to his friend, even if for a short while at a time.

Seeing Ronny had given Archie a real lift, he was only half way through his sentence, but seeing his friend again after all these years reminded him more about going home, oh he couldn't wait to get the fuck out of this shit hole and go home to everyone.

But, soon, Archie Parker's life would change in yet another direction, a different direction, a direction he was not expecting and a direction that would change the course of his life again, forever!

Chapter 21

On Wednesday June 1st 2013, word quickly spread around the old place that the young American fucker, who had raped and murdered his girlfriend on the Island of Koh Samui, had been sentenced to death by firing squad right here in Bang Kwang. I remember the date well as it was my old man's birthday. The day had started off in good spirits as I managed to speak to the old fella to wish him a happy birthday. He informed me that everyone was doing well, I'm sure he was blagging to make me feel a little better, that's what he was like, always thinking of others and putting his family's feeling first before his own, as did the old dear. I loved speaking to my family as it always gave me a little lift, but shortly after our phone call had ended, I heard the news of the young American's fate.

This was the first death row case since I had been here, and I don't know, it just didn't sit well with me. Sure, what he had done was terrible and unforgiving in every way possible, but there just seemed something so awful and sad and lonely about being marched to your death, knowing that it was coming, by a storm of flying bullets. Maybe he did deserve it, and I'm sure the family of the young lady would agree that he did, but it just brought an air of sadness into my already emotionally unstable mind. I just hoped that I didn't have to witness it when the time came, as I had heard rumours of past executions where inmates were forced to stand and watch as the death row prisoner was marched to the wall and gunned down to their very last breath, I mean how terrifying does that sound, watching people, some you may know and call friends, watching you die, awful mate!

The guards, led by Doctor Death, saw this as a time of celebration and on arrival from the court house, Mason was put in his ankle shackles, and one of the guards tied a long piece of rope around his neck, they then started to pull him through the prison grounds and through the yard like they were parading a big game catch, as they were pulling him along he would be losing his feet and falling over, but the guards just kept picking him up at the orders from their fearful leader at the front of this wicked procession, inmates were then encouraged to throw stuff at the young American, it only seemed to the Thais joining in to be honest, they were throwing anything they could get hold of, old bits of food, sticks and stones, I even saw one of the locals pull his trousers down, take a shit in his hand and throw it at Mason. Of all the violence and neglect I had seen in here, this was probably right up there with one of the worse things I ever had the misfortune of witnessing, proper dark!

When the guards thought that he had had enough, he inevitably ended up being thrown into the box to await his day of destiny. From what I could tell, he had spent more time down there, than he had anywhere in The Big Tiger, this place really was eating him alive.

I tried to push the incident to the back of my mind along with all the other terrible acts I had witnessed, but as I went on with my mundane day, I just couldn't get the picture out of my head of a grown man being treated like absolute shit in front of a baying crowd, but I had to keep reminding myself that this wasn't play school, this wasn't fun and free times, this man had brutally raped and murdered his own bird, this was as close to hell on earth as you could possible get, and I would soon be right in the thick of it, again!

Chapter 22
A month or so later

I had seen Mason around the prison a few times before his sentencing, when he wasn't in the box that was. He looked a more beaten and broken man every time I saw him. I had never said a word to him, and I didn't really want to due to the terrible things he done to that poor young Thai girl, but I did notice he spent most of his time in the box, he seemed to be down there for weeks on end. I wouldn't say I felt sorry for him, what he had done to his girlfriend was unforgivable, everyone hated him, especially the Thais, and rightly so, but everyone needs a friend, especially in this place.

The first time I approached Mason Stone he had just been released from the hot box from a four week stretch, after finding out he was indeed going to be killed by firing squad, I say released, but more like he was dragged up the steps and thrown out of the door and simply left battered in a bloody heap on the yard floor, God only knows what he had been through down there. I had only seen him a few times. He was laying in what looked like a pile of his own shit, and I almost felt a bit embarrassed by my first words to him…

'Hey man, you ok down there?'

Of course he was not OK, he is in a Thai prison 'thousands of miles from home for raping and murdering his own girlfriend. Anyway he didn't answer, he either thought I was too stupid to talk to, or he physically couldn't talk through the punishment he had received, but I saw the look his eyes for the first time, deep sadness, and that was the first time I thought that this kid didn't look like he was capable of what they say he did. He was in no fit state to talk, so I just sat with him, I am sure he welcomed it deep down, as I am pretty sure I am the first person since he had been here to say anything remotely nice to him.

I wanted to tell him that everything was going to be OK, but that would be a lie, everything was definitely not going to be ok, he was going to be executed very soon for what he had done.

I was on yard cleaning duties, so I shouldn't have really been sitting with him, but I was willing to take the risk if I could just give Mason even a few minutes of something, anything that would for the very brief of moments lift his spirits, and mine to be fair, this feeling was to be short-lived as minutes later doctor fucking death of all people walked past and saw me sitting with Thailand's current public enemy number one and split up the party straight away. I tried to protest Mason's innocence in the situation, saying that I had approached him, and he had not said a word to me, but before I knew it we were both being frog marched by his horrible little helpers towards the hot box, I shouted and I begged to just put me in but the sadistic bastard laughed it off and ordered us to be thrown in the box for two weeks along with a vicious beating.

'I'm fucking sorry man,' I said as we hit the cold and wet deck of the box, he didn't even look my way, he seemed so far out of it that I am not sure he even knew where he was.

Chapter 23

This wasn't my first time in the box, far from it, but it proved to be the most memorable, for good and bad reasons.

The box was rammed. I couldn't quite see how many people were down there as it was pitch black, but I guess there were about thirty men all together. All doing serious time for various crimes from Drug dealing to cold-blooded murders. You name it, we had them in here, but all that didn't matter, not down here in this pit of shit and desperation, there was an almost unwritten rule to live in harmony, it was literally too small and cramped for any trouble, keep to yourself and share the very little space you had with others.

I settled down next to Mason Stone, the guy who had brutally raped and killed his Thai girlfriend, who he had met in Koh Samui. I didn't say anything, but I was filled with guilt, the poor kid had literally been let out fifteen minutes ago from his latest visit to hell and here he was, straight back in, all because I sat down to talk to him. I whispered sorry to him, I am not sure if he heard me or not, but I then settled down in my little dark, hot, smelly rotten corner for what I knew was going to be one of the toughest few weeks of my life.

The only way to tell if it was day or night was if you were at the entrance end of the box and could see up the steps there was a couple of tiny little holes, which the sun either shone through, or at night time the little rays of light simply disappeared.

Day 1:

Eventually I had managed to settle down, and I think I even got a couple of hours sleep, when I came round and my eyes had adjusted to the light, or little of it, I could see Mason was sitting up, alert and wide awake. I wondered if he had slept? I could tell it was day light from the small tunnel of lights beaming into the box through a small hole in the roof. Mason was sitting opposite me with a couple of guys lying between us on the dirty wet floor. I was already counting down the days they get the fuck out of here, little did I know at this point what laid ahead. At one point, I thought I saw Mason look my way, I didn't attempt to make conversation, not just yet, but instead I gave him a little acknowledgement nod of the head. Apart from two feeding sessions from the guards, not much else happened on day 1.

Day 2:

I was woken by the guards hauling the big concrete door back, and the sun piercing through the dark like a sharp knife. What the fuck are they doing? I tried to squint through the bright light and watch the commotion up above. It turns out we had some new guests joining us, this caused all sorts of problems as it was already crammed, a few scuffles broke out for floor space, but the laughing guards up above us closed the door and darkness fell upon us once again, the trouble soon stopped, and we all settled down for another day in paradise. Through all of the commotion Mason had not moved a muscle, I couldn't work out at this stage if he was a stone-cold killer, or someone so scared that he didn't even dare move a muscle. Tomorrow I will try to start a line of communication with him, partly out of intrigue for his story and partly because I was bored and lonely down here. I may even start up my language school, I could do with an assistant, maybe Mason could help?

Day 3:

Day 3 started in the usual way, I woke up from a disturbed sleep and the tunnel of daylight was illuminating the far end of the box. Today I will try and talk to the young American they say killed his girlfriend. I have no idea how it will go. I won't go all in, maybe just drop a few simple questions.

At one point in the day, the afternoon I assumed as it was the hottest part of the day, I shuffled across the dirty skanky floor as much as I could and whispered over to Mason and said,

'Look man, I'm proper sorry about landing you back down here, you looked like you needed a friend up there, it's cool if you don't want to talk but, you know where I am if you want a chat, my name is Archie Parker by the way,' and with that I just patted him on the arm and moved back to my little spot. I still couldn't read him, he didn't respond in any way, his eyes flickered a few times, but no words left his mouth. He will talk when he is ready, I'm sure, either that or he would kill me; I still wasn't too sure which one yet.

Day 4:

Nothing happened on day 4, apart for some arguing at one end of the box between a few of the Thais, they seemed to be arguing about floor space, what the fuck else was there to argue about in here? I had made an attempt to talk to Mason, but so far, he had not been interested, so I would give him a bit of space. When the guards delivered our food, I could see from the clouds that a storm was brewing up above.

Day 5:

I am not hundred percent sure what time it was when I was woken by the god-awful noise of the large concrete door being dragged back as it was still dark, but within seconds we were soaking wet, we were in the middle of the monsoon season and the storm had arrived, it was as if someone had turned a big fucking tap on right above our heads, there was no escape from it, for a few brief seconds it was a slight relief from the sticky and stifling heat, but it soon became unbearable. I looked over at Mason and he hadn't moved an inch since before we went to sleep, had he been to sleep? Had he been to sleep since entering the box? When was the last time he had a good night sleep, not for a long time, I assumed?

Over the next few hours, we sat there like 'statues, not wanting to move too much, any movement was so uncomfortable. One of the Thai prisoners did try to make a run for it at one point, he darted up the stairs but was beaten back down into the pit of despair that is the hot box, he landed in a heap at the bottom of the stairs, and this is where he would stay for now. As day light arrived the rain slowed a little and the guards seemed to be bored of laughing at us, and probably wanted to go get nice and dry before they go home so they eventually pulled the door back over, darkness formed all around us again, but this time we were wet through and sitting in a puddle of dirty water a foot deep, I had to stand, sitting in that shit was not an option for me.

A little later on in the day, the water had drained away somewhat, so I took my seat back and tried to settle down and get some sleep when I caught Masons eye across the box, he seemed to come round from whatever trance he had been in for the last five days, he looked me straight in the eyes and for the first time I saw emotion in his face, he looked like he wanted to tell me something. I shuffled over to him, I had to bribe the Thai man sitting next to him with two packets of cigarettes when we get out of here to swap places with me, which took some effort, but as mentioned before, you can bribe any man in here with the right thing.

'Mason, isn't it?' I asked him, he slowly nodded 'Do you want to talk, mate?'

He said nothing for a few moments, but I could see he was building up to it so I gave him a moment before I said anything.

'If you want to talk mate you can, I won't judge you,' I said after a short moment,

Even with the bad light down here I could see his lips start to quiver as he started to try and talk…

'I didn't do it, man.'

It had taken him five days to pluck up the courage to say those five words to me; It through me, I wasn't expecting that. I composed myself and tried to replay over in my head what he just said, it was a shock, I hadn't considered for one minute that me may be innocent, and for some unknown reason I believed every one of the five words of what this stranger was telling me,

'I didn't do it man,' he said again in his thick New York accent, and from that moment, from the look of pure horror in his eyes that very moment, I knew Mason Stone was innocent, he suddenly looked proper venerable and way out of his depth in.

I took his hand and held it tight, he was shaking with fear and that was the moment he broke. I don't think he had cried or even spoken a word to anyone for six months, he had been to in shock for that, but at that moment I saw him break and crumble into a million little pieces on the floor of this fucking hell hole. I had seen some things that shocked me in prison, but nothing affected me the way this did, this poor bastard was innocent and yet, here he was, due to be executed, I wanted more than anything to help him, but what could I do? Nothing more was said that day.

Day 6:

I had now taken up a permanent residence next to Mason, thanks to my bribing skills. I am sure he slept, I heard him mumbling in the night, perhaps dreaming of distant memories, escaping from this place even if it was just for a few hours each night, dreaming was, after all, the only escape in prison. Perhaps his breakdown last night was what he needed to force his body into rest, so he could think carefully about how to fight this nightmare that was now his life.

The guards delivered our food shortly after we woke up, I hadn't seen Mason eat a thing and he looked terrible.

'Hey man, the food is shit, but you need something inside you, you need to keep your strength up,' I said to him, he half looked at me out the corner of his eye and looked down at his food, without saying anything he tried to eat a little bit of the slop, but by the looks of it he just couldn't stomach it. I made a promise to myself that when we get out of the box, I would use some of my money to buy him something half decent to eat.

He didn't say any more words to me; he just went back into himself and didn't look up again for the rest of the day.

Day 7:

I woke up on day 7 still in shock from what Mason had told me a few days ago. The mood in the box since the monsoon had reached an all-time low, people were ill, people were being sick and I'm sure pneumonia had settled in for a few folks. Mason looked terrible; I asked him if he needed anything? Did he need to see the doctor? He just shook his head, and said, 'no, thank you.' He spoke in such an innocent and polite manner that I knew he was not capable of the crimes they say he committed. I was told by the rumour mill in the yard that the evidence against Mason was overwhelming, there were no other finger prints or DNA in the beach hut where his girlfriend was raped and murdered, only her and Masons DNA was found at the scene. Mason also had severe bruising on his right hand, which was consistent with punch marks on her cheeks. I wasn't sure of the details of what happened, and I certainly wasn't going to ask him, at least not yet anyway, but of course I will be here if he wants to talk. The most action that day 7 saw was one of the Thai's being carried out by his hands and legs, I wasn't sure if he was dead or not but rumours from his end of the box was that he hadn't moved since the morning of the Monsoon, so it wasn't looking good. We were surrounded by death and misery, shit, piss and rats, and I was actually looking forward to walking around freely in the yard, yes, the yard felt like freedom compared to being down here, were we now half way through.

Day 8
By day 8 the box had dried up from the monsoon, but a terrible smell had since settled in, I couldn't quite put my finger on what it was, but it was a cross somewhere between mould and shit and it tormented my senses, the rats had also come back, big fucking rats as long as your arm, but twice as thick, I heard some of the Thai's talking about eating the rats, good for protein apparently. I was desperate for some meat and

127

a good feed, but I was not quite that desperate.

Day 8 produced the most productive day in my new friendship with a Thailand's public enemy number 1.

I was tucking in to my morning breakfast of slop and maggots and some other weird shit when I suddenly heard,

'What did you do Archie? To end up in here I mean?'

I wasn't prepared for this question, in fact, it had been the first time I been asked since being in prison, no one else seemed to give a fuck what you have done to find yourself in Bang Kwang.

"Silly really, Mason. I was caught with twenty ecstasy tablets at the full moon party in Koh Phangan, a couple of years ago, I promised my girlfriend that I wasn't going to score, but I couldn't resist, and here I am.

He pondered on that for a moment…

'Sorry to hear that,' he finally said,

'Yeah, me too man.'

He didn't reply any further, so I saw this as good time to tell Mason a bit about myself whilst he tucked into his breakfast, this might build up a bit more trust between us. I told Mason where I was from; I told him all about my best pal Ronny and co and of our clubbing adventures which ultimately led me here. I told him about my Holly, although I quickly went off that subject, as the reason he was here was for killing his girlfriend, I thought it would be a bit disrespectful, so instead I decided to tell him about the night I got arrested. He listened intently and nodded now and then and when I had finished telling the story he just simply said to me,

'I hope your family will one day forgive you Archie,' and with that he curled up into his little corner and didn't come up again for the rest of the day. Progress was made, but I still know very little about Mason Stone.

Day 9, 10, 11:

Over the course of days 9, 10 and 11 in the hot box Mason Stone opened up to me a little bit more each day. He told me off his family back home in Long Island, New York. He only talked of happy memories, there was no mention at all of what had happened to him that fateful night on Koh Samui, and that was fine, if he only want to talk of happy days who was I stop him? I swear I even saw the odd tiny smile, as if he was transported back home with his family, even if it was for the briefest of moments, he would snap back to reality, a feeling I know oh too well myself, I also found myself wondering off many times in a day to long distant memories of my family, friends and of course my Holly, you had to daydream, if not you would go insane.

Day 12:

Even though me and Mason Stone had only known each other for under two weeks, even less really as it had only been the last three or four days that he seemed to start trusting me and talking more to me. I felt like a very tight bond was growing between us. I was the only person in the world who knew of his innocence, I am sure his family knew it deep down, but they had not spoken a word to him for months now, so even Mason couldn't be too sure what they were thinking. Knowing of his innocence was a massive weight on my shoulders, and I felt as if I needed to protect him as much as I could. I started to look at him as the little brother I never had, and when we got out of the box in a few days I was going to do all I could for him. I had no idea at this stage how much that would be, but there was no way I was going to let an innocent man die and do nothing about it, but I had to be clever.

Day 13:

I finally plucked up the courage on day 13 to ask Mason what happened, what exactly happened that dreadful night all those months ago for you to end up in here, on death row, in this hell hole. At this point I still didn't know any details, and fuck me was I not prepared for what I was about to hear...

Part 2.5

Chapter 24

My name is Mason Stone, I grew up in the small town of Huntingdon, Suffolk County, Long Island, New York. My parents were well-off, not rich, but financially comfortable, we were a happy little family. My father owned a small law firm out of the city, and my mother was a doctor in the Local Hospital, Huntingdon Hospital, where me, my brother and sister were all born.

We spent endless summers sailing around Huntingdon Harbour on our Minor Offshore 36 Fly boat called MAY-STONE, named after me, my sister Annabelle and my little brother, Yann, we were happy, just the five of us living our own version of the American dream.

My father worked very hard to build up his business, but he always found time for his family, he seemed to work longer hours in the autumn and winter months, but he was around in the summer time to look after us all whilst our mother was working shifts at the hospital, and of course taking us out on the MAY-STONE.

After leaving Goosehill primary school, I studied business studies at Five Towns College in Dix hill. I still wasn't sure what I wanted to do with my life, but a business degree behind me would surely be a good start?

I'm your average twenty odd year-old American guy. I love sports, I had been in all of the school and college football teams, and I was a keen boxer, I had never had a professional fight, but one day perhaps I could pursue this dream, but, the only thing I knew I wanted to do first was to travel, my friends couldn't go but I was more than happy to go by myself, it would be a self-building and life learning experience, and I would make the most of every minute of it.

Mason worked down the harbour at one of the boat-hire shacks to save up money for his trip. His dad had promised that if he worked hard and saved as much money as he could for his travels, he would match what he saved, he saw this as a challenge and even had two jobs at one point, his second job was washing up and waiting at one of the exclusive harbour view restaurants, the tips would often be more than he took home in wages, but he saved every dollar of what he earned, and his father stuck to his promise and matched what he had saved.

Mason loved his life at the harbour and deep down this would always be home, but before he got married, had kids and settled down he needed to see the world, and that's exactly what he was going to do.

He had never really left the state of New York, and as he got a bit older, he started to read and hear more and more about the big and wonderful world. Some of his friends had been or knew people of had travelled to Europe and Asia, and before he started his real life (and he still didn't know what that was) he wanted to see some of the world.

He had worked hard all summer and into the autumn. As long as folk still liked to eat outside and hire boats the local shops were always open. He was now ready to book his flights, pack his oversized rucksack and head off on his travels.

My Leaving party on the 17th November 2013, which also happened to be my twentieth birthday. All of my family and friends were there. It was a chilly autumn evening but my dad still managed to fire up the BBQ and give me a good send off and a birthday party that I will never forget. I also got some very generous donations from friends and family for my travels.

20th November 2013, two days after his twentieth birthday, Mason set of from JFK Airport in New York bound London for a week before heading to South East Asia to travel around Laos, Cambodia and then to Thailand. He would miss home that's for sure, but he was also excited for his new chapter in his life.

Chapter 25

The next four weeks Mason spent travelling from London, which he absolutely loved with all of its history and culture, to Laos, which was a world away from London, and indeed a world away from his beloved homeland too, and then on to Cambodia.

Mason spent a week in London, taking in as many sights as possible before the long and tiring journey to South East Asia, where he finally arrived in Laos for some chill time. He loved Laos so much so that he ended up spending two weeks travelling the beautiful countryside and meeting some wonderful people on the way before making the long and difficult journey from four thousand Islands in Laos to Phnom Penh in Cambodia. After trying to avoid the Mafia in Laos and the 'medical team' trying to assess you for any bugs you may have, but actually just wanted to rip you off with charging you for their troubles he finally arrived in Cambodia.

It was there on his first night that he met a couple of unsavoury characters from his homeland which made him embarrassed to be from the same place as them, so he only spent one night in his first hostel before moving on to another road trip with some Europeans that he met in his hostel, then after a week in Cambodia it was time to move on, his new friends were happy where they were so they said their goodbyes over a couple of cheap beers on his last night, and wished each other the very best for the rest of their travels, wherever that would take them.

I had heard of the Paradise Island of Koh Samui as it was a Mecca for travellers who could stay along the beautiful beaches in the huts for very little money, they were basic, but that's what travelling was all about.

I arrived in Bangkok around four weeks after leaving home, but so much had happened it already felt like I had been away for years.

Bangkok was huge, a huge busy smelly machine that seemed to be alive, it never stops, it is 24/7 chaos and to be honest, I didn't really like it. Christmas was just around the corner, and I had no intention of staying in the big city all by myself on my first ever Christmas away from my family. I only hung around for a couple of days before taking the short flight over to Koh Samui, where I planned on staying for as long as my money would stretch me. Little did I know at this stage what lay ahead.

As a backpacker I had to stay in hostels and beach huts, which was fine, I didn't expect anything else, but for my birthday present before I left home all those weeks ago my parents had paid for a me to stay in a five-star hotel for a week when I arrived in Koh Samui. The Centara Grand Beach Resort, and it was in the hotel where I first set eyes on the most beautiful sight I had ever seen, it is where I met Kannika. She was serving drinks in the hotel bar. Her natural beauty stumped me a little, I fumbled around looking for the correct way to ask for a beer, normally a very simple sentence, but in this instance the words just didn't seem to come out.

He guessed she was around 5 feet 2 Inch tall, slim build but had striking blond hair, which so far, he hadn't noticed on any Asian girls, it made her stand out even more.

She seemed to pick up on my nervousness and helped me finish my sentence,

'Beer, sir?'

'Yes, yes please…'

'Will you be staying for some food? I can open a tab if you will be here for a while.'

Her delicate and well-spoken English voice just went straight through me, pull your together Mason.

'Yes, Yes I will be staying for some food, and yes, please can I open a tab as I don't plan on going anywhere just yet,' Boom, back in the game, pat on the back for me.

I found a spot at the end of bar and settled in for a few beers and a bite to eat.

I was trying my hardest not to stare at this beautiful young lady, but I just couldn't help it, every time she clocked me looking at her, I embarrassingly turned away.

It was quite late at night and the bar slowly emptied until it was just me and her, we soon got chatting and swapped basic details like name, age etc. I discovered she was working two jobs to save money to go travelling to Europe. When I told her I had spent a few days in London, she was most impressed as this was high on her places to visit. I could have sat there for hours talking to Kannika, but she had an early start in the morning for a taxi shift, she wished me a good night and said she would see me again another time at bar? I retired to my room and tried to rest my weary head, but something was wrong, I couldn't settle, I couldn't relax, I couldn't do anything but think of Kannika. I hope to see her again very soon, why was I feeling like this? I was scared and excited all in one emotion, shit, what was this feeling. I couldn't wait to see her again.

Christmas day was strange experience. I was eleven hours ahead of New York time, so I had to wait until later in the evening to call home and wish my family a very happy Christmas. I was a little sad being by myself, but let's be honest there are worse places to be, and I was pretty excited to see Kannika again in a few days' time.

Chapter 26

The name Kannika Means 'A Beautiful Flower', and she was every bit that, a beautiful flower through body and soul, and Mason fell head over heels in love with her. He hadn't had much experience with woman, but his time with Kannika was easy and natural. They spoke long into the nights and shared their dreams, he helped with her English and she was very grateful for it.

He had obviously heard of the saying love at first sight, but he had never really given it a second thought, he certainly didn't think it would ever happen to him, was that not just something that happened in the movies? Well, the day he met Kannika he did just that, her natural beauty blew him away, took his breath away, shit, is this what love felt like? Well, if it is he liked it, he liked it a lot.

Over the course of the next couple of days Mason and Kannika grew very close, she worked most nights in the hotel bar, and his days lazing around the pool were spent wishing the time away until her shift started. They spoke of their dreams, their families, their lives and it was on the 5th or 6th night as Kannika was closing up the bar that she leant over and gave Mason a kiss on the cheek, he blushed uncontrollably, and she picked up on his shyness and said to him,

'I have the day off tomorrow, and I want to spend the day with you, Mason Stone,' which happened to be New Year's Eve. He couldn't think of a better way to welcome in the new year.

Her confidence made him fall for her even deeper, and he went to bed that night with the biggest smile on his face, and of course he would spend the day with her, he would do anything for her.

Before he went to bed that night, Mason rang home, to ask his dad for some advise,

'Dad, I have met a girl and I really like her, what do I do?'

'Well Mason, just be yourself man, if a lady can't like you for being yourself that she doesn't really like you,' said his father

"Thanks dad, I knew you would say the right thing for me, I honestly think she may be the one."

"I am happy for you son, and I hope to meet her one day."

'Thanks dad, and happy new years to you, give my love to everyone, and I will call you again soon.'

'Will do son, Love you too. Stay safe and talk soon,' his father replied,

Of course, his dad didn't have the heart to tell his naive son, that she probably wasn't the one, more of a holiday romance, but his wished him all the happiness in the world and to come home soon as they all missed his dearly.

It was so good to hear his dad's voice….

Chapter 27
31st December 2013

The young couple's first full day together had started out as a truly magical moment in their lives and flowered into a perfect night, a night they wished could have lived on forever, but it ended in unimaginable horror that changed Mason's life forever.

Today was to be the first full day and night that me and Kannika had spent with each, I was super excited by the prospect of this, but terribly nervous too. I was up earlier than normal, around 7am, but I wasn't meeting Kannika until 11am, as she had some family duties to carry out first. After opening my beach hut door to the world for the first time of the very last day of year and marvelling in the spectacular view across the bay, I decided I would go for a morning run, not really because I was into running all that much, it was more to burn of some nervous energy, yes, I was very nervous about the day ahead, I was going to be with Kannika, was she my Kannika now? I wasn't too sure about that, but I certainly hoped she would be soon. I had those beautiful, nervous, butterfly feeling in my tummy, I had never felt like this before, I didn't really understand the feeling but I was extremely excited by it. I had four hours to spare before we met, this was plenty of time to go for a run, have a shower, have breakfast, and anything else I can find to fill the time.

11am:

There was a knock at the door, bang on time, I leaped off the bed and darted for the door, I stopped and stood behind it for a minute, not to act cool or anything, it was more to have a big deep breath and compose myself for what lays on the other side.

As I opened the door, the first thing I noticed was her shinny straight almost dark blond hair glistening in the sun directly behind her, she was looking away, perhaps she was getting impatient waiting for me to open the door and started to walk away. She quickly realized I had opened the door and tuned around to reveal her true and pure beauty, her smile, that was what really made her stand out from the crowd, it was infectious in every great way. She jumped into my arms and embraced in the most amazing cuddle I had ever had in my life (I was glad she did this as I was a little worried how to greet her, would it be a cuddle? A quick kiss? A big kiss? I was so inexperienced with this and it terrified me) she smelt amazing, I closed my eyes and took in a deep breath of her scent, her hair and her perfume seemed to galvanise together to create the most warm and welcome smell a man could wish for.

'I missed you, Mason Stone,' she whispered in his ear, even though they had only seen each the previous day,

'I missed you too, Kannika,' I said back, I really had missed her so much, what is happening to me?

She broke away and skipped down the path towards to beach and asked Mason what he had planned for their day? She was wearing a short denim skirt, a short sleeve blue and white flowered loose shirt and some loose white flip flops, this was by far the most beautiful he had ever seen her.

'Wait up,' I said as I hurried after her, 'I thought we could go for a walk down the beach first and pick up some water melon on the way, then spend the rest of the morning until lunch just chilling on the beach, how does that sound?'

'That sounds perfect, Mason Stone,' she said as she looked over her sun glasses and winked at him.

He loved it that she called him by his full name, the only time he had ever been called by his full name was on the fourth or fifth time of his mother asking him to tidy his room, this made him smile a little, his missed his family but right now, all these 'thousands of miles away from home, but he was happy.

Mason didn't have any plans for after lunch, he just thought let's see what the day brings, he didn't care what he was doing as long as he was with his Kannika, that was enough for him. After eating lunch in one of the restaurants along the beach front, they headed back to the beach via Masons hut to pick up some towels and some cold beers.

They soon found a quiet little spot on the beach and set up camp, it was another beautifully hot and perfect day in paradise, a nice breeze coming off the Gulf of Thailand, perfect beach conditions.

Kannika told Mason stories of when they were young when they came to the beach after school with her two brothers, sister, and mum and dad, they spoke softly as they swapped happy childhood memories together, memories from opposite ends of the world, but similar in so many ways, happy childhood memories.

They laid in each other's arms talking for a while longer until the conversation slowed down a little, and they both slipped into an afternoon kip on the beach, with the breeze in their faces and the noise of the sea breaking in the background, the smitten pair let themselves drift in to a happy quite place.

A short while later he came around and Kannika wasn't there, he jumped up but his shock was short-lived as skipping towards him with two ice creams in her hand was Kannika.

'Time to wake up, Mason Stone,' she giggled as she landed back at their beach camp.

They sat quietly eating their ice creams and watching the world go by for a few moments, there were people out on boats, people playing games up and down the beach and people messing about in the sea,

'I want to go swimming Mason Stone, Will you come in water with me?' she asked, I am more of a sailor than a swimmer, but I did not want to let her down or embarrass myself,

"Sure, let's do it,' I said with a fake authority.

Kannika started to get undressed, she first took her shorts off, then she elegantly took her blouse off, Masons eyes lit up and she revealed her petit little figure in her two piece all black bikini, he found himself staring at her until she caught his gaze and quickly looked away embarrassed by his behaviour, he didn't know what to say, but luckily, he didn't have to as she then said,

'Your turn now, Mason Stone?' he already had his swimming shorts on, so he just had to take of his t-shirt to reveal his well-looked-after torso, this time Kannika found herself blushing,

'Race you to the sea,' I shouted and ran off toward the crashing waves, 'Be brave, Mason' I thought, 'Don't look scared, just jump in, which is what I done, shortly followed by a splashing Kannika who launched herself on me and ducked my head straight under water, I came up for breath only to see her laughing.

The young couple spent the next half hour or so playing in the sea, kissing and cuddling before they both decided it was time for a drink back on the beach. By now it was well into the afternoon, and they spent the rest of the day chilling in the sun whilst swapping stories and sharing dreams, two young people completely in love with each other and nothing else in the world mattered at this point, nothing!

Chapter 28

Kannika didn't really drink beer so she sent Mason to the nearest 24/7 to get her a bottle of wine and some evening snacks, they moved their camp up to near Mason's beach hut, and as the sun said goodbye to another day in paradise, Mason made a little fire for them to sit beside to drink and eat the night away, this was a skill his father had taught him on one of their many camping and fishing trips back home, his dad loves the great outdoors and had always encouraged his kids to do so, he had taught them all basic survival skills, a skill she seemed to be impressed by, 'cheers, dad' he thought to himself.

The night was going along just as he wished it had, the beers and wine were flowing and the conversation steered from future dreams to family and anything else in-between, the young couple were tipsy, the flirting and giggling seemed to pick up a bit, was it because it was night time? Was it the alcohol? He wasn't too sure, and he didn't really care when all of a sudden Kannika said.

'Mason Stone, can we go to your beach hut now?' in her soft little voice, and straight away his heart started to beat a little bit faster. Was she cold? Was she tired? His inexperienced mind wondered, or did she want to have some private time with him, either way he was excited to finally get to be alone with her, he wasn't sure what was about to happened but it felt right, so he went with it.

When they got back to Mason's beach hut, Kannika went to the bathroom to freshen up a bit, he took this time to down another beer for some Dutch courage and to wish himself luck, he was sure the moment he had been waiting for, for a while now was about to happen. Him and his Kannika, all alone with no one around and no interruptions.

After a short while she returned from the bathroom, her hair was wet from having a shower, and all she had around her was a little white towel from her chest to the top of her legs, I stood up to greet her at the end of the bed and without saying a word she peeled my t-shirt off and asked me to kiss her,

'Kiss me, Mason Stone,' she whispered,

'Yes ma'am,' I replied.

Her towel dropped to the floor as she pushed me back on the bed to reveal her natural beauty in all its glory right in front of my eyes,

'You are the most beautiful woman I have ever met,' I said as she climbed on top of me,

'I love you, Mason Stone,' she said, take me now and promise to never let me go,

He was slightly a taken back by what she said, he felt it, he knew he did, but he wasn't sure until this point if she felt the same, no girl had ever told him they loved him before, this was his first, and all he could do was smile the biggest smile his life and reply with,

'I love you too, my Kannika, happy new year,' Mason replied.

With that they were off, they made the most passionate and intimate love of their young lives, for the next moments the whole world outside of their door may not have existed, it was just the two of them, making love in a beach hut on the paradise Island of Koh Samui in the middle of the Gulf of Thailand, this was the happiest moment of both of their lives thus far, they climaxed together, and Mason took her in his muscular arms and promised never ever to let go of her.

Chapter 29

After laying in each other's arms for a short while and not really saying much, they decided to get dressed and go sit near the fire for another couple of drinks. It was just gone 1am.

The fire was nearly out so Mason went looking for some more dry wood, which wasn't hard to find as their hut was in the middle of trees and covered in broken branches, he added his knew logs to the fire and took a seat next to Kannika on the beach whilst she opened another beer for him, he thanked her and they sat next to each other, not really saying much, but watching the night go by, the moon shining brightly above them, they didn't really talk about much just this and that, it was getting late and they decided to have one more drink then call it a night, when out the corner of his eye Mason saw a few people walking along the beach towards them, he didn't really think much of it to start with, it looked like your average couple of drunk tourists, which this place had plenty of, but one of them suddenly said,

'Look, it's the dweeb we met in Cambodia from back home who ran a mile when it kicked off in that bar.'

Oh no, Mason thought, it was the guys he met in Cambodia, what's the chances of meeting him out here?

'Hey guys,' Mason said,' Small world meeting you out here, where you been since Cambodia?'

They didn't say much, they just started at him and before he got chance to introduce Kannika to the two of them, one of them interrupted and said,

'Oooh look, he has picked himself up a little lady boy, what have you got under their darling?' As he tried to grab her skirt and lift it up,

'Hey, get off her,' Mason shouted at him,

'What the fuck are you going to do Dweeb boy,' he said as the now standing Mason placed himself between the two of them and Kannika,

'Look, please, we don't want any trouble, it's late, we are tired, and we just want to go to bed,' he said,

'He just wants to go to bed,' the leader said to his follower, 'isn't that cute, the Dweeb from New York wants to go fuck his lady boyfriend.'

Kannika stood slowly; she was getting scared as she had never seen such aggression before,

'You are scaring her, please just leave us alone, we don't mean any harm to you, we are peaceful.'

'They are peaceful Lars,' said the follower, he then remembered his name, Lars Baron, he didn't like him the moment they met a month or so back in Cambodia, he didn't like the way he spoke to people, tonight he was extra aggressive, he was high on something for sure, he grabbed one of Masons' beers out of the box, and Mason just told him to take them all if he wants,

'I will take what the fuck I want you fucking Dweeb,' he said whilst getting in Masons face again. He couldn't show fear in front of Kannika, she needed him to be strong right now. He backed off a little and turned to see if Kannika was OK,

'Go back to the beach hut darling,' he told her. 'It's fine, I will be back in a minute.' It wasn't fine, he was shitting himself, he was fit and strong, and he knew he could take the two of them if he had to, he had been boxing since the age of ten, but he was not a fighter and he was not a brawler, the leader, Lars, was a big unit, but he was off his head, and he would have been no competition for a young fit guy like Mason, but he did not want to fight them.

Kannika hurried back to the hut, she was really scared now, scared of what might happen to her man at the hands of these horrible people, but she didn't know that Mason could look after himself.

Since the age of ten Mason had been a keen boxer as well as a keen footballer. He inherited his father's strong DNA, so he was naturally big and strong. He never had a professional fight, but he'd had plenty of amateur fights, and he was undefeated in each age group as he got older. He was a natural sports man and strong as an ox, so looking after himself wouldn't be too much bother.

Lars pushed Mason in the chest, and it sent him stumbling backwards over the beer and fell onto the beach, the follower kicked out and caught Mason in the knee cap, Lars then joined in and tried to kick Mason in the head whilst he was on the floor, but with cat like reflexes he dodged the flying boot, but as he tried to pull himself up off the floor Lars swung and big right hand which clipped Mason on the ear, it didn't catch him full blow but it stung like crazy, Mason swerved a couple more of Lars's wild swings, he had no control over them, he swung so hard on one of the them that when Mason moved out the way he lost his footing, Mason took this opportunity to land one on the nose of the follower, he hit him just hard enough to scramble his senses and knock him back to give him enough time to deal with Lars,

'I don't want to fight you man,' Mason pleaded, 'please,

please just walk away,'

'Fuck you,' Lars shouted, and sprung himself forward but in one movement Mason diverted Lars right swing, took one step back, then planted a quick double left jab on the bridge of Lars Nose, Lars stumbled backwards, he looked at Mason with a look of anger and hatred, like a wild animal who has just missed out on his pray, Lars quickly pulled himself together and ran away through the tree line, the follower followed and within seconds they were out of sight.

Kannika appeared again,

'Kannika, are you okay, darling?' I said as I grab her and push her hair back away from the tears streaming down her face,

'I am okay,' she said, 'are you okay, Mason Stone,' she then asked me,

'Yeah, yeah I am fine,' I answered

'I am so sorry you had to see that, hopefully that is the last we see of those bullies,' I said.

We headed back to the hut, and Kannika was clearly shaken up by what just happened, I offered to take her home, but she wanted to stay with me, I told her that first thing in the morning I would move on and find somewhere else to stay, and she seemed happy with that. His ear was ringing from the whack he took, and his knuckles hurt from meeting Lars' nose, Kannika ran a hand towel under the cold water and held it to his ear and got some ice for his hand to try stop it swelling up, it stung and first, but after a while it seemed to help. The young couple stayed awake talking about the night's events for a while and then tried to settle down to get some sleep. I said a little prayer to myself that Lars Baron was somewhere else spark out from whatever he was on, and hoped that he would never ever bother us again.

Chapter 30

Kannika Devakul was born and raised on the Paradise Island of Koh Samui, Thailand. She was the oldest of four siblings with two brothers and a sister. Her father worked as a taxi driver ferrying passengers around the island, mainly tourists, plenty of drunk ones, which he always enjoyed, even though he couldn't understand a word most of them said, he always found them funny.

Her mother's job was looking after her family. She would work tirelessly keeping their little home clean, her family clothed and fed and making sure that all of her children had what then needed on the little spare money they had.

They were a simple but hard-working little family. They didn't have much, but then again, they didn't need much where they lived. As long as they had clothes on their backs and food in their bellies, they were a happy little unit.

As Kannika got older and left school, she decided to go out to work to help with the family duties. She followed in her father's footsteps by doing some taxi runs. At first her father wasn't too happy with it as she was a young pretty girl, and some of the European tourists could be a handful so she was only allowed to work day shifts, which was fine as she then got a second job working in the bar in the Centara Grand Beach Resort, where she would eventually meet Mason Stone.

The differences in family life from the Stones' to the Devakul's was a world apart, literally. Mason and his family were pretty well-off, they had a big five-bedroom house on the shores on Huntingdon Harbour, New York. They had their own boat. They were all schooled in the best schools available. Kannika and her family had a little two bed apartment, not too far from the Samui Airport. The four siblings did go to school, but it was a far cry from the private schools the Stones' children attended in Long Island. They also didn't have much money. But one thing both of the families had in common was they were both very happy families.

Chapter 31

Mason was suddenly woken by something, he hadn't been properly asleep after the night's events, he was closest to the door and as he turned to see what the noise was all he could see was a dark figure running at him, he had no time to react and was caught by a wicked blow to the side of his head, he felt liquid running down his face, and he was dazed and confused, was he dreaming or was this real, where is Kannika? He rolled off the bed and lost conscious.

Mason came around a short while later, he tried to pull himself up but the pain in his head was excruciating, he managed to get up, but his eyes were blurry, he saw on the bedside table clock that it was 4.37 a.m., he called out for his love.

'Kannika, Kannika where are you?' She was not in the room, what the fuck has happened to her? He wiped his head and his hand was now covered in blood, his head was pounding as he tried to gather his thoughts,

'Kannika, darling, where are you?' He called out; the front door was wide open. Mason looked outside, nothing. He made his way back inside and headed to the bathroom to see if she was there, and the scene that unfolded in front of him shocked him to his very core, without warning he was sick, he was sick everywhere,

'Kannika, Kannika,' he cried, but she didn't answer. She was naked and slumped in the bath in a none natural position, there was blood everywhere, her dark blond hair was now a terrible crimson red, her eyes were closed,

'NO, NO, NO!' screamed Mason, he slowly tried to lift her limp head, but the way she was laying, the way her neck and head moved, he knew she was dead! He held her head tight into his body and broke down, he cried like a baby, he held her tight and did not want to let her go, when he heard a voice coming through the front door,

'Hello, what happening,' an unfamiliar voice said, 'We got called to screams, what happening in there? Come out now.'

'In here,' I said,' 'help me, I think she is dead,' I screamed and with that, two police men burst into the room.

'Let her go, let her go' They screamed at me as I held her tight, but I couldn't let go, I could not let go of my Kannika, oh my lovely little Kannika,

'Let her go, let her go' they screamed again and eventually I carefully placed her head on the back of the bath and took a step back, the two police officers bundled me to the floor and were now shouting,

'You not move, you not move,' then I thought I heard them saying,

'Why you do this, you die for this.'

It took me a few moments to digest what they were saying,

'Hold on, officers, I didn't do this, she is my girlfriend, I did not do this I promise.'

But they bundled me to the ground whilst more police turned up to help their colleagues, what I assumed what the commanding officer came in and pulled a chair up in-front of me, I was terrified, I was shaking, I was covered in blood, both mine and Kannika's, and he said calmly to me,

'Tell us why you did this?'

'I didn't officer, I didn't do this,' I tried to explain what had happened earlier but then a stinging backhander caught me square on the cheek, and he then said again,

'Tell us why you did this, or your life become hell?'

At this point a million confusing thoughts ran through my mind that I couldn't concentrate, I couldn't think straight, I decided that at this stage to say nothing was probably the best thing to do, so I simply said that I would not say anything else until I have a lawyer, how American did that sound?

And with that for my troubles I received another wicked backhander and was bundled out of the room and into the back of a waiting police van outside.

Chapter 32

I was taken out the back of the van and frog marched into an old building, which I assumed was the local police station, it was now early morning, the sun was coming up for another day in paradise, a new year, a new dawn on the world, but this day would be like no other I had ever lived through, and I was terrified, I have never been so scared in my life. Why would they think I had done this to my beautiful Kannika? Oh, my poor Kannika.

I was thrown into what can only be described as a cage, a cage that would be used to transport animals. The two arresting officers slammed the door shut and quickly left the room, the lights went off, my life fell into darkness and silence, I held my breath, I was too scared to even move, then the silence was replaced by my pounding heart, a low quick thubthub, thubthub, thubthub, my heart had never beaten so hard in all of my life, I was on the cold floor in the middle of the cage, I didn't dare move, I couldn't move, just the low thud of my heart beating and my mind racing at 100 MPH.

The light came back on.

'Why you kill young lady? You die bastard for what you do.'

'I didn't do it officer, she was my girlfriend I would never have hurt her, somebody broke in and…'

'Confess or die, confess or die.'

They kept repeating to me, I took some deep breaths and

tried to tell them in a calm voice that she was my girlfriend and someone had broken in whilst we were asleep, they knocked me out, and I have no idea what then happened to her.

They either didn't understand, or they didn't give a fuck as the three of them starting beating me with their batons whilst they kept shouting,

'Confess or die, confess or die bastard.'

I am not sure how long they beat me but they suddenly stopped and left the room, and I was left in total darkness again, it was like a Scene out of a horror movie, but I was living it, I was actually living this nightmare.

I tried to pick myself up, but I was in so much pain. My whole body was throbbing, they had battered my arms, legs, body and head, it was pitched black, but I could feel the blood dripping, dripping into my mouth from somewhere on my head. I managed to pull myself up against the bars, I felt sick, I was sick, all over the floor, this couldn't possibly be happening to me, a couple of hours ago I was having passionate sex with my beautiful Kannika, then those fuckers came along to the beach and ruined everything!

A short while later the lights flicked on, and they stormed in again, they were so angry with me I thought they were going to kill me right there and then,

'Why you kill her you American fuck? We know you done it.'

I begged them to listen to me,

'Please officer, I swear on my life I did not do this, I had met the man who done it a few times, he is an American called…

BAM, more blows starting raining down on me, I screamed and begged them to stop, but they didn't and no one came to my aid. For the first time in my life, I was purely petrified, they are going to kill me I kept thinking, the more it went on, the more I wish they had killed me to get it over and done with, darkness fell upon me again!

I was being tortured, I was a twenty-year-old American man being tortured in Thailand, surely this sort of behaviour is prehistoric, barbaric and didn't happen in this day and age? But it was, it was happening to me right here and right now and I had no idea how to stop it, I was 'thousands of miles from home in a cage being tortured into confessing to murdering my own girlfriend.

The next time the lights come on, they brought a chair with them. One of them hauled me up off the cold floor and sat me down, finally I thought, it was going to stop and we could talk like adults to get to the bottom of this horrible mess. I wouldn't even report them to the authorities for brutalising me, I would help and corporate with the investigation all the way.

'Please, tell us why you killed young lady?

'I didn't do it officer, I swear.'

I saw his head drop slightly as if disappointed with what I said, he looked across to one of his colleagues who pulled my chair back, so I was now laying down staring up at the roof of the cage whilst another one put a towel over my face, my first thought was he was trying to suffocate me, but he started pouring water on my face, I couldn't breathe, I was panicking and I couldn't move, and all I could hear was the police men shouting questions at me.

This seemed to go on for longer than I knew I couldn't breathe, they would stop for a moment, release the towel, I would gasp for air then more questions, but I simply could not answer them.

This went on for a while, down, up, same questions same treatment, each time I couldn't breathe, the water was chocking me.

After a while they stopped and pulled me up. I was dripping wet, shivering, bleeding, I had been sick and was pretty sure I had shit myself. The lights went off.

From a young age, my father had told me to always tell the truth, never back down if you are right and never give in to bullies, and thus far it had served me well in life, but every man has his breaking point and mine was soon to come...

The door flew open and the lights flickered into action once again, but this time a ferocious force came flying through the door in the form of a sadistic looking Thai man who I had not seen until now, he came flying at me with a gun, pointed it straight in my mouth and in a total rage kept shouting,

'Sign the confession, or we kill you right now, no one knows you are here.'

I had never seen a man with so much anger in my whole life, and I had certainly never had a gun shoved in my mouth before. He was possessed, he was frothing at the mouth, pushing the gun deeper into my throat, I was gagging and I couldn't breathe,

'Sign confession, SIGN IT, SIGN IT, SIGN IT.'

'OK, OK,' I tried to say as he pulled the gun back slightly, I broke... 'I will sign the confession just please, please stop what you are doing, I cannot take any more of this!'

Chapter 33

I don't really remember much about the next day or so, I was in so much pain, both mentally and physically. When I did come round, I couldn't think straight, my mind and my body were numb. I was confused, and I just didn't know how to feel emotionally. A day ago, I was falling madly in love for the first time, and my life was the most exciting it had ever been, and now, I was sitting alone, in a cage, in a police station, someone in the middle of what was paradise a matter of hours ago.

The officers really did hate me; in their eyes I was the young American man who had viciously murdered a local Thai girl. I still didn't know exactly what happened to Kannika, how was she killed? How did she die? Perhaps, and maybe for the better, I will never know what happened in that bathroom whilst I was knocked unconscious.

Lars Baron was fucking fuming, he stormed back to his beach hut just a short walk from where the incident took place.

'Why didn't you fucking hit him whilst he was down?' He screamed at the follower,

'I tried Lars but he was so quick, he dodged it and smashed me on the nose,' the follower cried, he was scared of Lars Baron, Lars was unsteady and could burst at any given moment, he had seen it in Vietnam, he was petrified of him.

Lars Baron is a third generation US Marine, who had done his training in Camp Selby, Mississippi, as did his father, as did his grandfather for the 199th light infantry brigade ahead of deployment to Vietnam. He got kicked out of the army after a recent stint in Afghanistan for a third successive failed dope test. He was an all-round nasty shit of a man who had travelled to South East Asia, for nothing more than to do drugs, rob people and rape young Asian girls.

His Grandad was his hero, bit of a nasty bastard too, the nastiness must have skipped a generation as his father was high ranking, and very well respected, general in the US army to this day. His dad and grandad didn't get on too well, so it was no great shock that when his grandad passed away, he left all of his money and belongings to Lars. Having this money, would eventually lead Lars to Vietnam and then on to Thailand.

Lars Baron spent most of his childhood in and around army barracks, he was moved from school to school and never really settled in any friendship groups.

In his younger years he was a bit of a mummy's boy but, suddenly, and out of the blue one morning whilst making Lars and his father's breakfast his mother collapsed and never stood again. Heart attack they were later told, but that meant fuck all to Lars, all he knew was, his mother had been taken from him and the world, including his father, were to blame.

It was clear from an early age that Lars and his father, Corporal Baron, did not really see eye to eye. Before his mother died, she had tried her hardest to keep the family close, but after she passed, he turned into an angry young man, always getting in trouble and fighting in the playground, he quickly built up a reputation wherever he went as someone you didn't want to fuck with, and as he grew older through his teens, he only got more violent.

There was only one person he liked and respected and that was his grandad, a Vietnam war veteran who was as angry with the world as young Lars was. He often told stories to Lars of shocking brutality from 'Nam', which Lars seemed to thrive on, in his eyes his grandad was a war hero who deserved more respect that he got, from his country and his own son alike. But what Lars had failed to see in his young and inspirational years was that his grandad was nothing more than a classic bully, and he had been his whole miserable life.

No one was too sure whey Lars' grandad was so unhappy, not even his father, this was until his grandad's long-lost sister turned up at his funeral and explained that their own father had beat them senseless through their childhoods. She ran away at age ten and joined a traveling circus, Corporal Baron had never heard of her, his father never ever spoke of his past, but it was starting to make more sense why he was the way he was.

When his grandad died and left him all his money, he wanted to trace his steps through Vietnam, as if paying homage to his life in some fucked up way. Maybe he thought the war was still on in his twisted mind, the Vietnam war had ended fifty years ago but raged on in Lars' head all the same.

Whilst in Vietnam the follower saw Lars attacking a local man for no reason. He attacked this poor man with pure violence, violence that he had never seen before.

They were in a bar one night in the Ho Chi Ming City area, and Lars got into an argument with a local man, the man was much older and although the follower didn't see how it started, he certainly heard what was said afterwards. Lars was kicked out of the bar before it got too out of control, but he laid in wait outside for the old man to leave,

'I am going to fuck that gook up, my grandad should have shot the fucking lot of them, horrible fucking gooks,' Lars said to the follower outside the bar,

'Shall we just leave it Lars, and move on?' The follower replied,

'Are you fucking joking, you saw the way he went for me, man the fuck up or I will stab you in the heart, are you a fucking gook you little runt?' Lars Ranted.

'OK, OK, Lars,' said the follower.

They found a seat in another bar across the street where they could see where the old man was sitting, Lars and his friend waited patiently for the old man to leave. Finally, a couple of hours later they saw the old man finish his drink and leave the bar, they watched him say goodbye to his pals and leave out the front door,

'Here we go, get ready and follow me,' Lars ordered.

They followed the old man out of the bar and waited for him to go down a little side street. The rain was pouring down, Lars followed his victim, like he was acting out a scene from a war film, but this was no war, this was modern day life in the middle of Vietnam, there were no American troops patrolling the streets, the place was full of tourists having a good time. The old man turned down a side street, and he didn't stand a chance as Lars and the follower attacked him from behind. They sent him flying over rubbish bins in the street, and Lars pilled in, kicking and punching the poor man whilst he tried hopelessly to defend himself, the follower gave the odd kick, but he didn't really want to be involved. Lars continued to punch the old man, he was now out cold on the floor, the follower tried to stop Lars by pulling him back, but he just screamed back at him,

'THIS FUCKING GOOK TRIED TO KILL MY GRANDAD.'

The follower had no control over the situation, he was shit scared, so he just stood back and hoped Lars would finish soon. There was a shout of stop from the top of the alley and the follower screamed to Lars to stop as some people were coming. Lars stood back and took one last swinging right boot to the old man's head and then ran off, he was so excited he kept saying to the follower,

'Did you see his fucking head explode? He fucking deserved that the fucking gook.'

The follower was terrified, was the old man dead? He thought he must have been, but there was no way he going back to check.

They got back to their hotel room, and Lars announce they needed to get the fuck out of here first thing in the morning, they would leave for Thailand on the next possible flight out of Vietnam. Lars was covered in blood, his hands and legs, it was everywhere.

'I am going to have a shower then go dump these cloths somewhere, I suggest you do the same,' he ordered to the follower.

The follower wanted to pack his bags and get as far away from this mad man as possible, but he knew where lived, he would come and search for him for sure, he did not trust this man as far as he could kick him, so he decided to stick around for now, if not for his sake for the safety of his family.

After Lars and his little bitch follower got back to their beach hut in Koh Samui, the follower said around two a.m., whilst Lars was pacing around the room, that he had had enough excitement for one night and was going to bed. Lars was still proper angry, and he could see it in his eyes, he wasn't sure he would get much sleep being in the same room as this mad man when he was in this kind of mood, he needed to get far, far away from him.

Lars pulled up a chair, calmly placed it next to a small coffee table in their room. He proceeded to place a few beers on the table and rolled himself and cocktail spliff, which included Amphetamine, crack and weed, it was a potent cocktail of drugs, and he was a potent man with bad thoughts running through his twisted mind. He sat there with an unerring calmness about him for a man with so much hatred and class A drugs pumping through his veins. He sat until the time on his watch turned to 4am, action time he announced and loaded up his tools ready to go to work. A knuckle duster and a two by fours piece of wood he had picked up earlier along with a pair of US army military socks.

Lars left the beach hut quietly, but the follower was still awake, he heard him leave and thought the worse for the young couple from the earlier incident, but he did nothing about it, he didn't follow Lars, he didn't call the police, he just rolled over and wished it would all go away.

Lars Baron was in his element, he slowly made his way through the tree line on the edge of the beach, stalking his prey, the sun was slowly starting to appear over the horizon for another beautiful day in paradise, there was no one around, this was the perfect time to execute a mission.

It was now 4.35am.

Lars saw the opening in the beach he was looking for, his heart beat quick-end as the excitement grew, his mission rolling out in front of him, they had no idea he was coming.

167

He walked slowly through the tree line towards the front door, his target was in site, no one would get in his way, the anticipation of what laid ahead was killing him. He slowly walked the perimeter of the beach hut, checking for any life, there was no lights on, he looked though the bedroom window and could just about make out the figures of two people laying on the bed. There was only one way in and that was though the front door, breaking in would be easy, these huts are cheap with no security whatsoever. He pulled around to the front of the building, stood up, placed his knuckle duster on his right hand, his 2 by 4 in the left. He turned the handle down towards the floor and gave it a short sharp push, and to his delight the door flew opened, he was in. He could see the dweeb and the ladyboy asleep under a thin sheet on the bed, the fan spinning above their heads, this was his moment, he flew in the room with a ferocious pace, and as he did, the American dweeb sat up and with a thunderous right hand he caught Mason Stone square on his left temple with his knuckle duster, the dweeb fell onto the floor, and before the ladyboy could react, Lars flew across the bed and smothered her mouth with his big hand,

'Now you shut the fuck up ladyboy, you hear me?'

She nodded, scared shitless, whilst Lars pulled a sock from his pocket and tied it around her mouth, she tried to scream, but Lars gave her a backhander across the cheek with such force that the knuckle duster flew across the room, he then turned her over and tied her hands behind her back with his second sock, tight, so tight she couldn't undo it. She was small and petit, so he picked her up with ease and carried her toward the bathroom.

He carefully closed the door behind them and placed a

chair under the handle, so the dweeb couldn't get in if here came around.

'Right, you dirty fucking ladyboy, let's see what you've got,' Lars whispered, and with that he ripped her little shorts off and fully expected to see a cock flapping about, but to his surprise there was no cock, she actually was a lady. He smiled a sadistic smile and ripped her vest off, she now stood there fully naked, hands tied behind her back, the was blood dripping from her cheek from the earlier backhander, she tried to scream, but the thick sock in her mouth permitted her from doing so. He was so strong and overpowering, she could hardly breathe, let along scream, he punched her in the stomach, and she bent over in pain, and with that he turned her around so she was no bent over the bath, he pulled his trousers and pants down and starting raping her from behind, he was a vicious and out of control man, she prayed her Mason would come and help, but he didn't come, no one came. After a minute or so, Lars grabbed her hair to pull her up straight and tried to turn her around, so he could fuck her from the front. Her footing slipped, and she fell to floor. There was a loud crack as her skull hit the deck and followed almost instantly, but a pool of blood pouring from the back her head, Lars tried to pick up her, but her body was limp, he stood up and just simply called her a fucking bitch and threw her in the bath before calmly looking for his beloved knuckle duster and leaving the beach hut.

Chapter 34

I was flown out of the island of Koh Samui the next morning. As the plane took off, I was in immense pain from head to toe, I couldn't think straight, and as I peered out of the window, I could see paradise disappearing down below me, and I couldn't help but think I was now on a one-way, non-refundable trip straight to hell. I sat back in my chair and closed my eyes and wished this horrible mess would go away.

Shortly after touching down on the runway, I was put in a waiting police car and driven through the busy streets of Bangkok. I had no idea where I was going but I was sure it wasn't going to be a very nice place. It turns out I was being driven to a courthouse to be officially charged with the murder of Kannika, a murder I had confessed too, so there was hundred percent no way I was going to get out of this mess.

I was taken through a side entrance to the courthouse but after being charged, now not only murder but rape too, I was escorted out the front of the building, and to my horror I was confronted by a commotion of photographers, reporters and TV cameras. Word has soon got around that a young American man had murdered and raped his girlfriend, and overnight it had become big news.

My first thought was would this be shown on American TV and would my poor family see what was happening to me? Surely, they would come and help me in my hour of need? Surely, the American embassy would help me in my hour of need? I desperately needed help from somewhere, but there was no one and nothing coming to my aid. I was transported in the back of a beaten-up old transit van with open bars, so the world and his friend could see my demise happening right here right now. I was told I was heading to Maha Chai prison where I would stay until they set a sentence date for me. There was no need for a trail as I had confessed to the crimes.

Upon arrive in Maha Chai, I was taken into a room that can only be described a blacksmiths workshop. It was a dirty room with rotten and rusty chains hanging from hooks, as you might see in some cheap horror movie, but this was no horror movie, it was real life and it was pure and simple horror in the lowest of all forms. I was ordered to sit on a battered old wooden bench and lift my legs onto a small stool. I wondered how many poor folk, had sat on this bench over the years? Plenty I assume by the state of it. A blacksmith appeared from a small cupboard in the corner of the room and proceeded to introduce me to three big thick chains and four horrible rusty buckles around my ankles and wrists that would be with me day and night for the rest of my life, so the blacksmith got off on telling me.

I guess that I had lived a relatively normal and comfortable life back home for the twenty years I had been living on earth, and maybe I was a bit naive to what goes on in the big bad world, but I had never seen so much hostility between human beings before my arrest. The police officers in Koh Samui, the officers in charge of my transfer to Bangkok, the guards in my new home Maha Chai, they all hated with me such force and anger that I dared not to talk through pure fear of another beating. It seems that it was not only humans that were angry in here, even the mosquitoes and cockroaches were hell bent on destroying anything in their path. This place breathed and bred anger, and I felt that all of it was coming my way.

The first week of my stay in Maha Chai, I was in building two, the punishment block. I guessed straight away that however long I was going to be in here and alive, that the prison authorities were going to make my life hell. I was so down, I was in so much pain, both physical and mentally. My heart was broken for my Kannika and both of our families. I honestly didn't know how much of this I could take, maybe it wouldn't be for too long as every person I met told me that I was going to die for what I had done. I was petrified of dying so far away from home, all alone, but I was also petrified of living in these conditions, maybe the latter more so, and my journey deep into hell was about to get a whole lot darker.

One morning in my second week in Maha Chai, and without warning or explanation, I was marched away from building two and told I was going to the dark room for the foreseeable future. I had no idea what the dark room was, but it didn't sound good at all, but I was too afraid to argue or question the reasons. I would soon find out why it is called the dark room though, and that is because it's exactly that, a pitch-black room with no windows. The door opened and I was thrown in, literally. I landed in a heap. The room was hot and the rotten smell invaded my senses like never before. As my eyes slowly adjusted to the darkness, all I could see was eyes, lots of eyes all looking in my direction, blinking, there must have been twenty odd men down there. I was pushed from one side to the next until I had been forced across the room and finally, I hit a wall and couldn't move any further, so I slid down the dirty wet walls to the floor. There was no talking;

just noises of grown men cramped together, and most of them were in considerable pain by the sounds of it.

As I sat as still I could, I wondered who I was in here with? What had these people done to deserve being locked up in total darkness with a room full of strangers, they must have done some unspeakable things. Were they murderers, or rapist, child killers or drug dealers, I wasn't too sure, but I knew I did not belong down there with them, but what was I to do? I had confessed to the policemen back in Koh Samui. The realization of what was happening to me began to sink in, and there was absolutely nothing I could do about it.

I wondered if my family back home knew anything yet? Surely, with all the press coverage they would know, were they here in Thailand? Were they trying to help me? Did they still love me? All I knew for sure was that my once innocent and happy life had gone, and I was now in a dungeon, deep underground, with no light and only thick dirty air to breath in. I had hit rock bottom. And the only way up from this hell, that I could see, was death.

Chapter 35

I remember watching some old war films back home when I was younger with my grandpa. The inmates in the prisoner of war camps across German occupied Europe were ordered to make every single movement by the guards, they were not allowed to move unless told so, they had to eat and wash when told so they couldn't even go to the toilet without the say, so of the German guards. That was of course during the 1940's in World War Two, but this sort of treatment for prisoners still exists to this day, as I soon found out on the first morning after one of the longest nights of my life upon arrival in the darkroom in Maha Chai.

I was pretty sure, I hadn't slept a wink. I was too scared to close my eyes. If I was awake, I could at least try and defend myself if one of the other inmates went for me, which I was sure it would only be a matter of time before I had to use some of my boxing skills. But suddenly the door that I had come flying through some hours ago flew open and startled everyone into covering their eyes to protect them from the sudden surge of light, and an awful high pitch whistle echoed through the small room and everyone sprang to life. I had no idea what was happening, so I got up and followed the other guys towards the shouting guard at the door. He seemed to be speaking a mixture of Thai and English, so I just about managed to understand that it was morning wash time. Upon exiting the darkroom, it took a while for my eyes to adjust to the extreme change in light, but when they finally did, I saw for the first time the look of absolute despair and deep misery on the faces of the other guys down there. They all looked local from what I could tell, some of them were so badly beaten they literally crawled out of the darkroom in agony and pain, but the crawling didn't last long as the rotten guards would beat them into standing up and walking. I wondered how long some of them had been down here? I wondered how long I would be down here? I wanted to help these men, but my instinct kicked in and told me that would not be a good idea.

We were first ordered to wash ourselves out of some small plastic bowls that were on the floor, but the water was so horrific, I was sure it was actually making us even dirtier than we already were. I tried to wash my hands and that was as far as I was willing to go. One of the guys next to me said something in Thai to the guards, I had no idea what he said, but I assumed it was something about not wanting to touch the disgusting water, and for his troubles the horrible guard who seemed to be in charge pulled his bamboo cane high above his head, and brought it crashing onto the augmentatives prisoners back, once, twice, three times, and on and on and every blow tore away a little piece of his already severely damaged skin, blood was splattering everywhere, until he was laying on the cold dirty floor, after a minute or so he was carried away, and I never saw him again. I stood there and watched the whole scene unfold, and I done absolutely nothing about it, the pure horror of what I was witnessing had me glued to the spot. The high-pitched whistle then blew again, and we were now ordered through to another room where breakfast was waiting for us. I waited, then took place at the table and although the look of the food made me reach in my own mouth, I still managed to get a few mouthfuls in, there was no way I was going to disobey the guards, especially after what I just witnessed.

This would be my daily routine every day for the next couple of months or so, in which time I kept my head down and done as I was told. Time, days, weeks, it all meant nothing to me now, but I guessed it had been around two months since my Kannika had been brutally taken from me, and my life had turned completely upside down. One morning out of the blue, I was told I was to leave the darkroom. That had been by far the worst couple of months of my life, but was it about to get any better? Far from it, I was told that I was being transferred to Bank Kwang prison. I was told that this would be the end of the line for me, as it was for most of the unfortunate men who get sent there. I was told that I would die all alone in one of the most feared prison on earth.

Chapter 36

I was transferred to Bank Kwang prison on the Wednesday 8th April 2014. It had been one hundred and thirty-nine days since I left home, left my family, on what was meant to be the trip of a lifetime and which turned into a living hell.

I had not spoken a word to anyone from back home since the night before I was arrested, when I called my father to tell him I was in love and to ask for some father to son advise. God, I hoped he had believed me, I hope he had not thought this to be some kind of cover up, knowing I was about to kill Kannika, surely my own family didn't think this?

The truth is, I had no idea what they were thinking. I had been allowed zero visitors and zero letters into or out of the prison. There was no way I was going to die with my friends and family back home thinking I was capable of such crimes. I knew they wouldn't, but without talking to them and knowing exactly what they knew or what they were thinking was breaking my heart every single minute that went past.

My life in Bang Kwang prison was not going to get any easier, quite the opposite in fact, at least to start with. I was taken straight to the governor's office to be told what was expected of me. I later found out the man in charge around here was called doctor death, and for good reason too.

I entered the office and doctor death was standing still and stern, looking out of an open window, a fan slowly ticking around in front of his face. He was wearing military style clothes and boots with a pair of black, aviator sun glasses. He didn't say a word at first, for what seemed like an eternity as I stood still and didn't dare move, motionless. I was in pain from head to toe, I was desperate to sit down, I was tired, I was desperate to sleep, I was lonely, and I was desperate to talk to someone. When he finally turned around and said,

'Ahhh, the American, murdering, rapist pig.'

I said nothing,

'You think you big, tough man?'

I said nothing, but inside I was trembling,

'You rape and murder young Thai girl, I own you now, I own you right up till you're very last breath, you fucking understand?'

I said nothing but gently nodded my head.

He was now right up in my face, he slowly took his sunglasses off and for the first time I saw his deep, dark, soulless eyes, I could feel his breath on my face,

'Can you not talk, you American fuck? Why you not talk? Did someone cut your fucking tongue out?' He carried on, and for the first time in months I opened my mouth to talk, I was going to say that I was innocent sir, and that I was forced into confessing, but before I had chance to open my mouth I was caught with a wicked blow to the side of the head. I didn't even see it coming, he was so close to me that I had not seen him take his right hand out of his pocket and unleash it towards my head.

I crashed down to the floor in an almighty heap, the blow took me by surprise and knocked me straight off my feet, he made his two guards who witnessed the unprovoked attack pick me and sit me on an old wooden stool in the middle of the room. I was terrified again, the last time I was lifted off a cold dirty floor and put on an old wooden stool, I was being tortured into confessing to a crime I had not committed. Surely, it was not about to happen again? He bent down as if doing a squat and said to me,

'I watch you twenty-four hours a day, I own you, I own everyone, if you step out of line just once, I will open you up from head to toe in front of every single person here.'

I said nothing,

'Do you understand me, Stone?'

I nodded, and with that he ordered me straight to the hotbox for two weeks. I had no idea what the hotbox was, but surely it couldn't have been any worse than the darkroom back in Maha Chai? But little did I know, as I was marched with my shackles clunking at my feet that I was now heading straight into the jaws of hell!

Chapter 37

The hotbox was much like the darkroom back in Maha Chai, it was small and dark, cramped and hot, it smelt of rotten sewer and it was home to some pretty desperate looking people, including myself, but the differences with the hotbox was that you never left. There was no marching us out every morning at the order of the high pitch whistle for your morning wash and to eat, you simply did not wash, which added to the already desperate conditions in there. At food time it was delivered to you, well actually sometimes it was just thrown down as if feeding time at the zoo, if you were lucky, or unlucky, whichever way you want to look at it, there may have been some food left in the serving tins by the time they landed. At least being able to leave the darkroom, albeit for a very short time, gave you something to do, something to look forward to even, to break your extreme mundane and torturous day up, to stretch your legs a little, even with these god-awful chains on, but staying in one position, pretty much day and night for weeks on end, apart from when I walked 3 metres to the hole in the floor, was by far the worse experience of being in the hotbox. One other difference with the hotbox is that as an extra punishment, the guards would sometimes open the large concrete door high up above our heads and let god's elements rain down on us, either as scorching heat, which would pick at our blistered and already broken skin. Or on the flip side, they would open the big door in torrential rain, which was by far the worse of the two extreme punishments, as within seconds you are soaked to the bone and depending on how severe the storm was, and how long it lasted you could sometime be knee deep in dirty, horrible, disgusting, brown water forcing you to stand up until it drained away, which would often take a day or two, and you were then left with a mass of dirty black slop inches thick under your body, and the smell would invade your senses, and you just couldn't escape from it. This was surely up there with some of the most horrific human living conditions in the world.

I spent a whole month in that desperate and disgusting underground pit before I was ordered out one day in the mid-afternoon heat. As the big door up above was drawn back, I wondered what was coming my way this time, but to my shock my name was called out and for the first time in a while I was soon walking, which was particularly difficult, as the only motion I had done recently was standing up and sitting down and the very short stride to the toilet. My legs were so sore and the apparently simple job of moving my legs one foot in front of the other was proving to be anything but simple. I was mid-way between the entrance and the far wall, only around 10 metres or so to walk, but it seemed to take an eternity, especially as I've still got these rotten chains on. The guard calling my name was obviously getting impatient, as he soon stormed down the stairs to meet me at the bottom on drag me up to the outside world. When we reached the top, a scene presented itself that I had not been expecting, or prepared for. There was a crowd of people all standing around trying to get a look, like a group of people trying to get a look at a celebrity or something. There were guards and inmates together, all staring at me, I tried not to look into any of their eyes, did they feel sorry for me or did they want to kill me? The latter I assumed, so I just kept my head down in an almost submissive motion and continued to do as I was told.

At the front of the mass gathering was doctor death, he calmly walked over to me, lifted my head up and said,

'You go to medic, but when you come back you are mine again, I will do what I want with you, I own you, Stone.'

I just nodded my head, too scared to talk. I was led away past the crowd and towards to medics' room, where I was to be assessed.

When I got to the medic room, I was ordered to lay on the bed, which wasn't too easy, but once I was on it was somewhat of a relief to be laying down. It had been a long time since I'd had enough room to actually lie down and stretch my legs out. The medic started to do a full examination of me. I guess him looking for any broken bones or other injuries. I was so hungry, I was in so much pain, I was so tired, and I closed my eyes and felt myself drifting off…

It was a sunny July morning in Huntingdon, New Jersey, the height of the summer, the temperature was going to be in the high 80's today, the car was packed with food and drink for the short journey down to the harbour to embark onto our beloved boat, the MAY-STONE. Mom had the weekend off from her long shifts in Huntingdon Hospital, my father was already at the harbour giving the MAY-STONE a quick clean ahead of the day. Annabelle and Yann were in the back of the car. I was up front with my mother as I called shotgun, and therefore it was my turn to navigate us to the harbour. It was only a five-minute drive, but it had become a family ritual for the lucky one of us who called shotgun first to be the side seat driver of the day and to be the navigator to get us safely down the water front. As we parked up at the harbour, my father was there to greet us with wave and a big smile us and help unload the car. Me, Annabelle and Yann would help our father with getting all the bags of goodies onto the boat whilst our mother had already boarded and was unloading the food and drink to their temporary home in the little kitchen area. Dad then completed his final checks, and we were ready for the off, we were ready for another magical day, the Stone family at their very happiest on their beloved boat.

Shortly after leaving the harbours edge, our mother would smoother us in sun cream, she loved us so much, and she would do everything she could to look after her little ones, much to our dismay at times, especially Yann, he hated sun cream time. But as soon as it was done, me and Yann would head off to the back of the boat where our father had already set up and baited three fishing rods, one for me, one for Yann and one for himself. Our father loved nothing more than fishing with his two sons. Annabelle on the other hand, had no desire to get her hands dirty with such activities, no, she was more than happy laying in the sun and reading whatever latest teen novel she was half way through. We anchored up a couple of miles downstream from where we started. The three boys were fishing, my sister was happy reading and our mother was preparing our food. This was the five of us together, doing what we loved doing — Happy Days....

I am not sure how long I was laying there for, probably not that long, but for the briefest of moments I had escaped reality for the first time in months, I felt free, but it was short lived as the medic who was treating me soon saw an end to my dreaming, with some short sharp slaps on my cheeks to bring me round. He helped me sit up and gave me some pills to take for the pain. I had no idea what he had given me but I didn't care, he told me that I would need to come back every morning and every night for a top up of the pills.

As we left the medics room, I was told by a new guard who was now escorting me that I was not going back to the Hotbox, at least not yet, but I would instead go to a single cell in the punishment blocks. He seemed nice, almost like he felt sorry for me, but I still didn't trust him so I kept quiet and done as I was told. He went on to tell me that the medic had told doctor death that I was not to go back in the hotbox, not at least for a few weeks or so until I was looking a bit better, and that for my own good, I should be put in a cell all by myself, which I was more than happy with.

After the guard has escorted me to my new cell, I gave him a thankful smile and crawled on in. The cell, or cage, was barely big enough for one person, but I could lie down, so it was an almighty upgrade from the hot box. There was an old straw mat in there that I managed to roll up to use as a pillow. I had no idea what time or day it was, but I didn't really care, the pain killers were kicking in and for the first time in months I was chilled and relaxed. So I decided to lie down and close my eyes again. In some ways I wished that my exhausted mind would give up and my tired eyes would never ever open again.

Chapter 38

Everything in prison works like clockwork. In Maha Chai, it was the whistle at the exact same time of day which started wash and feeding time, day in day out, the exact same routine. In the hotbox, the guards would pull back the big concrete door at the same time every day, twice a day, to deliver our food. Now I had a new routine, which was slightly better than my previous two. I was to be escorted from my cell at 6.30am every morning, before the other inmates, this was due to my own projection apparently, but I didn't mind too much. I was led into the wash room, had a quick rinse down with a fresh batch of dirty water. I was then taken to the eating area, where I had five minutes to eat whatever mixture of red rice, some kind of brown liquid, and a glass a water before I was escorted to the medics' room to pick up my next dose of pills, but this time I had two daily walks, which I had not had so far as I also needed my evening supply of drugs, before being taken back to my cell at 6pm for another lonely night in the punishment block.

As much as I like being alone, my health soon started to take a serious turn, and I quickly became very unwell. I had contracted phenomena in the hotbox and the symptoms were terrible. I started to lose all sense of reality. One minute I was sweating buckets, and the next I was shivering to the bone. I am not sure if it was the drugs or not, but I soon started hallucinating. I would see terrifying black shadows weaving in and out of my cell like a flying silent devil. Or maybe I wasn't hallucinating; there was so much death in this place that I could be haunted by past occupants of these evil cells. Sometimes I would come round, and I was standing up in the cell, and I had no idea how I had got there, or how long I had been standing for. I was losing my grip on reality, and something I struggled to tell the difference between was sleep and reality. I was living in a real-time nightmare, so I didn't really see the difference between the two. Sometimes I wouldn't even remember going to see the medic, that was until the drugs would kick in and I would relax somewhat. I still had no idea what I was taking, but I really didn't care.

Other times I would come around from whatever lost trance I had been in and doctor death would be standing at the entrance to my cell, tapping his knuckle duster on the bars and saying this like,

'I miss you, Stone,' before walking off laughing.

I am not a violent man, but I was once a strong young man who could look after myself in a boxing ring. If only I could be giving the change to go one on one with that despicable man, he could even bring his knuckle duster along if he wanted, but I would still put him down, not only for the way he treats me, but the way he treats everyone in this place. I was sure that one day he would meet his match, and I hoped it would be sooner rather than later.

During these terrible times I would often wonder what my family was up to? Had they giving up on me for the awful crimes I had confessed to? Or did they deep down know that their little boy was not capable of such acts on violence? I truly hoped the latter, but I had no way of knowing, so one day on one of my morning trips to pick up my daily supply of drugs,

I spotted a small pencil, the type your dad would have in his golf bag to keep his scored card topped up on his Sunday morning round. I casually slipped in into pants, and on my next visit I will try to find some paper. I needed to write a letter home to my family. I had no idea at this stage how I was going to get it out of the prison, but I would figure something out, for now I just need to get the letter written and to keep it hidden from the guards. If they found it that would be the end for me and my family will never know the truth of what happened back in Koh Samui. I was tempted, of course, to sharpen the pencil as much as I could, lay in wait for when the evil doctor shows his miserable face at my cell bars and jump out of the shadows to plunge the pencil deep into his eye, oh yes that was tempting, but I need to at least try and get this letter to my family, maybe when I was finished, I could dispose of the pencil in his eye, just maybe.

I kept the pencil on me day and night. At first, I hid it in my pants but it moved around too much, and I was scared of losing it, so I then decided the hide in my rectum, I had no other choice. I now needed some paper.

I got lucky, for the first time in what seemed like a lifetime, as the next time I was in the medics' room I noticed a small notepad right next to where the medic kept his sample tubes. Perfect, I managed to rip a few pieces of paper from the pad whilst the medic and guards were chatting, I forced them down my pants along with a sample tube, which would keep the letters dry whilst inserted inside me. It was not going to be pleasant but if it meant my family knowing of my innocence, then I was more than happy to go through with it.

The problem I soon realized was that every time I went to the toilet, I had to retrieve the tube from hole in the floor in amongst not only my shit but half of the residents of Bang Kwang. I tried to clean it every time as best I could, as I was sure I would contact every disease going by entering it back inside me, but to be honest, I was going to die so I didn't really care either way, perhaps it would bring death to me quicker.

Chapter 39
Sentencing

I'd had some pretty dark days in the last year, but none more so than my day of sentencing. I was so poorly, both physically and mentally. I think the pneumonia had cleared up, but I had severe malnutrition from the lack of a good meal since God knows when. I must have lost around four or five stone, I was literally half the man I used to be. I am sure my family wouldn't even recognise me any more. My hair had grown, and my face was a mess with stubble and scars.

I was woken by a guard one morning and told to get up and smarten myself up, as today I would be going to the courthouse for sentencing. I started to panic, I couldn't control my breathing, I was sick on the floor, but the guard insisted I move quickly, for my own good, he whispered in my ear as he helped me up.

I was taken to a room I had never seen before and was ordered to sit on a chair in the middle of the room. I was soon joined by another Thai man, who without introduction pulled a hair brush and a pair of scissors from his bag and proceeded to start trying to tidy me up for my big day.

Once he trimmed my hair and slicked it back with some gel, he started to give me a wet shave with a cut throat razor, the type your grandad once had. I was again tempted to free him of his tool and start swinging aimlessly at any one who got in my way, but I just didn't have the energy for it. After finishing my shave, I was stripped down and for the first time in nearly a year, these god-forsaken chains were removed from my ankles, it was such a relief to have those things off me. I was sure it wouldn't be for too long, but it was a welcome brake all the same. Once I was stripped naked, I suddenly remembered the little packet in my rectum, I had almost finished the letter and there was no way I was going to lose it now, so I clinched them cheeks as hard as I could and prayed they would do an internal search of me, like they did on my arrival, which thank god they didn't. There was a large tin bucket, big enough to bath a small child in, on one side of the room which had the nicest cleanest water in that I had seen for a very long time, I was ordered to use the water to wash myself, which again was such a nice feeling to place some clean cold water on my face, a procedure I had taken for granted thousands of times in my life, and only now did I fully appreciate what clean water meant and felt like. After washing, I was ordered to get dressed in some black jeans and a plain white shirt that was sitting on the table waiting for me.

I was then escorted by four guards towards the entrance of the prison. Walking without my shackles on was almost a joy, until I saw the beaten-up old van that I had been delivered to Bank Kwang in some months back. I was placed in the back of the van on a wooden bench with one guard either side of me and two sitting opposite me on another bench. The back of van was open, but with a cage over the top to stop anyone getting out, or in. As the big iron gates opened at the entrance of the prison grounds, I saw two police cars. Upon leaving the gates both of the police cars sounded their sirens, one pulled off in front and the other one was to follow in behind, I couldn't help but think did they really need all this fuss just for me? What was I going to do anyway? With no outside contact, and the fact that only an hour ago I didn't even know this was happening, I could hardly have plotted an escape plan.

For the last couple of months, I had been in isolation, pretty much twenty-three hours a day, with very little movement, but I now found myself travelling at what I thought was a pretty high speed through the intense streets of Bangkok. It was terrifying. I held onto the wooden seat with every bit of muscle I could muster up, it was like the sensation of being on a rollercoaster. The streets were busy, people were looking at me. I was so paranoid that every single person in Thailand wanted me dead that I couldn't look in any direction but down at my feet, I closed my eyes tight.

We suddenly screeched to a halt, and I instinctively lifted my head to see where we were, and the first thing I saw was a mass of people and flashing cameras, storming their way towards the old van. There was shouting from every one of them, some looked foreign, American or British, I wasn't sure as it was hard to tell with all the noise, some were local, but one thing they shared in common was their desire to get the best picture possible, and perhaps a few words for the cameras.

I was terrified.

The four guards opened the back of the van and escorted me through the baying crowd. Some people without cameras were trying to get to me, objects we're flying through the sky, I think they were being aimed at me. I kept my head down and wished it would all go away. I really was a hated man, and my story was big news, bigger than I thought it would be. There seemed to be cameras and people from all over the world, were my family here, I wondered, in the melee, I hoped not.

On one hand I would have done anything to see my

family. I could shout to them that I didn't do it, and perhaps that would be enough for the authorities to re-open the case, but on the other hand I did not want my family to see me in this terrible state. I was not a well man, and I looked awful. I actually now looked like a man capable of committing the horrible crimes I had confessed to. Oh, why did I confess? I had to, I had very little choice, I could not have handled any more of the punishment they were dishing out to me, but maybe they would have stopped in the end and believed me? I guess I will never know.

Finally, after what seemed like an entirety, we were off the streets, and I was being ushered through to my designated courtroom where I would be sentenced. As we entered the room, I was expecting to see more people, I was expecting to see some journalists, maybe some more Thai authorities, maybe even my family, but all I saw was my lawyer who I hadn't seen heard a word from since being charged for rape and murder, great lawyer. The room went quiet; it was just me, my lawyer and the four guards who had escorted me from Bang Kwang.

A door to the left sprung open, and a Thai official entered the room, shortly followed by a judge. I was made to stand until the judge sat down. He was presented with some papers and documents from his colleague. The judge took his time looking through the papers, evidence I assumed. Before asking me to stand and prepare myself for sentencing.

My heart skipped a beat, I started sweating, I was petrified of what words were about to come out of the judge's mouth. Perhaps, just perhaps some new evidence had surfaced and they would re-open the case? Perhaps that horrible American man who actually done this has come forward. Perhaps, the

American embassy had asked for a trial? All this was of course my last ditch and desperate attempt to try and somehow reassure myself that my life was still worth living, that my life as it once was, was now over and for whatever remained in my life, I would be living a real-life nightmare.

Then, in his broken English I heard the following words...

Mr Stone, you have shown no remorse or compassion and have given no explanation to the crimes you committed on Kannika Devakul in Koh Samui on the morning of 1st January 2014, so I therefore sentence you to death by firing squad in Bang Kwang prison on date that will soon be set for you...

Chapter 40

The words didn't seem to make any sense to me. I was in shock, pure shock to my core, I couldn't move. I had been repeatedly told that I was going to die in prison for what I had done but honestly, I just thought they were trying to scare me and break me as much as they could, how naive was I?

My lawyer, a complete waste of time he was, just turned to me and simply said, 'Sorry, Mr Stone,' before gathering his papers and disappearing out of the room quicker than he had entered. The four guards, two on each side, started escorting me out of the courtroom again. I still didn't speak, I still didn't lift my head. They were marching me back toward the exit of the courthouse that I had entered around 20 minutes ago. I could see day light up ahead, out of that door was freedom, perhaps I could make a run for it and disappear into the wilderness of Thailand and never be seen again. But when the door flew open the mass of bodies rushed in my direction again, one of the guards told me to keep my head down, and we would soon be back in the van. The noise was deafening, people were shouting and screaming in my direction. The hatred towards me was terrifying. I had gone from a young, curious and ambitious American man travelling the world in the hope of finding love and peace to Thailand's public energy number 1 overnight. Bottles and other objects were hitting me from every angle. The guards, and now some police officers, battled with the crowds, and I was soon in the back of the van again. As I took my seat on the old wooden bench, heart pounding, an American voice caught my attention from outside of the bars at the back of the van,

'Mason,' shouted the female voice,

'Mason, why did you do it, Mason?' the voice was repeating, and I turned around to see a young American reporter with a microphone in her hand accompanied by her camera man. The van fired up its old engine, this was my opportunity to say something, would this be the newsfeed my family would see, I was just about to the say something, when the van screeched away. I tried to stand up and look back at the camera but the two guards either side sat me down as quick as I stood. I tried to turn my head whilst sitting, was she still there? Would she hear me if I shouted, but it was no good, we shot off and within seconds we were well out of sight from all the cameras. I sank back into my chair, put my head in my hands, and prayed for forgiveness for what I have put my dear beloved family through.

Chapter 41

I don't remember any of the journey back to Bang Kwang prison, my head was in a desperately sad state, it was official, I was going to be killed for the crimes I had been tortured into confessing, trying to get my head around this injustice was mind blowing. I just couldn't believe this was happening to me, maybe I had done something in my previous life to deserve this? Maybe it was somehow my fault!

I was ordered out of the van and marched straight back to the room where I'd had a haircut and a wash before setting off to the courthouse. My old dirty overalls were still where I left them. I was told to get undressed, and put the overalls back on, and wait for the blacksmith to come, and put my awful chains back on. I sat in silence, I didn't move, I didn't dare, and I had nowhere to go and nothing to do, I miss my family so much.

The locksmith turned up shortly after and reunited me with my chains. When he was finished, the next person I saw walk through the door was the evil dictator Doctor Death. He walked into the room slowly but authoritatively, at first, he didn't say anything, he didn't even look at me, he actually made an effort to stand in front of me, but looking the other way, for what seemed like an unusual amount of time, showing his strength and power over me I assumed. I could have easily wrapped my wrist chains around his scrawny neck and strangled the miserable life out of him, what did I have to lose after all? I would maybe become some kind of cult hero in the prison, and my time left on planet earth could maybe be a little easier, but I didn't. Instead, I sat patiently and waited for him to make the first move, I was sure he wanted me to say something, but there was no way I was going to.

I listened carefully as I could hear a quite noise coming from him, I soon realized he was starting to laugh, ever so quietly at first, but it soon became quicker and louder, but he still didn't look at me, he was mocking me by laughing at me, but facing the other direction. I thought this was a bit strange, but then again, this man clearly wasn't hundred percent human. Some of the things I had seen him do were so inhuman, that a normal man could simply not do, to other living, breathing people.

The laughing went on for 2, maybe 3 minutes, there was no one else in the room. The laughing finally started to slow, as it had sped up a few minutes ago, it slowed to a stop. He then slowly turned around, so he was standing over me whilst I was sitting down on the chair. He took his sun glasses off to reveal his deep and troubled dark eyes, he bent down so his eyes were level with mine and said,

'I now hundred own you till your very last breath, Stone.'

His breath stunk horrible; I was so tempted to spit in his face. He went on,

'Prepare yourself for a one-way trip to hell, you will not return, not ever.'

He paused and stood up, never once taking his gaze off me, I stared back at him, I would not be blindsided by this horrible man again,

'Do you understand you Rapist pig?'

I nodded, I wasn't prepared to talk to him, not now and not ever, that is one fight he will never win against me.

'Good,' he snapped as he rubbed his hands together and

called out for one of his guards. I wasn't sure what he said, but within seconds the guard was standing at the door and ready for his next order.

'Please escort, Mr Stone to the hot box where he will stay until I see fit, oh and spread the news that he will die here soon, the way we do with all of the other death row scum,' was the next order.

The guard then proceeded to tie a piece of rope around my neck and dragged me off in the direction of the yard whilst shouting at the top of his voice,

'Death row to the American rapist, Death row to the American rapist,' on and on, and on he kept shouting.

I kept losing my balance; he was pulling me faster that my shackled legs could move. Crowds were gathering, doctor death appeared and started leading this cruel ritual. Everyone knew that I was now officially sentenced to death, and I would never again leave these grounds. Doctor death seemed in his element, he soon started shouting in Thai at the locals. I couldn't understand what he was saying but the excitement grew, the excitement grew from his voice and the excitement grew from the locals, and they soon started throwing objects at me. I couldn't see what they were throwing as I closed my eyes, and put my head down, some objects were dry and hard, they were hitting me from every direction, some were soft and wet, I had no idea what they were but from the terrible stench I could of guessed. I kept my head down. I couldn't be too sure, but I think they were walking me around in a large circle, like parading an animal at the zoo, but much crueller and degrading. I kept my eyes shut. I didn't want to look at anyone, especially doctor death, I suddenly regretted not strangling him with my chains when I had the chance back there. If I get the chance again, I will take it for sure, if I had the strength that was.

The crowds and commotion soon slowed down, and I was stopped and ordered to stand still. I had my eyes closed tight, I was shaking, was it coming now? Was this my end? I was waiting for the bullet, almost praying for it. I could smell his horrible breath right in front of my face again,

'Open your eyes, Stone,' ordered the doctor.

There was no way I was going to do as he said. I was sure this was a bad idea, but it was the only power I had left. I stood strong and kept my eyes closed tight, shaking.

'Fine,' he said, I then heard the unmistakable sound of the large concrete door of the hot box being pulled back by the guards. I knew what was happening, and where I was heading but I stood strong.

I then received a sudden wicked blow to the stomach, all the wind and air rushed from my lungs, and I instinctively leant forward, and was then all in one motion pushed backwards down the entrance and in to the hot box, I was sent tumbling head over heels, chains rattling, I kept my eyes shut, within a few brief seconds I smashed into the floor at the bottom of the steps. I kept my eyes shut. The large concrete door up above me slowly closed; although I had my eyes shut, I could see the natural day light disappearing up above before my life ascended into darkness once again. I shuffled in my spot to try and sit up straight and slowly opened my eyes, it took a few moments for my tired eyes to adjust to the darkness, but when they did, I could see the dark silhouettes of around twenty other men, not one of them seemed bothered by the commotion of my entrance, maybe they were too broken and battered to care about me, which was fine. I settled down to try and gather my thoughts and to get as comfortable as possible, as I was pretty dam sure I wasn't going anywhere, anytime soon.

Chapter 42
4 weeks later

The first time I met Archie Parker was the moment that my life took a slightly different turn. I hadn't spoken a word to anyone for as long as I could remember as I was too scared to open my mouth to talk, but shortly after being released from the box around four weeks after my sentencing, Archie approached me and asked in his strong cockney ancient 'hey man, how's it going.' my initial thought was, how the hell do I look man? I am sure he approached me out of sympathy, and although at first, I didn't show any sign of wanting to talk to him, deep down I was desperate to talk to someone, my heart was broken from the loss of my girlfriend and the injustice of being sentenced to death for her rape and murder, but I just wasn't ready to talk to anyone. What happened next though did change my prison life, not much, but slightly for the better.

For his polite efforts, Archie got us both thrown back in the hot box for another two weeks. During our time together down there, I slowly started to trust Archie Parker from London. I am not sure why he wanted to talk to me, no one else did, I was public enemy number 1 in Thailand. Perhaps he saw through all that and felt sorry for me as a man, perhaps he was lonely and wanted to speak to another westerner, perhaps all of the above, I didn't really know but I was desperate to talk to someone. At first, we spoke very briefly, he said sorry for landing me back in the box and introduced himself, but at that stage I was still deep in shock to how my life had spiralled out of control. Archie was very patient with me, time is one thing you have in Prison, even more so in the infamous hot box as there was nowhere to go and nothing to do.

Since being tortured into confessing to the rape and murder of my Kannika, I hadn't spoken a word to anyone, not one word, I didn't know what to say to be honest, I wanted to scream from the top of my lungs that I did not commit these horrible crimes, but I was so terribly scared after what the officers had done to me on Koh Samui that I just didn't dare talk, but soon I started to trust Archie Parker and after four or five days together I open my mouth and spoke my first words for the first time in months, and I told him that I had not done what they accused me of. I saw the look in his eyes, the look of pure shock and horror, for some reason he believed me straight away, if only the Thai authorities had believed me, I would be a free man now. He didn't ask me any more questions at that stage, perhaps he was too shocked with what I had told him, or perhaps he just couldn't find the right words to say to me.

As our time went by in the hot box, I slowly started to open up more and more and Archie took me under his wing, he forced me to eat some food, if you can call it food that is, he told me that I needed to keep my strength up for when we get out of the box.

On our last day in the box, Archie finally asked me what happened, what happened all those months ago for me to end up here, on death row, in this hell hole. I had built up an undisputed trust by now with Archie so at this time I decided to tell him my story, from the beginning to the now. I don't think he was mentally prepared for what I was about to tell him, he sat back and listened intently to every word I said, and at the end of my story he broke down and cried like I had never seen a man cry before.

Chapter 43

On what was meant to be our last day in the hot box, I was numb from what Mason hold told me the previous night. He completely opened up and told me his story from his happy life back home right up till the moment we met. I thought my story was tragic, I thought I'd had it bad the last couple of years, but Mason Stone had been through more punishment and heartbreak in the last year or so than any man will ever deserve to go through in a lifetime. At least I still had a family who I could talk to, friends I could write to, a loving girlfriend who against all odds will still be waiting for me when I get home, but Mason had nothing, he wasn't going home, he would never see his family again, and his bird was dead, murdered by a fucking pig who just simply walked away into the early morning sunrise as if nothing happened. I had no idea what to say to the poor kid, there really was nothing I could say to him, the Thai authorities wouldn't listen to me, I would probably just take another beating for trying to help their public energy number 1, but I didn't really care about what would happen to me right now, I just had to try and help him, I wasn't sure how, but I needed to think of something.

One morning the guards opened the big concrete slab up above us, as they did every day, but this time they called out my name, followed by a couple of the Thai prisoners and ordered us out of the box,

'C'mon mate, it's time to go and work out what we're

going to do,' I said to Mason as I offered him a hand up. We started to walk up the wet and dirty stairs behind the Thai prisoners. I was in-front and Mason was just a few steps behind me when one of the guards stopped us with his baton and said,

'Just you Parker, he stays for longer.'

'No fucking way, he is coming with me, look at the fucking state of him, he needs to see a medic,' I screamed at the guard and with that he dragged me out of the hole in the ground and threw me to one side whilst another guard appeared from behind and kicked Mason in the chest and sent him tumbling back down to hell and within seconds more of the guards dragged the door closed,

'Let him out you fucking dogs, he is dying down there.'

'He died in Bang Kwang you English fuck,' he screamed back and began severing me up a brutal beating along with a couple of his mates before they dragged me off to one of the other punishment blocks, where I was left battered and bleeding in a heap on the floor.

I was woken up by one of the guards called Punyaa sometime later with a bowl of food. I liked this particular guard, as he seemed to want to help people rather than kicking the fuck out of them.

'Punyaa, help me man,' I begged.

'What can I do, Archie?'

'The American, the one they say raped and killed his girlfriend, he didn't fucking do it man, he honestly didn't,' I tried to explain to him.

'But he caught doing it Archie, the police caught him with that poor young girl in his hands.'

'He found her like that, he was set up by another American

he'd met.'

'Even if true, Archie' he went on, 'What can I do about it?'

'I need to get a letter out of here, can you help me out man?'

'I don't know my friend, let me think about it, if they catch me, they kill me,' Punyaa said,

'I will pay you, you know I will, you know I have money',

'Ok, let me think about it, I come back to you,'

'Thanks man, appreciate it, and I will make it worth it for you,' I told Punyaa.

At this stage I didn't actually know who I was going to write a letter too, but this was the only hope of helping my friend out, fuck I hope he is OK down there by himself?

The next morning, I was woken up by Doctor Death tapping his knuckle duster on the bars of my new cell in the punishment block. That's one scary motherfucker to see first thing in the morning, and I was pretty sure I was in for a shit day if it started like this,

'Wakey, wakey, Parker. Wakey, wakey,' he kept saying.

What the fuck did this knob head want from me at this time of the morning? Was it even morning? I didn't know and I didn't really care to be honest,

'What do you want?' I snapped.

'Why you friend with American rapist?'

'He didn't fucking do it, look at him, does he look capable of doing that to someone?'

'Ha, ha, ha, ha,' he laughed with a sadistic laugh that only a mad man can carry,

'No one in here is guilty, but I own every fucking one of you,' his voice getting lower and more authoritative, 'I fucking own you all, and you all do as I say, two weeks in punishment with no letters, visitors or phone calls, just you down here with the rats and cockroaches,' and with that he stormed off and the punishment door was slammed shut, there was no windows, it was hot and humid and stunk of shit and piss and my cell was only just big enough for one person. In some ways it was worse than the hot box, but in many other ways it better. I settled down to think about how I could help Mason Stone. I just prayed that Punyaa would come good for me.

Over the course of the next couple of days, my health took a seriously nose dive, both mentally and physically. I was struggling to deal with the injustice that my friend was going through, and I left the box with severe dehydration and pneumonia, not a good combination, trust me.

When I came round one morning, my breakfast of slop had been delivered whilst I slept and under the bowl was a piece of paper and a small pencil, Punyaa, you legend. I started to write my letter which I had decided I was going to send to my parents, this was my only hope of getting a letter to the American embassy, as I guessed this would be the best place to start.

'Mum and Dad,

Sorry I haven't been in touch recently, but I just wanted to let you know I am still alive and doing OK, but I need your help.

I am not sure if the news had reached the UK about the young American chap who raped and murdered his Thai girlfriend, but he is in here with me, and he did not commit those terrible crimes that they say he done, he was set up.

I have got to know him well recently, and he told me

everything that happened and I believe him, the Thai authorities would not believe his story, but long story short; Mason and his girlfriend were attacked in the middle of the night in their beach hut in Koh Samui, and the man who done it was long gone by the time the police turned up and found Mason Stone trying to save her life. They arrested him on the spot and tortured him into confessing, and he is now on death row. They have not let him have any visitors or send any letters or make any phone calls, the treatment of him has been barbaric, but I need to try and help him. He is a desperately sad, lonely and a very poorly young man!

I am also on a letter and visitor ban, but one of the guards is helping me out a little bit. Please, can you get in touch with the American embassy, or Mason's family and get word of his innocence out there, I am begging you for help on this?

I love and miss you all dearly,

Archie xxx.'

I wrote the letter and hid it in my clothes until I next saw Punyaa. This was now my darkest hour in prison. I was not well, but writing this letter gave me a little bit of hope, hope that I could help my friend. God, I hope he is OK!

Chapter 44

Punyaa grew up and lived in one of the suburbs near to Bang Kwang prison. He was twenty-three years old and had his whole life ahead of him. His uncle had also worked in the prison, and had got him a job there shortly after his father had died of a heart attack a year or so earlier. His father had been a poor man for many years with heart conditions and numerous other illnesses. Punyaa was his carer whilst his mother was out working all hours of the day with two different jobs, so she could feed and clothe her little family, but when his father passed away, he decided it was time to get a job so he could help his mother, and so his uncle got him the job in Bang Kwang Prison.

It came naturally to Punyaa to look after people, he had done it at home for so long that it became second nature, and this was to be no different in the prison grounds. Everyone liked him, the inmates and guards alike. Although he wasn't violent like most of the guards, they still liked and respected him. Some people took advantage of his good nature, but he didn't mind, he was there to help, and when inmate Archie Parker reached out to him, he was more than willing to oblige, it was risky, but he only ever saw the good in people, and he'd always help if he could.

Punyaa didn't work the punishment blocks, as he was regarded not strong enough to do so, but he did have access down there and would often go and visit the helpless and desperate folks in the depths of hell. The inmates liked his visits as they would often go for days without talking to anyone, any little bit of conversation would lift the spirits of those in punishment blocks, even if just for while. After he left the paper and pencil for Archie Parker, he would go back in a few days and check on him.

'Archie, my friend, how you doing?'

'Not too good man, but hey Punyaa, thank you so much for the pen and paper. I have wrote the letter and the address you need to send this to in on the back, can you send this out ASAP?'

'I send letter for you, no worries my friend, I be careful, don't worry.'

'Thank you, from the bottom of my heart, thank you, and I will sort you out as a thank you when I get out of here, I promise,' Archie said to Punyaa.

And on that Punyaa took Archies letter, stuffed it in his pocket and carried on doing the rounds with the other inmates.

As Punyaa was about to clock off after another long day at work in Bang Kwang prison, one of the blueboys approached him and said a few of them had been invited to Doctor Deaths office to have a drink as a thank you for all their hard work. Punyaa thought this as a little strange as he'd never heard of this happening before, but he always saw the good in people so he assumed the miserable bastard had had a change of heart.

As Punyaa and one of the blueboys were heading in the direction of the office the blueboy said,

'Just quickly come in here Punyaa, I want to show you something, it's a little surprise'

And led him through a closed door in the main building,

as they entered the room, he was greeted by the sight of Doctor Death standing in the middle with four other blueboys,

'Ahh, Punyaa, my friend, come in, close the door, we need to chat,' said Doctor Death as one of the blueboys slammed the door shut,

'Now, what have you been talking to Parker about?'

'Oh, you know boss, I checked if they OK, and if they want to talk.'

'Hmmm, so what did he hand you and you put in your pocket earlier today?'

'Oh, nothing boss, really nothing.'

'Empty your fucking pockets, now,' but Punyaa refused to do so, he was getting worried, he knew full well what this horrible man was capable of,

'Search him now, strip off all of his clothes' order Doctor Death,

The blueboys done as they were told without hesitation, they would never disobey him, and they wrestled Punyaa to ground, ripped off all of his clothes and left him laying naked on the floor. Doctor death searched the poor man's pockets and pulled out a piece of paper and proceeded to read the letter Archie Parker had written,

'You silly boy Punyaa,' laughed the Doctor and pulled out his beloved knuckle duster from his pocket and without warning he started smashing Punyaa in the face with fast wicked sharp blows, Punyaa was screaming for help and begging him to stop, his face instantly opened up, blood was sputtering everywhere, he finally stopped and with Punyaa barley moving on the floor, he ordered the blueboys to finish him off, they pulled out there batons and mercifully beat the poor man to death then and there on the cold concrete floor!

When the attack was over, Doctor Death ordered the blueboys to carry his limp body out into the yard as a show of strength and to send a message, once again, that if you fuck with Doctor Death this is what will happen to you. They would then alert the authorities and say they found him like that after a few of the lifers had attacked him out of the blue and left him for dead in the yard. Fucking savages!

Chapter 45

Pneumonia had settled in once again, one minute I sweating buckets and the other I had the chills, I am sure there is no good place to have pneumonia, but solidarity confident in a Thai prison must be one of the worse places to contract this horrible infection. I was coughing up phlegm and other rank shit that I didn't even know the human body could make. I had fever, and I struggled breathing. I couldn't eat properly due to swelling in my mouth from the dehydration, all this together, and I was in a pretty dark place. The medic would visit me once a day, usually in the afternoon, I think. He would give me some tablets to take, I didn't know what the fuck he was giving me, but to be honest I didn't really give a shit. I was desperate so I would have taken anything.

After a couple of days, I hadn't seen or heard from Punyaa, I thought this was strange as he usually done his daily walks to check on the inmates in the punishment blocks, maybe he had a few days off? Was he OK? Had he managed to post my letter? Was word finally on the way to getting Mason a fair trial?

I wasn't sure what day it was, or how long I had been down there, or even how long ago it was that I gave Punyaa my letter, but one morning shortly after breakfast was served for another day in paradise, I looked up to see Doctor Death of all people looking through my cell bars again.

'Tell me Parker, why you think you could get one over

me?'

'What you talking about man? I'm not in the mood for your mind games.' It was risky talking to Doctor Death in such a way but fuck him, I was too ill and tired for his shit.

'Have you not learnt by now, this my prison, I have eyes and ears everywhere, nothing gets past me, I fucking own every single person in here,' 'EVERY SINGLE PERSON,' he said through gritted teeth, he then pulled a piece of paper out of his pocket,

'Do you recognize this?'

'What the fuck, man?' I sprang into life,

The piece of paper in question was the letter I had wrote to my family asking for their help, and it was covered in what looked like blood,

'Your friend, Punyaa, he silly boy and now he pay for helping you'

'WHAT THE FUCK HAVE YOU DONE?' I yelled at him through the cage,

'You not see Punyaa again, Punyaa is weak and pay for what he done'

And with that I lost it, I managed to grab doctor death by his scrawny little neck through the bars, and I swear for the briefest on moments I found an inner strength I never knew I had, and I actually lifted him off the ground,

'DIE YOU FUCKING BASTARD,' I screamed in his face and with that two more guards appeared from nowhere, stormed my cell and started kicking the fuck out of me, the last thing I remember was the two of them picking me up and Doctor Death looked me straight in the face and said,

'Punyaa now dead, and your friend Stone join him soon,' then it was lights out after he struck me in the temple with his fucking knuckleduster, and I was left in a heap on the floor, maybe left for dead for all they cared.

I came round a few days later in the medics' room where I was told that I have severe concussion, and I had been on drip to try and help the dehydration and pneumonia. The medic tried to tell me that I was lucky to be alive, but as soon as I came around, I would be sent straight back to the punishment cells, and still no communication with outside world. I asked him to help me and tell the guards I was simply to poorly to go back down there, but he said it was more than his job and life was worth to help me, and after what happened to Punyaa, I wasn't going to beg him, I had seen enough death and depression for one life time so I just accepted it.

Chapter 46

Since arriving in Bang Kwang, Mason Stone had a price on his head, he was a target for the Locals and guards alike, they look at Rape and Murder as the ultimate crime and he had to be punished by death, whether it be by execution in the prison by lethal injection, or the firing squad, or by being beaten to death.

He was a category A prisoner, and the only reason we ever met was due to being thrown in the box together, and this is where I learn the true horror of how he ended up here.

The last day in the box Mason opened up to me, he told everything, everything about his happy family life back home, he told me of the family boat called the MAY-STONE which they sailed around Huntingdon Lake in endless happy and carefree summers as children and into their teens, he told me of his Brother and Sister and of course his parents, he told me of his dream to travel which ultimately lead him on to meeting the love of his life, he told me of this Love, the young and beautiful Kannika, he told me how they fell head over heels in love with each other in the short time they shared. He then told me what happened the night Lars Baron confronted them on the beach and how he bravely fought them off, and that his last memory of the night was seeing a dark shadow figure running at him in his bed in the middle of the night. The next thing he knew he came around and found Kannika dead in the bathroom. He told me of being arrested and tortured into confessing to the crime which made my stomach churn. Did this shit really happen in modern times? This is barbaric, it angered me, he then told me of how he was sent to Maha Chai prison to await being charged and then moved on to the infamous Bang Kwang prison to await sentencing, where he was going to be sentenced to death. All of this and he was not allowed any contact with family and friends outside of the prison.

I mean, fuck me, you couldn't make this shit up. I had to help him somehow, I am not sure what I could do, but I was going to give it a damn good go. Mason asked me not to get involved as he didn't want to see any harm come to me, but there was no way I was going to let this poor kid die without a fight!

The medic on duty was called Rama. I had seen Rama a few times over the years and although he couldn't speak much English, he always seemed nice, by nice I mean that he smiled a lot, which around here was uncommon, so it stuck with me. My guilt for what happened to Punyaa forced me not to ask Rama for any more help, but shortly before the guards turned up to take me back to my cell he opened my hand, slipped some extra pills in and closed my hand tight before sending me on my way with an extra smile. It wasn't until I got back to my cell and opened my hand, I realized that he had given me about twenty extra pills. To this day, I am not sure if he gave me the pills simply as extra pain killers, or did he slip me the pills so I could top myself and end my hell? Either way I appreciated his gesture, but there was no way I was going to top myself and die in a dirty Thai prison, no fucking way, I needed to help my friend, or if I couldn't help him, I needed to speak to his family, and one day I will do just that.

Chapter 47

I hadn't seen Mason for two weeks now. I had been beaten, starved, I had pneumonia and dehydration, but since the kick in by the guards, I had been given extra food and water so I was slowly pulling myself together. Sometime during my third week in Punishment, I was disturbed by some commotion coming from in the corridor. I looked up to see what was going on as not much happened down there, to see the door come flying open and in stormed Doctor Death and his merry men, 'oh here we go again,' I thought, but I could hear these harrowing screams coming from behind them, and I soon realized they were dragging someone by their feet, their head bouncing along the floor like a football, they suddenly stopped outside my cell and Doctor Death looked me in the eye and said,

'You like American Rapist so much, you look after him.'

It was then I realized it was Mason they had dragged in like a hunters kill, he was withering in agony, and I'm sure he didn't really know where he was. The guards opened up my cell and dragged Mason through the open door,

'Careful, watch his head you fucking dogs,' I shouted, when one of them gave me a wicked backhander for good measure,

'He your problem now, Parker, but he die soon,' The sadistic bastard laughed and they all left the room.

'Mason,' I lightly tapped his face, 'Can you hear me,

man?' He slightly opened his eyes and tried to talk but not much came out,

'Mason, take a few of these Pills mate with some water, they will help, I promise.'

It took a while but I managed to get him to swallow a couple of the tablets, he was in so much pain. I would help him as much as possible, and right now all I could think of to do was lay down and cuddle him whilst stroking this hair and whispering to him that everything would be OK, as you would to a child who was poorly. I knew everything was not going to be OK, but I also knew that Mason Stone right now just needed some love and comfort, and that I could help him with. I even felt his arms tighten a little around me, maybe so he could imagine I was his mother and father for a brief time.

The cell was barley big enough for one person, let alone two grown men, but over the course of the next few days, I let Mason lay down in as much space as he could whilst I sat at one end of the cell. Behind all the scares and bruising, I could see that he was once a good-looking chap. He was far too young to be here, he should be living his life up somewhere out in the world as a free man, this made my blood boil, but there was fuck all I could do about that, so I put the little energy I had into nursing him better. I tried to water him, feed him, kept him topped up with pain killers and even tried to give the fella a little clean.

Trying to sleep sitting upright on a cold and dirty floor isn't easy, but I did manage to drift off at times. One morning when I came round, I could see Mason had sat up on the other end of the small cell, he was staring at me, it startled me slightly but I sprang into life,

'Dude, you're awake?'

'Hey, Archie, how did I end up in here with you, and where are we?' He asked.

I proceeded to explain that the guards delivered him down to me four or five days ago and left me to look after you. I told him that I had been giving him pain killers and food and water, and I told him he looked great for the first time I had known him. This was a lie, he looked utter shit, but I didn't want to tell him that. He didn't say much else, and I told him he didn't need talk and to just rest as much as he could,

'I have no idea how long we will be down here, but at least it's kind of dry and slightly better that the box,' I said to him,

'Thank you, Archie, thank you for believing in me when no one has, and thank you for looking after me.'

'No worries, man, some fucker has to look after you,' and for the first time I saw him smile, only for the briefest of moments, but it was nice to see. After that he laid back down and drifted off, so I left him to it for now.

By the end of the first week after joining me, Mason was slightly on the mend, and he started to tell me what happened after I was taken from the box. He told me that the guards would only bring him food every other day, but a couple of the other foreign inmates would share small parts of their food with him. He couldn't really eat much as he too had severe dehydration, and his mouth was swelled up making eating very difficult. He went on to tell me that word got around of an upcoming official visit to the prison by some Thai authorities, and that all inmates would soon be released from the hot box and back into the normal grounds of the prison.

He had no idea how this was going to impact him as he was not the favourite inmate with the locals, but as least he could see a medic and get something for the pain.

On the day of the inmates' release from the box, Mason was told to wait at the end of the line, and he thought the worse. Had his day of execution arrived? He was petrified of dying, but really, what could he do? But when the guards finally came down for him, they pulled him out by his arms, dragged him across the yard, chains rattling together, he eyes stung in the sun light as he had seen little of it for over a month now, he was marched towards the punishment block, where he was to receive a proper good kick in by the guards, then dragged into my cell and dump for me to look after, which I told him I was more than happy to do so.

'Archie, I know I am not going home, there is no way I am going to get out of this,' Mason said out of the blue one morning,

'Mason, I honestly don't know what to say bruv, I want to help you, I need to help you, but I really don't know what I can do now,' I didn't tell him about what happened to poor Punyaa, I felt bad enough as it was about that, I didn't want him to feel bad too.

'It's OK Archie.'

'No, no it's really not fucking OK man, this fucking country has done you a proper wrong'n,'

'There is one thing you can do for me, Archie,'

'Anything man, just you say the word?'

'I need my parents to know of my innocence.'

'Of course, what can I do?'

'When you get out of here, please somehow pass this letter to my parents?' Mason pulled a little package from the back of his pants.

'I've had this hidden, I didn't really know what to do with it to start with, but now I have met you, and I trust you more than anyone in the world right now, perhaps you could deliver it?'

'It would be my pleasure mate, if it is the last thing I ever do, I promise you I will do this for you,' Archie said to his friend,

'Thank you, Archie, it is my only hope for my family.'

'Hey, I promise I will do this, I will hide it somewhere where safe when I get out of the block.'

'Thank you, Archie Parker, I am so happy I met you, we would have never met in different circumstances, so every cloud...'

'Just don't give in yet man, there is always hope,' Archie pleaded to his friend.

With that Mason sank back down to rest his battered body, and for the first time Archie realized that there really was fuck all he could do for this poor lad, at least not in here, but he would one day deliver the little package to Mason's family, that he was sure of.

Chapter 48
2 months later

Death row inmates in Bang Kwang are not given a date for their day of destiny. It could come at any moment, day or night, the poor fuckers just never knew when it was coming. I think that is the thing Mason dreaded the most, one day just simply being marched to his death. This must have been terrifying for him, it was terrifying for him. It was terrifying for me too! The guards would taunt him on a daily basis saying that today was his last, and when the day came and went, and he wasn't looking down the barrel of a gun, it was another day that me and Mason Stone became closer and closer. We had been together in the confines of the punishment block for what seemed like a lifetime now, pretty much every minute of the day squashed together in our new home, apart from every day at some point in the afternoon they took us out one by one for a walk for the briefest of exercise. Every time they took Mason for his walk, I never knew if he was going to come back or not. There are some pretty long hours down there with nothing to do, but that hour every day for the last couple of months was without a doubt the longest hour of my day.

In the short time I had known Mason, he became like a little brother to me. A little brother I never had. He was like a terminally ill family member who was living out his last days, which was affectively what he was doing, but instead of living in some kind of comfort, surrounded by loving family and friends and doctors and nurses with medication to ease the pain, he was living out the last of his days in what can only be described as a dungeon, a small, dirty, hot and disgusting place on god's earth. I guess the only confort he could take from it was that he was not all alone, he had me with him, imagine going through this all by yourself. I nursed him the best I could since he arrived down here with me. I fed him as much as I could, I washed him, I even managed to buy some Vaseline to ease the pain on his ankles from the fucking shackles those dogs put on him. But nothing I could have done would really help an innocent man facing the death penalty in a foreign prison 'thousands of miles away from home, not really.

The more I got to know the young chap, the more I loved him as one of my own, his American accent reminded me of my Holly, who I missed dearly, but at least I would see her again, but if truth be told, I couldn't worry too much about my own messed up life right now, I miss Holls madly, my family and my home, but they could all wait for now. Mason was my focus and time was running out. If I couldn't help him, I would do my upmost to love and comfort him in his final days.

We were woken in the middle of the night on 15th February 2015 by the cage door being opened and straight away I saw Doctor Death, he was accompanied by four of his most feared and trusted guards, and behind them I could see Snipper, as he was named by the locals, the man who carried out the executions with his beloved rifle. I knew what was happening straight away when I saw Snipper lurking in the background.

'Wakey Wakey American rapist,' Doctor death ordered,

'No, no, NOOOOO', I screamed out, 'please fucking no, he is innocent, and you fucking know he is'

'Shut fuck up Parker or you go with him.'

'Take me, if you have to kill someone, take me you bastard, I am guilty of my crimes but he isn't, take me you fucking cunts.'

'Get that English fuck out of my way,' The doctor ordered to his sidekicks and two of them stormed the small cell and dragged me out by my legs, I fought with everything I had, but I was so weak and they beat me to the floor with their batons before tying my hands and legs together as they both sat on my back on the floor so I couldn't move. I screamed out. I begged them not to hurt my friend any more, I started to cry, I lost it, the day we were both dreading was here. I wasn't ready for this shit.

What happened next seemed to go in slow motion, like I was watching a film, but Mason slowly got out of the cell and stood up by himself, he didn't resist and he didn't complain, he stood up and walk out of the cell calmly, he knew what was happening, and it was as if he had finally made his peace with it. He whispered something to Doctor Death that I didn't hear, but whatever he said the Doctor had one very small bit of compassion, and he nodded his head. Mason then knelt down next to me on the cold wet and dirty floor, he lifted my head, he wiped the tears from down my face with his thumbs, and he looked me in the eye and said,

'It's OK, Archie Parker, from London, I will be OK. Thank you from the bottom of my heart for everything you have done for me,' before giving me a kiss of the head, and he wrapped his young and once strong arms around me for one final embrace before being led away, and just before he went out of sight for the very last time, he turned around and whispered,

'I love you, man,' and I said it back through tears streaming down my face again, those were to be the final words that Mason Stone ever spoke, and with that he disappeared through the door and on to the final moments of his life.

The guards threw me back in my cell. I broke down like I had never broken in my life. Everything I believed in, everything I trusted in mankind, in the human race, every single good fucking thing that had ever happened to me suddenly seemed a complete fucking waste of time. I wanted to die there and then on that cold floor, then it got worse about 10 minutes later as I heard the unmistakable sound of a low faint noise somewhere in the distance that will live with me every day for the rest of my life, POP, POP POPPOPPOP, POP…

Part 3

Chapter 49

Life after Mason died for Archie spiralled out of control into an abyss of depression. He just couldn't come to terms with how his young American friend had died. His own life sucked right now, but how a human can be put through an injustice like this and to die in the most horrific way was just too much to take.

The last memory of his friend was the peaceful smile he gave Archie, as he was being taken away by the guards for his final moments on earth. He prayed that his body and mind simply gave up before the bullets rained down, but he very much doubted it happened that way!

I can't really describe the feeling I had after Mason was gone, never in my life had I ever felt so sad and lonely, even more so than when I got arrested myself. We had only known each other for a short while, but inside these walls that felt that an eternity. I was numb, that feeling you get when dumped by a girl you loved with all your heart but magnified by a thousand percent, but the difference being I had nowhere to go and nowhere to hide, or scream out in pain behind closed doors. It hit me proper hard; I had nothing in me, no life, no dreams, nothing. I literally found myself staring at concrete walls for what could of been days at a time. Days, nights, awake, asleep, it all rolled into one, and I began to loose sense of reality.

I had always been a sociable guy, I love meeting new

people, even on the inside in the early days, I went out of my way to make new friends, I gathered that if I had friends I could do the time better but, after Mason had gone, and for the first time in my life I started hating people, even people I had befriended along the way, I just wasn't interested, they were all cunts as far as I was concerned, and I just wished they'd all leave me the fuck alone. Holly came over to visit during this time, but I hardly said a word to her, I didn't reply to any letters from good wishers back home, including friends and family, I couldn't, I just couldn't muster up the effort or the energy. I had nothing to say to anyone in the whole world, I desperately missed my friend. I even contemplated suicide a few times, but something in the back of my mind stopped me every time.

I was like this for around the next six months or so until I finally decided to look at the little package Mason had given me. I wasn't meant to see this until I got out, but I was desperate for something, I needed a lift, perhaps it would help somehow? One of the last things Mason ever said to me was hide this until you are a free man. He said one was for me and the other was for his family, and I promised him that one day I would deliver it to them. Shortly after Mason was gone, I was released from the Punishment block and I set about burying the package out in the yard. I sat against one of the walls, I sat there for hours and slowly dug a little hole under my leg with a stick I had found. The ground was gravely, so it was fairly easy to move around as long as I took my time, and time is what I had, I just prayed no one saw me do it, as I had promised my friend that I would one day deliver his package.

I am not sure where Mason had got the little plastic tube from or where he had hidden it all the time, although I had a good idea where it had been by the smell of it. I was fairly confident that I had dug it deep enough, so it wouldn't resurface, and I was also pretty sure it must have been waterproof, I just needed to remember where I put it.

The only way I could be sure of this was to count the paces from the nearest building, which wasn't too hard to do, prisoners often walked up and down the perimeter wall, either out of boredom or trying to imagine what was on the other side. Either way I worked out, it was sixteen paces away from the building and the distance of the top half of my leg in from the wall. Getting the package back out of the ground wouldn't be that easy, but I didn't need to worry about that just yet. I made this little walk every day for the rest of my sentence; I could do it blindfolded, easy.

I did not want to read the letter to Mason's family as this was for their eyes not mine, but the little package for me was a very small handwritten note rolled up in a small plastic tube, it had two lines in the letter, the first was only five words, and the second was only four words and three numbers, this total of nine words and three numbers was the game changer I needed, and it instantly pulled me out of my depression and focused all my rage and energy on my next plan.

Thank you, my English brother.
Lars Baron from Memphis — 29/11/84.
The next few months we're a bit of a blur, I survived, I am not sure how, but I just did.

Chapter 50

I'd never really been one for holding grudges and wanting payback on people, but then again, no one I had ever know before and been killed in a Thai prison for the rape and murder of his girlfriend, a crime that he did not commit. But I was now presented with such a situation that I could not let it go, this man had to pay for the life of my friend, a life he lost so young, a life he didn't deserve to loose, but it was not only what he went through, I could hardly imagine what his family back home in Huntingdon, Long Island, New York went through. Did they know deep down that their son, their dear sweet little boy was innocent? I truly hoped they did, but would this make the situation any different? I mean which scenario would be worse for a parent to deal with? The thought of their son raping and murdering a young Thai girl for no apparent reason, and sentenced to death, or for their son being sentenced to death by firing squad, but he was innocent all along? Both situations were just awful, but I intended on somehow fulfilling my promise to my friend and telling his family that he was innocent all along.

After a long and very tough six months or so after losing Mason, maybe the toughest emotionally of my life, I finally started to pull myself together. There had been whispers and rumours through the prison of the upcoming king's pardon, and I couldn't help but wonder if my time in Bang Kwang prison could be nearing an end? I needed to focus and start planning, planning revenge for my friend. I was energised again and my body and mind were fuelled by rage. There was no doubt that prison life had changed me, I was no longer the chilled, easy going, and down to earth geezer I once was. I have been through too much to come out the other side that same person, prison changes every man, some for the better, some for the worse, it had certainly done a lifetime's worth of physiological damage on me. I was determined to try and rebuild my life one day, to rebuild mine and Holly's life. I often dreamt of marrying her and having her beautiful children but, I would never really be same again, deep down, and there was one thing I needed to do way before I could think of rebuilding my own life.

At this stage I didn't know if I would get sent home to serve the rest of my sentence back in the UK, but I needed to get a plan in place, or at least start a plan, and I knew exactly who could help me. My friend, Maggie Rose.

Chapter 51

Although in recent times I had not written many letters back home, Maggie always wrote to me, and I always read her letters. She was my best friend, Ron's rock, she kept him together the whole time I had been inside, and Holly, too. Maggie is everything you could wish for in a friend. She is only small, around 5' 1 inch, but she's a feisty little thing, she is insanely loyal, and she would literally do anything for one of her own.

I knew very little about this cunt called Lars Baron, all I knew was his name, date of birth and that he was from Memphis, Tennessee, USA, but Mason knew his basic details and he must have trusted that I would do the right thing by him.

I needed an in to America, it seemed obvious to use Holly as she is after all an American, but I didn't want to involve her. I didn't really want to involve Maggie too, but I had no one else. I didn't want to involve Ronny, and I knew he would understand my thinking. The reason I knew I could ask Maggie for a little help was she had some family in the states, she had some cousins around the same age as us, Liam and Benji, I had met them a few times when they had been travelling through Europe, safe as houses the two of them. We gave them their first pills one night at Ministry, Maggie loved popping the cherries of new bee's, and they in turn proper loved her back for introducing them to the narcotic world of the London

Underground scene. They hung around for a while and raved with us as much as they could before they went of partying around Europe, the last I had heard of them was they were living back in the states, one of them was now a DJ on the circuit, and Maggie was proud as punch that she started the journey for them,

'Bread in London, flowered in New York,' she would often say of her cousins.

I set about writing a letter to Maggie, I didn't outline a plan, as to be honest I didn't really have one yet, I just needed to get something moving and see where it takes me.

'Maggie, you old tart, how the fuck are you? Look, I'm sorry I haven't written back recently, but it's been pretty full on over here, I was down and nearly out for a while but I'm back now.

Listen, there is a reason for this letter, I don't really want to go into details yet, but I need your help. You are the only person I could come to with this, Not Ron, and certainly not Holly. Before we go any further, I need to know if you are cool with that? I don't want them to know anything, at least not at this stage.

Hit me back little Mags,

Miss you all like crazy,

All my love

Archie xxx

I knew she would be cool, but I just wanted to check, as what I was going to ask her was a big favour, as much as I hated keeping things from Holly and Ron, on this one occasion I would turn my feelings the other way.

A couple of weeks later, I received my reply from Maggie,

I knew she wouldn't let me down, the superstar.

'Hey Archie, you fucking knob head ;)

Where you been man? I have been proper worried about you. Holls said you've been on a bad one over there for a while. I hope you got all my letters, but I understand why you don't reply, so no worries m'dear.

Of course I will help you, just name what you need. I am not sure what I can do from all the way over here, but you know I've got your back, right? Just say what you need, and Mum's the word with the others. I am sure you have your reasons for not wanting to involve them.

Already waiting for your reply

Luv ya

Mags :) xxx'

What a star, I replied straight away...

'Mags, you legend, I knew I could rely on your help.

I need a contact in America to do a little research for me. Are your cousins still working the scene and touring round over there? I need contact details for them. Don't worry, I just want some digging.

Buy yourself a burner phone from down the market, send me the number as I have access to a mobile this end, when I get the number, I will text you as it will be easier and quicker to chat that way, in the meantime could you reach out to Liam and Benji and say they may hear from me in the coming weeks or months? Burn these letters after you have read them ;)

Nice one Mags

Archie xxx

A couple of 'weeks later I received a letter back form Maggie saying she had spoken to one of her cousins and they would be more than happy to help with whatever I needed. I had looked after them good when they were in London, me and Ronny took them under our wings and showed them the very best the London Nightlife could offer, from Ministry to Camden Palace to The Cross to Turnmills, these American lads sure could party hard, harder that we first gave them credit for, dam we had a good time, and for that I knew they would want to help me out.

Mags was originally from South of the river, but she moved up to our little pocket of North London shortly after meeting her Ron, we took her in with open arms, and she soon became a core member of our little crew.

I now had Maggie's burner number. I just needed to get hold of my own, this shouldn't be too hard. My family had been sending me money since the beginning, and my prison account had been building up nicely, I had hardly touched it over the last 6 month or so, but now I was getting back on my feet so I started to use it to my advantage.

One of the Blueboys called Loki could pretty much get you whatever you wanted if you had the cash, and this is who I turned to for my new purchase. For 300Baht I could get a pre-paid mobile phone. I would get a new one every week to hide any evidence. And even better for a mere 200Baht a week, Loki would look after my phone for me, he would bring it to me at a certain time of the day, around 8am, which would be 9pm on the east coast of USA, this would be the hour of day we could open up communications.

We kept the conversation short and sweet, I didn't want to

tell them too much, and they didn't ask any questions. I simply told them that first of all I needed to locate a man called Lars Baron, he was originally from Memphis, his date of birth is 29/11/84, and he is an ex, US Marine. I don't want him contacted, I just need to know his whereabouts at this stage, or even if he is still alive?

They said it could take a while, but leave it with them.

Archie checked his phone every morning at the same time, there was the odd update saying that they had found nothing yet, but between touring the US they would keep searching. At the end of the day, they were not private detectives, and they did have their own lives to live, Archie knew this and fully respected it could take some time, time is what he has so that was no problem.

One morning a few months later, Archie picked up his phone from Loki as he did every morning, he turned it on and it flashed into life, three texts came through straight away, he knew something had happened as if he was lucky there would sometimes be one text, but not three. The first one read,

ARCHIE, WE HAVE FOUND HIM.

My excitement grew, the second one read,

HE LIVES IN A SMALL RENTED IN MEMPHIS AND SELLS GEAR TO THE LOCAL CRACK HEADS.

Oh my god, these two are fucking brilliant, the third text blinked into action… It was picture of Lars Baron…

I held it in my hands for a few minutes. I stared at him, I hated him. I had a picture of this man in my head from what Mason told me, but this was the first time I had seen the man who had killed my friend. He had deep, dark and disturbed eyes, a shaved head which I assume was from his US Marine days, a nasty looking scar on his left cheek. If I am honest, he looks pretty fucking scary, and every bit of a cunt what he is. I replied to the brothers thanking so much for their help, and that I would destroy this phone, and I will be in touch at a later date from a different number. I took the sim card out and put it down the toilet whilst I gave the phone back to Loki to destroy and paid him an extra 500 Baht for his troubles, which he gratefully accepted.

Chapter 52

It was around this time, that one morning I heard the sounds of screaming and shouting, but something was different, it wasn't screams of pain and despair and desperation that you would normally hear in the big tiger, it was screams of elation and happiness, noises I hadn't heard on this level for many years now, noises of excitement and joy.

I was going through my normal, mundane morning ritual of having a wash in dirty shity water and brushing my teeth when the commotion started. People were dancing and cheering, as if their footy team has just won the cup final. Some of the inmates I had never seen smile before were jumping for joy as word soon spread like wild fire that Doctor Death had finally met his match! The old miserable twat had been killed somewhere outside the prison, after he finished his shift last night, and his battered and bloody body had been dumped like a piece of trash outside the big entrance gate to the prison, the guards coming in for their dayshift had found him in a pool of blood. I swear on my fucking life that even the guards and blueboys were joining in with the celebrations. It was like the whole of Bang Kwang prison has finally escaped the evil claws of Doctor Death, it was like Independence Day in there, even though some people were in here for life, there was a feeling of freedom in the air. I hoped Mason was watching down from the heavens with a big fucking smile on his face.

Over the next week or so, word got around that one of Punyaa's uncle's closest friends, who still worked in the prison, had heard some months later after Punyaa had been killed; that it was Doctor Death who orchestrated the attack and not some of the lifers as it had been reported at the time. The uncle's friend in question, Tamirye, had never liked Doctor Death anyway and hearing what he had done to poor Punyaa was the last straw, he had witnessed that evil bastard ruin to many people's life, and he had to put a stop to it once and for all.

Tamirye, along with a couple of Punyaa's friends, pulled together 20,000 Bhat to pay a local mobster to brutally torture and kill doctor death, and word has it that he screamed like a little girl all the way until his very last breath, justice served if you ask me. Rest in hell motherfucker!

Chapter 53

March 2016

Even though we were in one of the most feared prisons in the world, there seemed to be an air of optimism around the old place. People were still celebrating Doctor Death's passing, and there was also growing excitement about the rumoured up-and-comingking's pardon. It is said that the King of Thailand would grant royal pardons to some of the inmates to give them a chance to rebuild their lives and become good citizens. Some of the criteria for eligible prisoners would be for those with disabilities or chronically ill people, or some inmates who have a year or so left of their sentences, more so for foreign prisoners, which luckily, I fell into. I was trying not to get too excited, as I had seen so much let down and disappointment over the years, but maybe, just maybe my time in this hell on earth was coming to an end. I would happily serve the rest of my sentence on home soil. I missed home so much, I missed my family, I missed Holly, I missed my friends, I missed my old life, but that old life was long gone and before I could begin my new life, I had one thing to do.

After the low six months after losing Mason where I wasn't interested in talking to anyone at all, the last six or so months, I had begun trying to communicate with people again, I guess I was trying to rebuild myself after an all-time low, I had even started up my English lessons again for any of the locals who just simply wanted something to do. Holly and my family had been out to visit me a few times, which was proper nice. I was in the right head space to see them again. I had been writing to Mags, and I had also been talking regally to Liam and Benji. Although I was trying to rebuild, deep down I still had a raging anger in me for what happened to my friend, Mason Stone.

One morning whilst doing my cleaning shift in one of the blocks, one of the Blueboys came running up to me all excited,

'Archie, you must come now,' he said to me,

'Whats up man, what's happened?' I answered, but he didn't say anything back, he took me by the hand and led me to the main office where Doctor Deaths predecessor was sitting behind his old wooden desk, where he stood up and simply said,

'Mr Parker, you go home to finish your sentence, pack your stuff, you go now.'

I literally stood there, like a statue, everything seemed to go in slow motion as I tried to replay in my head what he said, and all I could say was,

'Sir, sorry?'

'Get out of here Parker, and never come back,' he said through a slight smile.'

I can't really remember much of what happened next as my head was in a spin, was this really happening to me? Completely out of the blue one morning whilst I was cleaning shit and piss off the floor, next thing BANG I'm going home. It was a little overwhelming, and I honestly didn't know what or how to think. I was excited and petrified all in one. I had been here for so many years, I'd had so many deep lows then suddenly I was on a real high, my body and mind didn't know how to cope with the sudden change in emotion. So many questions flew through my mind, could I cope outside? What would I do? Would my family still love me how they use to? I was institutionalized to prison life, and I had no idea how I would survive out there in the big world I had once thrived in. Then I realized that I wasn't actually a free man yet, I still had another year to serve back home. What would prison be like in England? I am sure it would be easier than here, but I couldn't tell for sure. But I would be able to start properly planning my mission. It was on, time to go home and never ever come back to this fucking country ever again!

Within an hour of being told that I was going home, I was ordered to clean myself up, gather my few belongings, then I was taken to the entrance of the prison that I had gone through all those years ago, handcuffed and put in the back of a waiting car. I was still shit scared, until I was on that plane heading for home I wouldn't relax. I hadn't seen a car since the days of my sentencing all those years back, and I was suddenly in the back of one weaving through the busy streets heading towards Bangkok International Airport. It was terrifying, the world was moving at 100MPH and my mind struggled to keep up, I sat back in the car and closed my eyes and didn't dare open them until I was ordered out at the airport.

It had now been just over a year since they wrongfully took my little brother away from me. The pain is still raw. I don't even know what happened to his young body. Did he get returned home for a proper burial, or did his body get dumped like some of the horror stories I'd heard of? I didn't really want to know if truth be told, all I knew was that I was now going home, and my mission to avenge Mason and to try and clear his name was on!

Part 3.5

Chapter 54

Upon arriving back in the UK, Archie was taken straight to HMP Brixton, a category C prison. He was home, back in his beloved London, although he was far from a free man, he was buzzing to be back on home shores, he set about planning what to do about Lars Baron, the motherfucker who had his friend Mason Stone wrongfully imprisoned and killed in a Thai prison.

Archie had nine months to serve in HMP Brixton before his release, plenty of time to create the perfect plan.

It was on his second day back on UK soil that Archie bumped into an old friend.

'Archie fucking Parker,' I heard through the hatch in my cell. It took me a few moments to realize who was standing in front of me,

'Is that you Jimmy? Bromy? Fuck a duck, I haven't seen you for years bruv, probably gurning my face off in Camden back in the day, what the fuck are you doing in here?'

I hadn't even realized at this point that he had a guard's uniform on, I thought he was one of the inmates,

'I work here, you fucking prick.' he laughed

'I heard what happened with you a few years back Archie, you silly fucker, you just couldn't resist could you? You daft brush, I still see your crew about from time to time, and I always asked after you, when I heard you were coming here, I made up you were back in the UK, and you were finishing your time in Brixton, I am sure this will be easy time compared to what you went though over there?'

'I hope so, mate.'

'Keep your head down, and you'll be out in no time,'

'I hope so, mate,' Archie said again,

'Listen, I will never forget what you done for me and my sister back in the day, if there is anything you need, anything Archie, just give me a shout I'm here most days, when I'm not here I'm out raving and praying... I don't end up in here with you cunts, ha ha'

'Cheers Bromy, I might just take you up on that.'

This got Archie thinking...

Chapter 55

On the surface, especially after being transferred back to the UK, I looked and acted like I was in good shape, all things considering, but deep down I was far from OK. I was angry, and the anger was growing each and every day. I was only really angry with one person, so I tried my hardest to hide it from other inmates, friends and family and now Bromy, no one knew how angry I was and the plans I had, it was tiring work holding onto to all of this anger by myself. At night time, I would often squeeze my pillow as hard as I could and scream into it whilst covering my face just to release some energy. I also worked out as much as I could to burn off all the excess anger energy flowing through my veins. One day I will seek help and talk about it, for sure. I will seek professional help if that is what it will take, but I wasn't ready, not yet. I was also a deeply sad man, I cried myself to sleep most nights, all alone in my cell, even though I was now so close to home, I felt a million miles away from any love and comfort. I didn't tell Holly how I felt, I couldn't, maybe one day, but not yet. I was sad for my friend being taken away from his life at such a young age, A life that promised so much, I'm sure of that. He would have been hugely successful, and he would have raised a good family, I knew this for sure, but his future wife will never be met, his children will never be born, those memories will never be made and that broke my heart. His family will never see him again, and they will never truly know what happened to their dear, sweet boy after he left their shores and never returned. Death and sadness are all around us, every day of our lives, but this one was close to my heart, and I was struggling to deal with it, big time.

I tried to turn all of my anger into energy for my plan, it kept me going, it was the only thing that kept me going. I worked out as much as I could, there was a decent gym back in the UK compared to the makeshift gym the Germans had built in Bang Kwang, all of my energy went in to working out and going over my plan over and over in my head, so I hundred percent knew what I need to do, and how I would execute it.

Chapter 56

Most of the inmates got on really well with James Bromwich, yes, he was a screw, and most of the screws were power tripping pricks, much like in Thailand but not as brutal, well not all of them. Although I knew Bromy from the old days and most inmates knew this, I didn't want to be seen talking to him too much as I didn't want to get a reputation as a suck ass, or worse still a grass, that would be a nightmare. I needed to work on him slowly and in private as much as possible. This was going to be tough, but it was my only hope although I thought I could trust him, I wasn't hundred percent sure as if he got caught this would have been his career over. At the end of the day, I only needed him to do one little job, then turn the other way.

Jimmy popped his head into my cell one Monday morning.

'Archie, how was your weekend man?' He asked with a kid like grin on his face,

'Yeah, banging Jimmy, proper good weekend.' I replied with a hint of sarcasm.

'I saw Josh and Lens in town Saturday night, Lens was off it as usual, and Josh weren't too far behind, I told them you were at my gaff now, and they both said hurry the fuck up and get out so we can have a proper good welcome home sesh.'

The thought of seeing my friends was nice but my life had changed now, I am not sure I could do a sesh any more, I am not right in the head for it, my emotions aren't right, it could be dangerous, I thought, but didn't say that to Jimmy,

'Ha, ha, them tossers, always on it, not sure how they are still alive to be honest,' we both laughed,

'Tell me mate, how the fuck did you end up working in here, surely you could be in here with the rest of us if they knew the half of it,' I whispered.

'Keep your fucking voice down, Arch,' Jimmy said whilst coming further into my cell,

'You probably don't remember Arch, but the old man was a screw. He spent all of his working life around the London Prisons and I don't know, I didn't really leave school with much, the old man had always tried to steer me away, but it just kind of happened and here I am.'

'Fair one mate, and of course I remember you, silly sod, me and Ronny took you under our wing,' I replied, and with that he gave me a wink and told me to keep my head down and nose clean, and I'll be out of here soon.

Over the course of the next couple of months I started testing the water with Jimmy, testing how far he would be willing to go to help an old friend out. He was a proper sound guy, and the more we spoke, the more I knew he would do this little favour for me.

Chapter 57

It was probably inevitable that Lars Baron would end up back where he started, he had little else anywhere in the world, he didn't really have much at home either, his dad was the only family he had left, but that ship had sailed many moons ago. His father tried many times to make an effort with his only son, but he always threw it back in his face by telling him things like,

'My grandad was a war hero, you didn't give him the respect he deserved... you fucking bastard.'

And he tried to explain that his grandfather was not all that, and he did not want him to turn out the same as his grandad did, but Lars didn't listen, his grandad was his hero and that was that.

After leaving the scene of the crime in Koh Samui at around 5am on that fateful morning in Paradise, Lars made his way back to his own beach hut, he looked in the room where the follower was asleep, tutted to himself and murmured 'fucking pussy' under his breath before packing his bags and preparing to get the fuck off the island. He figured the police would be after him soon, so best get away whilst he can.

Lars Baron did not show any guilt, he casually had a shower, packed his army edition rucksack that he took everywhere with him, he didn't try to wake the follower, who had actually been wide awake the whole time, but laid there as still as could with his eyes closed, he was too scared to get up and see what Lars was doing. When he was ready, he simply threw his backpack on and left, he left the door wide open and made his way up to the street where he would flag a taxi down, and make his way to the airport to start his journey. He decided in the taxi that he's had enough of travelling and would make his way home, he may have to wait a day or so to get a flight to Bangkok, but he had money so this wouldn't be a problem.

The next morning Lars was on a plane out of the Samui International Airport and bound for Bangkok, where he would stay for a night or two. He had never really liked the Asian girls before, but after seeing how beautiful the geek's girlfriend was, he had only one thing on his mind when arriving in Bangkok, he wanted more of that!

After checking in to a hotel he couldn't wait to get out and find some young Thai girls to play with. Just over a day ago he had raped and murdered a young girl and left her boyfriend for dead, but he showed no remorse what so ever, if anything he was buzzing from it, she wasn't his first victim and sure enough she wouldn't be his last, but he knew he couldn't stay in Thailand for too long, in fact, he was done with Asia, he had one more night to wreak havoc then he was out of there.

It didn't take too long to find some action in Bangkok, Lars knew what he was looking for, he headed straight to the Patpong area in the city and soon found himself sitting at a bar in some seedy, neon lite joint, this was right up his street, he was feeling greedy tonight and was quickly approached by a young-looking Thai with jet black straight hair and dressed in a school uniform outfit, small and petite, just the way he liked it, he was getting excited. A westerner sitting by himself in bar like this was only after one thing. He had to do 'the check' first to see if it was a boy or a girl, he had no intention of sucking on any cock, not tonight and not ever. He grabbed the crouch area, a little too hard as it took her back, but he was happy with his findings.

'Find a friend you fucking whore' he ordered her.

'Go, go bring another one over then we will talk,' he barked again,

Off she went and within two minutes she was making her way back over with one of her colleagues, a small, petite local looking girl with bleached blond hair and a perfect little body. Yes, he thought, two of the fucking whores together, he had never had a threesome, and this was the perfect time to do so.

They took him into a little back room away from the crowds, the room was everything you would expect to see in a Thai whorehouse. There was a velvet cushioned seat in the middle of the dimly lit room with a small table next to it, he ordered the two girls to start dancing for him whilst he racked up a massive line of coke on the table, he took the whole lot in one big hit up his right nostril, and sat back to wait for the rush through his bloodstream. The two girls continued to dance, and he ordered them to sit on his knees and kiss each, he pulled one of them back by her hair and started aggressively kissing her, then followed by the other one, they seemed to go along with it to start with, they seemed to enjoy the roughness. He then ordered them to strip off completely, showing their pert little bodies. Next, he stood up and made them take his trousers off and start performing oral on him, whilst saying to them,

'Take it all you fucking whores,' but he was getting more aggressive with every second that passed, the girls started to get a scared, he was so much bigger and stronger than them, he easily overpowered the both of them. Lars pushed one of them so she was bending over the chair and started banging her from behind, the other one tried to stop him by climbing on his back whilst shouting 'STOP, STOP YOU ANIMAL,' he swung her off his back and she landed bang on the table, the table broke and glass went flying everywhere, the other girl tried to escape, but he grabbed her by the arms and landed a full blown head-butt to the bridge of her nose, blood splattered everywhere and she collapsed to the floor, the second girl had managed to get loose through the curtain, he realized she was gone and flew through the curtain, but he was met by and angry mod of Thai men, the pimps he assumed, he flew straight at them in a rage but there was too many of them, they picked him up by the arms and legs and carried him out of the front door, Lars was trying to escape their clutches, tables and chairs and glass was flying everywhere, he was thrown to the floor outside, more tables and chairs were sent crashing, he managed to picked up the leg of a broken chair and confronted the mod,

'COME ON YOU FUCKING GOOKS,' he screamed at them, more and more people were gathering and something inside his mind told him this is one fight he couldn't win, he scarpered through the crowd and ran for safety, he was not followed. Lars made his way back to the hotel still buzzing from what just happened, and decided his time was now over in this fucking country. Lars Baron would return home to Memphis tomorrow.

Chapter 58

'Archie, this is not going to be easy, and I am not going to ask why on earth you want to tell your friends and family your release date will be five days after you officially get release from prison, in fact I really do not want to know,' Jimmy said.

'Geezer, I know what I am asking is big and believe me I have no other options, and don't worry I will not tell you why I need to do this, and nothing will ever come back on you, you have my fucking word on that Jimmy, OK?'

'I trust you with my Life Arch, I really do, let me have a think about it, I might be able to call in a few favours.'

'Thank you, Jimmy,' Archie simply said as they said their goodbyes again for another day.

James Bromwich, or Jimmy as he was known, was teased and bullied from his early teens in school. He was a bit of a geek. His old man was a screw in Pentonville prison, North London, and the self-proclaimed cool kids at school would pick on him by calling his old man a grass, just because he worked in a nick. Most of the bullies' own fathers had been in and out of prison most of their adult life, but what they failed to see was that Jimmy's old man didn't put them there in the first place, he wasn't old bill, he was just a hard working father trying to support his family. What the bullies also didn't seem to know, which I am sure they would have, if they'd spoke to their own fathers now and then was that David Bromwich was one of the most respected screws in Pentonville. Typical bullies looking for an easy target!

Around this time, just to make matters worse for poor little Jimmy, his mother contracted lung cancer from years of smoking forty fags a day and passed away in the summer of 95 just before Jimmy went into year 11. So he was now called the grass with no mother, brutal bullying by some horrible little cunts. Jimmys's old man worked all hours in the prison so when his mother passed away, Jimmy and his little Sister were home alone for long periods of time and having to fend for themselves, Jimmy became his little sister's, Sarah, pretty much full-time carer. Making sure she got up for school, and had breakfast and lunch sorted, and also made sure they both had a good dinner inside them every night. It was safe to say that James Bromwich's teen years were not the happiest of times!

Archie Parker was a known face around town, he was a couple of years older that Jimmy and was well respected in the area; they lived in the same street and spoke now and then and about this and that.

'Hey man, I'm Archie from down the road.'

'Hey Archie, what can I do you for, mate?'

'Oh, nothing really, I just wanted to pop by as I heard about your old dear and wanted to say how sorry we all are, and that if you need anything, you know where to find me.'

'Appreciate that mate, I really do, I think we are OK for now but will keep that in mind.'

'How's the old man?'

'Oh, you know, he seems ok, he doesn't really talk about it, he works most days or nights so it's just me and Sarah, you know?'

'Yeah, I hear you Jimmy, well like I said, you know where I'm at chap.'

'Nice one bruv,' answered Jimmy and they shook hands and said their goodbyes.

Jimmy thought that was a lovely touch, not many people had offered him help throughout his life, so he was chuffed with Archie coming around, but he didn't want to bother him too much with his own problems.

A couple of weeks later, Archie was pulling up outside his house after another days of work, he had Ronny with him as it was thirsty Thursday, so they were getting ready to hit the town for a cheeky warm up session ahead of the weekend, when they heard some commotion and shouting coming from down the street, they didn't like the sound of it so they went to investigate.

Poor little Jimmy had already had a pretty shit day. At break time, three of the cool kids had nicked his lunch money when he was in the line for the ice cream van and then at lunch time whilst he went for a shady fag down the thicket, the same three cool kids had followed him and nicked his ten Superking, which he had brought with the previous days lunch money, and his day was to get even worse after school.

When Archie and Ronny approached the scene, they could see three boys trying to attack Jimmy, right on his own door step, what a fucking liberty,

'C'mon Ron, that kid needs our help,' Archie stressed to his best mate,

'Right behind you, bruv,' answered Ronny,

'What the fuck are you doing?' Screamed Archie, 'Get the fuck off him.'

Archie and Ron streamed in by throwing a few punches

and kicks in the direction of the attackers, the three cool kids from school, they later learnt. Archie grabbed one of them by the throat,

'If I ever see you round here again you little pikies, we'll kick the fuck out of every one of you, now fuck off,' Archie screamed in his best hard man voice. Archie and Ronny were not the violent type in any way shape or form, but if push came to shove, they could look after themselves, and they proper hated bullies too, so seeing off these little cunts wasn't too much bother.

"I was just about to get and kick the fuck out of them, Arch,' Jimmy said with a little smile on his face,

'You OK, mate?' Ron and Archie asked,

'Yeah, I'm all good, cheers, I proper owe you one,' Jimmy said as Ronny helped him to his feet,

'Ron, this is my neighbour Jimmy, Jimmy, this is my best mate, Ron.'

'Nice to meet you, Ron.'

'Likewise, man, who were those pricks?'

'Oh, just a couple of the cool kids from school.'

'Don't you worry about them any more, they won't ever touch you again, and if they do just let us know, mate,' Archie reassured his friend,

'You wanna come for a joint mate?' Ronny asked Jimmy,

'Erm, yeah sure if you don't mind?' Jimmy nervously answered,

'C'mon, let's go get stoned chaps,' Archie announced.

From that day on two things happened. The cool kids never ever bothered little Jimmy again, and Jimmy became good friends with Archie and Ronny. He was a bit younger than the two of them so he couldn't go out raving with them, not just yet anyway, but they would often meet up at each other's houses after school and work to chill with a few joints. Archie even invited Jimmy and his younger sister round for diner a couple of nights a week whilst their old man was out at work all night. A good little bond was formed and James Bromwich would forever be in debt to Archie Parker for the kindness and generosity that he showed him through his dark times.

Chapter 59

Five days after the rape and murder of the geeks Thai girlfriend, Lars Baron was back on home soil, as if nothing had happened. He had no home as his dad had kicked him out before he left so he needed somewhere to stay. As soon as he landed in Memphis International Airport, he made his way to his ex-girlfriend's apartment, he had loved her once upon a time, and he was sure she would look after him for a while.

Jessi was from the deep south, and she was a desperate Junkie living in small rented near the Parkway Village in Memphis, USA, she had no money, her little boy had been taken away from her last year, she had been in and out of prison for possession and robbery charges, so she was more than happy to take Lars back in, he had money, and she was desperate.

It didn't take long for the two of them to get up to old tricks, and start robbing places and people. Not that Lars really needed the money, he just liked being a naughty cunt' and then change 'just enough money to feed their addictions' to 'but there was no way on gods earth that Lars was going to feed Jessie's addiction out of his own money, the bitch would have to earn her hits'. He also beat the fuck out of her on a regular basis, but she seemed to accept it as she had nothing else.

For robbing people and holding up shops, they had a collection of different masks raging from the classic Jason masks to any Halloween costumes they could find. One of their favourite and easiest jobs was robbing people at cash machines, they weren't after much money, just enough to feed their addictions. It was easy money, and they drove all over Tennessee robbing poor people of their hard-earned money. The deranged couple would scope out machines for days on end sometimes, looking to stay clear of any CCTV, they would more often than not rob the elderly who could not fight back, desperate people can be very dangerous, especially ones like Lars Baron, who had two addictions to fulfil, his drug addiction and his rage, put these together and people will get hurt.

On one of their morning raids in Arlington, North West of Memphis, they attempted to rob an old man of a mere 30 Dollars, the old man tried to fend them off, and Lars beat the poor old fella to within an inch of his life with his own walking stick. Although Lars was a raging drug addict, he was also very smart and never wore the same mask twice in the same town. After attacking the old man, it was now time to move on.

They lived like this, up and down the road, robbing folks for around a year until they nearly got caught one day.

They never tried to rob any more whilst high as this would cloud their judgement, but one day whilst Lars had just jacked up, he came round with Jessi screaming at him to drive. He didn't really know what was going on at first, but she was hysterical so his instincts kicked into gear just as he saw a police man running towards the car, he threw his mask on and he screeched off down the road, and they managed to get away just in time, but they now needed to dump this car and get another one, and with a man of Lars' skills would be too hard.

'What the fuck are you doing you stupid whore,' he screamed at Jessi as they hit the highway and headed south,

'Oh, but baby, he was just an easy target,' she said back.

'What have I told you about going out by yourself and when you are high,' he shouted and threw a wicked backhander across her cheek.

They turned off at the next junction, 'I am going to have to ditch this car now you fucking bitch, I love this fucking car,' he screamed at her. They skidded to a halt down a little country lane which led to a farm up ahead. He opened his door and in one movement he grabbed her by the hair and pull her across the driver's seat and out of the door, a big clump of her stayed in his hands.

'You fucking useless bitch,' he screamed as he started kicking her in the stomach against the car, he was in an absolute rage, this was Lars at his most dangerous, Jessi was shaking with fear as she tried to cover herself. He eventually stopped kicking her, he knelt down next to her and calmly said,

'Now you wait here like a good girl whilst I go get us another car.'

Lars returned ten minutes later with a new car, he had simply walked up to the farm and stole the first car he came to, god forbid anyone that got in his way today. As he drove back to towards Jessi, he managed to take a deep breath and compose himself, Jessi was laying on the floor being sick and not in a good way, he pulled up her...

'I'm sorry baby, it's just you know what to do and what not to do by now down you?' 'Are you sorry for what you done, Jessi?' He asked,

'Yes baby, I'm so sorry, it will never happen again.'

'OK, let's get you up, this car will do for a while, let's get the fuck out of here, and go home, shall we?'

'Yes please, baby, if you could just serve me up, I will be

just fine baby.'

Lars served Jessi up, and she slept for most of the journey back home, they dumped the car and got the train back to Memphis, Lars was fed up of being on the road, it was tiring work, so he decided to try and get clean and instead serve all of the down and out junkies of Memphis, there would be plenty of business for the horrible pair to make some easy cash.

Chapter 60
January 2016

For nine years and six months I had been locked up, both in the notorious Bang Kwang prison in Thailand and here in HMP Brixton, in this time my life has changed forever. I will never ever be the same young and carefree Archie Parker that left these shores all those years ago for a two-week dream holiday to Thailand with my Holly and my best pals, but here I stand at the gates to Brixton Prison, armed with a small bag of clothes, £1000 cash that I had saved from various places and a fake passport. For the next five days I shall be known as James Tanner.

I said my goodbyes to anyone I slightly cared about, and made my way out of the front door. I'd dreamed of this moment for so long, but it was not what I had expected, there was no family and friends waiting for me with a bottle of champagne and a bag of Charlie. It was cold, it was raining, it was bleak, but I had a job to do and only five days in which to do it in.

After leaving the main entrance on Jebb avenue, I took a left then headed North on Brixton Hill for a few hundred yards before crossing the road, and taking a right onto Fairmount Road where saw what I was looking for, my old mate James Bromwich sitting in his people carrier, engine running and waiting for me.

Everything seemed to be going in fast forward.

'Quick, jump in Arch and keep your head down,' he said,

'I'm in, let's go,' I pleaded,

'I hope you know what you're doing, mate?' Bromy asked

'Oh, don't you worry about me Bromy,' I replied 'but you will never know how much I appreciate this.'

'I wish I knew what the fuck you are up to, but then again it's probably best I don't know,' he said through a cheeky smile, 'Just don't end up back in the nick, OK?' he demanded.

'I will try not to, mate, I promise I will try.'

'Check the glove box,' Bromy said.

I am going to drop you off at Clapham Common where you can jump on the underground, and make your way to Heathrow.

'Perfect man, nice one,' I said as I opened the glove box and good to his word there was an envelope with a single flight to Memphis, USA and an underground ticket,

'You're a fucking legend Jimmy, you know that, right?'

'Don't be silly Arch, I owe you from the old days, I will never forget what you done for me man, just be careful!' Bromy said whilst shaking my hand,

'Remember the meeting point for when you get back?'

'Absolutely, my friend,' I replied as I was exiting the car at the tube station.

It had been nearly ten years since I had moved anywhere at any great pace as free man, and if I'm honest, I was shitting myself. I was about to board a plane by myself, no one watching my every move, no one telling me what to do, I wasn't sure how I was going to cope. Apart from when I was moved from Thailand back to England, my life had moved very slowly, everything just seemed to go in slow motion, I mean, why rush when there was nowhere to go, everything was so slow paced, but out here in the real world it was totally different, everything and everybody seemed in such a rush to get somewhere. Was my life like this before prison? I couldn't remember, but it was scary being out by myself.

The first panic attack I had was when I entered the airport doors. I was suddenly greeted by a wall of people rushing this way and that, it confused me, I felt under so much pressure, I was being knocked sidewards by the rush, it was horrible, I needed to get away from it. I managed to fight my way through the surging crowds and found a toilet, I ran in to the first empty cubicle and locked the door, my heart was pounding, I was sweating, I tried to compose myself by taking some deep breaths, 'Pull yourself together, Archie,' I whispered to myself. I sat there for around 5 minutes to calm down. Deep breaths. I went over the plan in my head again; it seemed to take my focus away from what I was actually doing, as if reading a book or something.

I managed to get myself checked in and headed for security with a confident stride that told me I knew exactly what I was doing, which was far from the truth. In the past I'd always felt guilty going through security in airports, but never more so than I did today, I just hoped I could pull it off, under my clothes I was sweating my arse off, it was winter but that didn't seem to help. I put my sultry bag in the little tray provided along the contents of my pockets which consisted of my fake passport and my dollars, that I had just exchanged shortly after my panic attack, my whole life belongings trailed off through the little X-ray machine. I am sure the security guys were looking at me funny, or what this just me being paranoid? I wasn't sure, so I just politely said my hello's as I passed them through the metal detector without setting any arms off.

Phew, I thought. It wasn't as if I was actually carrying anything that could have got me stopped, well apart from travelling with a fake passport but that would have been picked up at check in, surely? I was through and by now, I was fucking starving so I made my way to the food hall, it was like Christmas day down there, there was McDonalds, Burger King, I was spoilt for choice and it was little overwhelming, I hadn't seen such marvellous food choices, for ten, long years, McDonalds in was, get in!

After ordering my food I set about finding my gate. I was travelling to Memphis, Tennessee via a quick stop in Chicago, Illinois. My Chicago flight was will boarding at gate 24 at 12.15pm, I made my way to the gate and found a quite little corner to sit it, and go over the plan again before my long journey to Memphis started.

Chapter 61
2 weeks earlier

Whilst seeing out the last of his days on the inside, Archie had weekly visits from Holly and his family, the chaps had even been in a few times, which was nice. Archie seemed OK to all of his loved ones, but inside he was a mess. It was on a visit from Holly a few weeks before his release where he asked her not to come any more, this was all part of his master plan.

'Oh Archie, a few more weeks and this nightmare will be behind us, you coming home, babe.'

'I know, Holls, it almost seems too good to be true, nearly ten years since we left for Thailand,' sighed Archie,

'Listen, none of that matters now, none of it at all, you're coming home back to where you belong, and we are going to start life again, start our life together again,' said Holly,

'I can't believe you have stuck around all these years darling,' smile Archie,

'I love you, Archie Parker, from London, I would wait until the end of the world for you, you know that right?'

'Of course I do, babe, if I didn't we wouldn't be sitting here having this conversation right now would we?' They both laughed and shared a nice moment together.

Archie loved Holly more that he had ever loved anyone, he will be forever grateful for sticking around and waiting for him, and for all of her help whilst he has been locked up, both by helping him and helping out with his family back home whilst he was in Bang Kwang. He just hoped that it wasn't a waste of time, and that when he got out that he could still love her and look after her the way she deserves to be loved and looked after.

'Listen, Holls, don't take this the wrong way, but I don't want any more visitors until I'm out of here.'

'OK babe, no worries.'

'It's just, I want to get my head down and concentrate on getting out of here in one piece, you know what I mean?'

'Yeah course, I will give your parents a call tonight, and let them know too, shall I?' ask Holly,

'Please babe, they will understand. I just need to get my head right before I leave those doors, you know?'

'I will call them tonight, they will be fine, they just want you home, as we all do.'

'Thank you, Holls, really thank you so much, you will never know how much you have helped me, I am not sure what I would have done without you on the outside, you are my rock, and I fucking love you,' Archie said whilst welling up, and with that they had an emotional moment together there in the visiting room in HMP Brixton. The next time they see each other, Archie Parker will be a free man, hopefully.

Chapter 62

Whilst Archie was in HMP Brixton prison, he kept in touch with Liam and Benji. It was as easy to get hold of mobile phones as it was back in Bang Kwang. He regularly changed burner phones and deleted every message ever sent, there was only two pieces of information that he needed to remember, and that was what the cousins sent in their last ever text to Archie. It was an address and a six-digit number, not too hard to remember as Archie had gone over every step of the plan over and over multiple times. The rest of the information would be waiting for him in a secure location in Memphis.

Chapter 63
Wednesday

After arriving in Memphis International Airport, I jumped in a cab and headed for my hotel. The Fairfield Inn Marriott on Memphis I-240 & Perkins. The nice taxi driver informed me that it was only a 10-minute drive as the Wednesday mid-afternoon traffic wasn't too bad. I was proper worn out, the journey had been long, it had been hard work on my poor head, and all I wanted to do was sleep, so I grabbed a bite to eat and checked in to my hotel. Wow, I had not seen a bed like this for years and years. The beds in HMP Brixton were a little better than the big tiger, at least I had a pillow there but this, this was the stuff of dreams. I didn't have much to unpack, so I grabbed a quick shower. It was only early evening by the time I had eaten, but I didn't care, my belly was full, and I was tired so I simply passed out on the bed, within seconds I was fast asleep.

Thursday

I awoke the next morning after the best sleep I've had for ten long years, there was no shouting and screaming from outside the door, there was no clattering of keys and people moaning, there was no slamming doors and being ordered to do this and to do that, it was just me, in silence, on the biggest most comfortable bed I had ever seen. I was rested, and now it was time to action my plan. Firstly, I need to find some shops to get myself some new clobber. The nice hotel manager informed me that just a mile or so down the road, I would find the Parkway Village where I could find plenty of shops and good food outlets. I tipped him $10, and he kindly ordered me a taxi.

It felt good to buy a decent t-shirt, some decent underwear, a pair of jeans and nice baggy hoody. I brought enough clothes to last me a few days and also some toiletries. Next, I needed to find the address that I knew of by heart, so I jumped in a cab and headed ten miles or so west to the secure location in downtown Memphis.

The safety deposit box was in the bank of America Financial Centre, just off the famous Beale Street in Downtown Memphis. All I needed was my passport to access the room, James Tanner. I had remembered the six-digit code to access the box. I went through security and was led to the secure room where I was shown to my box. I opened it up and was greeted by an A4 size brown envelope, I took out my package, closed the box, and got the fuck out of there, and jumped in another taxi, and headed back to my hotel.

I was tempted to hire a car for the few days I was here, it would be under the name of my fake passport so there would be no paper trail with my name on, but I hadn't driven a car for ten years, and I had never driven on the wrong side of the road, so I guessed it best to just use taxis.

When I got back to the hotel, I checked the contains of the envelope.

1 x Single flight ticket from Memphis International's airport to Heathrow, UK.

600 Dollars Cash,

1 x recent Picture of Lars Baron, a mug shot it looked like,

1 x letter detailing Lars' address etc. He lives in a small rented on Wooddale Avenue, Memphis and conducts most of his business in a sports bar on Winchester Road just around the corner from this house.

I had no idea how Liam and Benji had tracked down Lars Baron, and how they found out so much about him, and to honest I didn't really care, and I certainly wasn't going to ask them questions about it. I now knew where to find him and that was all that mattered. They knew how much I appreciated it, and that was all that mattered to me. It was a shame that I couldn't see them to thank them in person, but I'm sure one day I would have the opportunity.

There was nothing else to do today apart from to chill at the hotel and have bite to eat, maybe hit the gym to burn off some excess rage that still burns inside me, and go over the rest of the plan again. I had three days left in America before hopefully going home to try and rebuild my life, I wasn't sure If I was doing the right thing, I wasn't sure if I could actually go through with it, but I had come all this way so I wasn't going to give up now.

Chapter 64

As it also turns out it is fairly easy to source a fake passport in a UK prison. I didn't want to involve Jimmy with this part, he was already doing me the favour of a life time, so I didn't want to burden him any more. But there are plenty of geezers in prison who can get hold of pretty much anything, for a small fee of course.

The thing about junkies, is that they will do almost anything for money, and therefore they know all types of savoury characters from all corners on the underground, and there was once such junkie called Beaver who was just two cells down from me. I'm not really sure why he was called Beaver, and I didn't really give a fuck, but what I did know was for a couple of hundred quid he could get hold of a fake passport, and better still have it smuggled into Brixton Prison for me, and to show my appreciation I chucked in an extra fifty notes just for him. I am not sure how much crack that could buy you on the inside, but it was like all of his Christmas's had come at once, so happy fucking days to all parties involved with this shady little deal.

I arranged for Beaver to have it smuggle in the day before my official release. I didn't want to hang on to it for too long as I couldn't risk it being found. Even Bromy didn't know I had it. I received my gift the night before I was released and hid it down my pants where it would stay until I was well away from this place. I paid Beaver his £50, and he skipped off in the direction of his next hit. James Tanner was, albeit for a brief moment in history, born. I love it when a plan comes together!

Chapter 65
Friday

I woke up Friday morning with a clear but nervous head. Today I shall go back to the Parkway Village to buy some supplies. I hit the hotel gym at 7.30am, mixing it with some corporate looking knob heads who were away from home, and were trying to look like they knew what they were doing on the various cardio machines whilst sweeting out last night's client brought dinner and beer, probably a full-blown Memphis style BBQ somewhere, before getting showered and going off to meetings all day long where they would bullshit this and bullshit that whilst trying to seal the big dollar contract, no fucking thanks, mate!

After showering in my room, I made my way to the buffet in the canteen. Couple of bagels and a couple of strong coffees later, and I was ready and out the door in a taxi by 10.30am. Whilst at the shops I needed to buy a rucksack, or some kind of travel bag, some more cloths and some gloves, and anything else that I may need.

After a successful shopping trip, I clocked a KFC across the road and thought it'll be rude not to. After devouring some greasy chicken, the next part of my plan was to scope out the road where Lars Baron lives, and the sports bar on Winchester Road where I had been informed that the fucker done most of his business.

In my best American accent, I asked the young chap

working the till in KFC if he knew how far Wooddale Avenue was, and he kindly informed me that it was a brisk 15-minute walk if you were a quick walker, or if you were lazy like he was, a good 30 minutes. I thanked him and headed south on S Perkins Road. I was in no rush, so I decided it would be a lazy 30 minutes, like the lazy young geezer has just told me.

Around 20 or so minutes later, I came to the cross roads of Wooddale Road running east to west and S Perkins Road running north to south, I was heading south towards Winchester Road. I stopped for a moment on the corner of Wooddale and wondered, was one of the houses I could see Lars Barons house? I gathered he was a known face in the area, especially by the old bill, but what did the locals think of him? Was he liked? Was he hated? The latter I suspected.

I carried on my walk south towards where I was hoping to find the infamous sports bar on Winchester Road. On my right was now what looked like a gated community of some sort, there were multiple apartments all joined together. One and two bed places I assumed, maybe some bigger, some maybe even had swimming pools. I took a sharp right turn, the gated community was still on my right, now behind a wire fencing and wooden fence panels, on my left was what looked like some kind of auto repair shop with old beaten-up US style picks ups gathering rust in the yard. I carried on straight. I could hear some music up ahead. It was Friday afternoon by now, the weekend celebrations were probably already underway for the lucky early Friday finishes. This took me back fifteen to twenty years, where we would all be down the pub at opening time on a Friday lunch time for a good old fashioned all-dayer, good good times, but times gone by for sure.

As I approached the building where the music was coming from, there was a man emptying some glass bottles in the wheely bin out the back, this must be the place. I started to panic a little, but I had to keep walking, I couldn't stop down and have another panic attack in a dusty yard at the back of a bar in Memphis. I took a few deep breaths and carried on moving forward. I needed conformation that this was the place I was looking for, I followed the line of the building to my right and within thirty odd yards I was at the front of the building, I could see the sign for the sports bar. Bingo. Found it. Now what? I felt panicky again, so I headed along the front of the row of units to try and act normal. There was some kind of beauty solon, some kind of cash advance/loans place and a few BBQ joints. I carried on to the end of the units and double backed behind them, and passed all the different shape and sized bins and recycling skips you would expect to see at the back of working units, and towards the back of the sports bar again.

Those bins got me thinking.

That was enough for one day. I now knew where I needed to be. Tomorrow is a big day; I would hopefully come face to face for the first time with Lars fucking Baron.

Saturday

As part of my plan, I needed to look like a junkie. I purposely hadn't shaved for a couple of weeks, my hair was a mess, and I had brought some clothes and shoes from a second-hand charity shop in the Parkway Village, which I had scuffed up a little. I looked the part and was ready to go looking for some gear.

I was told that Lars conducted most of his business out the back of the sports bar on Winchester Road in the Oakhaven area of Memphis. I got the taxi driver to drop me off at the donuts and coffee shop a few units down from the sports bar, where I entered and ordered myself a coffee. I paid for the coffee, then left out of the front door with my travel bag over my right shoulder. I turned right out of the coffee shop, then right again at the end of the row of units, so I was now heading behind the units where at the far end the sports bar was situated. There was no one around. It was Saturday lunch time. I started walking the 200 or so yards from one end of the units to other, somewhere in the middle of road. Still no one around. When I approached one of the big blue metal recycling skips at the back of a liquor store, I had a look around, and quickly threw my travel bag in the skip, I tried to bury it the best I could. I assumed that as it was the weekend; there would be no recycling collection until Monday morning at the earliest, I hope I assumed correctly!

Since I had been in Memphis, I had been trying to fit in and not sound like the cockney that I am, so I had been practicing my US accent by watching some American shite on the TV in my hotel room, it was far from an Oscar winning performance, but I'm sure I could pull it off.

I entered the bar via the front door and ordered myself a beer as took my place on a bar stool. I purposefully sat all twitchy and constantly moving, like any decent and respectable crack head would do. I had been there for an hour or so when Lars Baron turned up. I recognised him straight away from the couple of pictures that I had seen. He turned up alone, he sat alone, and he drank alone. My heartbeat went into overdrive when I saw the man in front of me for the very first time, it was all a bit too much, my mind started racing in so many different directions, my hearing seemed to go a little bit funny, high pitched. I felt sick, I tried as calmly as I could to stand up and made a dash for the toilets, where I stumbled into the first cubicle I got to and puked my guts up! What the fuck am I doing? I thought. I needed to compose myself, which I managed to do after a few minutes. For the third time in as many of days, I was having a panic attack in a toilet, but this time I was on the other side of the world. I sat there breathing heavy, and I suddenly felt horribly alone, again. Until now my mind had been so pre occupied with my plan that I had hardly given anything else a thought. But as I sat on that filthy toilet somewhere in the middle of Memphis, this time 'thousands of miles away from home in the other direction, I was as sad as I had back in Thailand all those years ago. I gave myself a few more minutes to chill and pull myself together, and to tell myself that this will all soon be over. Hopefully.

After composing myself, I managed to make my way back to the bar and ordered another beer, it was more out of trying to build up some Dutch courage than anything else.

I sank a few pretty sharpish.

It wasn't long before Lars took a phone call; it was a quick sharp conversation. I couldn't hear what was being said from my end of the bar, but he disappeared out of a back door which was in my line of sight. I watched as he opened the door, he took something out of his pocket and handed it over to a scruffy looking man who quickly approached the back of the bar from the right side, he took what I assumed was some cash from the other man, put it in his pocket and made his way back into the bar, the whole transaction took less than 60 seconds. Next time he goes out, I am going to follow him and enquire about some gear.

Around half an hour later, and a few more beers, Lars took another call. He took a sip of his beer and coolly started the short journey past me at the end of the bar, down a little corridor where the toilets were and out of the back door, I saw another new client approach and within a matter of seconds the deal was done, now was my time, be brave, Arch!

I was shaking, I was about to talk to Lars Baron for the first time. I made my way down the short corridor, as he was turning around in the door way to head back to the bar,

'Hey man, you got any score?' I said in my best American accent,

'Who the fuck are you?' he barked,

'Sorry man, I was told I could score down here, and, I, I, I saw you out the door,' I said in a shaky voice,

'You fucking saw what?' and with that he grabbed me by the arm and pushed me through the toilet doors, fuck fuck fuck, I was shitting it.

'Don't you ever fucking blind side me like that again, you fucking bastard,' he raged as he grabbed me by the scruff of the neck and threw me against the wall,

'I'm sorry man, I'm sorry, I'm just after a score, can you sort me?'

He loosened his grip a little' I haven't seen you around here before, what's your game?'

'Does it really matter you haven't seen me before, I have money, and you have what I want, there is fifty Dollars in my jeans pocket with your name on, take the money, give me my hit, and I will be on my way man.'

Lars searched through my pockets and found the money,

'Why shouldn't I just rob you now and leave you for dead

on the floor?' He sniggered,

'Because I am in town for a while, and I can be a really good customer for you'

He pondered over that for a few seconds then took the money and casually placed a little wrap in my pocket.

'You got a phone you dirty fucking junkie?'

'Yes, yes it on my inside jacket pocket.'

Lars made me take the phone out of my pocket and tap in his number to my contacts along with his name. It was hundred percent him. Lars Fucking Baron.

'If you ever approach me like that again, I will open you up you fucking junkie, now fuck off and call me first next time,' he said as he threw me towards to door. I left the toilets and ran out of the open backdoor where Lars had done his earlier business and ran as fast as I could until I was well out of sight. My heart was racing quicker than ever as I reached the corner of Wooddale Road, I knelt down on the grassy verge and was sick again. I had made contact with Lars Baron. Tomorrow I shall end this. I threw the wrap away and made my way back to the hotel to come down from the adrenaline which was pounding through my veins.

Chapter 66

The day had arrived, I had been thinking of this day for two long years. I was so nervous, I hardly slept a wink last night. Today I will do something that I never thought I would do, and I still don't, but all I had to do was remind myself what happened to poor young Mason Stone, Kannika, and their families and the rage would boil again. I was going to do this, I needed to do this, I have to do this, I will do this.

The riskiest part of the plan was that it will need to be done in day light as the last flight out of Memphis on to O'Hare International Airport in Chicago and then to Heathrow was 18.20pm, and I wanted to be on that plane way before anyone knew what had happened.

I have never been religious and to be honest, I didn't really know what I believed in any more after all of the injustice I had witnessed, but today I decided for the first time to say a little prayer to the almighty as after today my fucked-up life will never ever be the same again. I knelt down at the end of the bed in prayer motion whilst holding the bible that was in my room.

'God, or whoever you are, if you are up there? I know I have hardly been a model citizen in my life, but if you are there, for just this one time, and I promise never to bother you again, can you watch my back, man? I know you won't agree with me, but I feel I am right in my decision to do this. I will go home and try my hardest to rebuild broken bridges, but I have to do this mate, I just have to. Amen'

11:30am

After hitting the gym again, as I had done each morning, and trying to eat something in the buffet, as I had done each morning, I checked out of the hotel wearing the light zip up jacket and grey tracksuit bottoms and with a pair of cheap knock-off Wayfarers I found down the mall. Spoke in American Accent. One bag had already been taken care of; the other a small hand-held bag, there was no room for excess baggage today.

The concierge at the hotel ordered me a taxi to the Parkway village, as he had most mornings, I tipped him with a $20 and thanked him for all his help during my stay, which he was most thankful for. The mid-day Sunday traffic was moving at a nice pace, and I made my way south on S Perkins Road. I paid the taxi driver and thank him in my best American accent, again. I took my bag and headed for the shopping centre just round the corner, where the next part of my plan was to find a toilet and loose the light jacket, and tracksuit bottoms I had on over the top of my black hoody and black jeans and ditch them in a bin, done. It was now 12.50pm.

To complete my plan, I had to find my inner demon, an inner demon I never knew existed, or maybe he was always there, lying dormant until called upon, and that time was now. I raised the demon inside me to the surface with the rage that ran wild through my veins at the pure injustice of what happened in Thailand, everything that took place in Thailand gave me rage. Doctor death and his relentless brutality, and what he done to poor Punyaa for trying to help me, the fucking bluecoats and their wicked ways at doing the guards dirty work, and getting off on it, horrible little cunts! The fucking cops in Koh Phangan. I even raged at my own stupidity at wanting to be the hero and going after some gear, when I should have just settled for what I had, after all I wouldn't be standing here today if that had never happened. I let my family down in every way possible and for that I will never forgive myself. But most of all I raged at Lars Baron, the motherfucker who raped and murdered Young Mason Stone's girlfriend, Kannika, and then left the scene without a trace of anyone else ever being there. Mason was then arrested for these sick crimes, he was tortured into confessing, and for his troubles he was sentenced to death by firing squad in the most feared and vial prison in the world, Bang Kwang — AKA — The Big Tiger. All of the rage inside me would avenge both Mason, Kannika and their families.

I hung around the shops for a while longer. I tried to have something to eat and to act as normal as possible, but I couldn't eat a thing, I was too nervous and anxious, but I did manage to sit for a while and have a few coffees. It was just over a mile from the shops to the bar, I had to time this right, I had done the walk yesterday, so I knew how long it would take.

I was dressed in all black, a black hoodie, black Jeans, the same black scuffed trainers I had on the other day, black gloves, and black woolly hat on as it was a bit chilly. I seemed to fit in, or at least I thought I did.

I was two blocks away from my destination. I couldn't see the bar yet, but I could see the sharp right turn up ahead, this was it, all I had planned and thought of for the last two years or so was unravelling in front of my very eyes. Was I crazy for doing this? Sure, I was! Would I regret doing this? Only time would tell! But I had come this far and I wasn't going to back down now.

The phone was in my pocket, my left hand was ready to hit call on my mobile as soon as I made the sharp right turn and was heading behind the car repair shop. My other hand was up the sleeve of my hoody. My cold breath hovered and danced in front of me along the road as if leading the way, I couldn't feel the cold though, the adrenalin was seeing to that. I felt alive and terrible and excited all in one go, I had never thought in all my days that I would one day do this to another human being, but in my eyes, he was no human being, not one with feelings and love and compassion.

The night that Lars and Masons paths first briefly crossed, Lars made a mistake that would one day be his downfall. The day was 29th November 2014, and it was the birthday of the unpredictable and unstable Lars Baron.

Lars was having a drink and drugs session in the bar across the road from Masons hotel in Cambodia.

Mason had just endured a mammoth thirty-two-hour trip from the UK to Laos, he was weary and tired from travelling, but it was early evening, and he was excited to get out and meet some people, so he headed for the nearest bar across the street. As he approached the entrance to the bar, he accidentally bumped into a drunk man outside,

"Sorry, my Friend,' offered Mason.

'Hey don't worry man, it's my fucking birthday, and I'm wasted,' the drunk guy replied,

Mason shook the man's hand, and wished him a happy birthday and said that he would buy him a drink later,

'American, hey?' said the drunk,

'Oh yes, my name is Mason, I'm from Long Island, New

York, let me guess you're from down south?'

'Lars Baron, Memphis, ex-marine,' replied the drunk as his voice and manner suddenly took a cold turn,

'Well, like I said man, I will grab you a drink when I've had something to eat.'

'Yeah, make sure you fucking do,' barked the Lars.

The sudden change in the birthday boy's manner shook Mason a little, it confessed him, almost scared him, but he just wanted to have some dinner and get on his way.

After Mason had eaten his dinner, he ordered a couple of fresh beers, he was a man of his word, and he had promised his fellow travelling American a birthday drink, and that was what he was going to do. He just assumed the guy was drunk, and didn't really know what he was doing so he gave him the benefit of doubt.

As Mason approached Lars table, all of a sudden Lars sprang off his chair and literally flew over the table and planted a full on headbutt on the poor guy sitting opposite him, splitting is nose wide open, a full-on fight broke out between Lars and another guy V's 5 or 6 others, Mason had no idea what the bother was over, but he wasn't interested in any of that so he turns away, put the beers down on an empty table and left the bar. He had never seen such violence break out in front of him before, and he hoped that he would never see the drunk American again.

It had been nine days since Mason left home so he decided now was a good time to call in and have a catch up with his family.

I was 80 yards away, I could hear some music coming from the bar, I couldn't make out what it was, some country mix I assumed. I was approaching from the rear of the bar so, I couldn't see how many cars were parked out front.

70 Yards away, I could see that back door where Lars meets his clients,

60 yards away, my heart was racing, I was sure I was walking at a normal speed, but the world seemed to be going in slow motion,

50 yards away, my left hand took the phone out of my pocket and got the required number on the screen,

40 yards away, I hit the call button and slowed my walk a little,

'OK' said the voice at the other end of the line and the call cut off,

30 yards away, the phone was back in my pocket,

20 yards away, my right hand primed for action,

10 yards away, I saw the back door of the bar open, Lars entered the outside world, I'm sure he was walking in slow motion, like I was watching a scene from a film. I had a quick look around, not one person in any direction, the world was defiantly going in slow motion, my right hand was behind my back by now and was gripping the handle as tight as I could.

5 yards away, my left hand reached into my left pocket and pulled out the cash, this was to take away any distraction from my right hand.

3 yards away, this was it, my world would never ever be the same after this moment. I was about to commit the ultimate sin, and if I got away with it, I would have to live with this for the rest of my life, through good and bad... I will always carry the burden with me.

2 yards away, I pulled the cash out of my left pocket with my left hand, and I saw his eyes look towards the cash, I

wondered how many junkies he had served in this very spot before today, this would be his last though, I would be Lars Baron's very last customer.

1 yard away, as he went to take the cash with his right hand, I could see the baggy full of white crystal in his left hand, and in one full motion I pulled the knife down from my sleeve with my right hand and came around his left side and plunged the 6-inch blade deep into the side of his stomach, and the little speech I had prepared over and over in my head came out in my brood cockney accent...

'Got ya, ya cunt, that's for the Thai girl you raped and murdered in Thailand two years ago, and left her boyfriend to take the blame, he was my friend and he died for what you did, this is for the both of them.'

He fell to the floor, he didn't try to struggle, I think the pure shock of what was happening to him didn't register, so he couldn't fight back.

I pulled the knife out of him and pushed it in again, two, three, four, maybe five times I was not sure but I looked him square in the eye the whole time.

'How. The. fuck...' 'were the only words he could muster up before his eyes rolled into the back of his head, a little trickle of blood swam down his cheek, as the life left Lars Baron for the very last time. I stood up, had a quick look around, there were no witnesses, I spat on him whilst he lay in a pool of blood on the concrete floor. I ran off behind the five or six units which the sports bar was connected to and towards the wheely bin, where I had left my bag yesterday and prayed it was still there.

I promptly found the bag I had left in the recycling skip, thank fuck it was still there, it was slightly buried under some bottles but was fairly easy to find. I jumped over the 5-foot wire fencing at the end of the row of units, some 200 yards from where Lars Barons dead body was laying, there was no one around, so I ducked down between another wheely bin and a wooden fence and quickly got changed into another pair of jeans and a clean top and hoody and my new trainers. I double checked, I had everything. I threw the old cloths in the wheely bin I was ducked down next to, the hoodie, the joggers, the hat, the gloves, scuffed trainers, it all went in, I double checked again that I had everything else that I needed, my fake passport, my flight ticket, a toiletry bag, and some more clothes were all in the bag I'd hid yesterday.

I made my way out from behind the building, which turned out to be a petrol station and headed as calmly and coolly as I could towards Winchester Road and then west towards the airport. Within a few minutes, I heard some sirens coming towards me, my heart skipped a beat, but I carried on walking as if nothing had happened. I was in danger being out in the open, then two American cop cars drove straight passed me at speed and east towards the bar, had someone found Lars and called the police? An ambulance soon followed, for sure this must have been for him. After another minute or so a taxi drove passed, which I flagged down, I jumped in and again with my best American accent I asked the driver to take me to the airport, my hands were trembling.

I sat in the back of the taxi, heart pounding, I didn't dare look back, I didn't want to look back, I just wanted to look forward and get the fuck out of there. I took a massive deep breath and sat back in my chair. In a few hours, I will be on a plane heading home to my beloved London.

The journey to the airport was only 10 minutes, I knew it

wasn't far, but was just long enough to calm myself down with some controlled breathing. I couldn't contemplate on what I had done just yet, I still had work to do. Even though I was sure I had pulled off the perfect plan and no one would be looking for me, I was still paranoid as fuck, so until I was safely home across the pond, I would not be happy.

I entered Memphis international airport, and I felt panicky again. There were crowds of people, not as many as at Heathrow four days ago, but still way too many for this to be comfortable. There was security, there was police officers with big fucking guns, I was sure they were looking at me, did they know what I had just done, although it was a completely different situation, it took me back to that frightful night on Koh Phangan all these years ago, was I going to get taken away again? I needed to get the fuck out of there, I ran towards to nearest toilets and was sick again in the first cubicle I got to, for the fourth time in five days I found myself having another panic attack in a public toilet, was this what my life would look like now? Had so much happened over the last ten years that I actually can't cope with life on the outside? Would I miss life on the inside? It was certainly less confusing than being out; maybe this would change when I get home? If anyone can help me, my darling Holly can.

After spending a good ten minutes composing myself in the toilets, I made my way to the check in desk. I got checked in and through security without too many problems, I made my way through to the shops to act like a tourist and mix in with the crowds the best I could.

My adrenalin was still pumping.

Within an hour, I was in the air for the short flight to O'Hare International airport. I only had a two hour turn around, so I quickly got off in Chicago and made my way to transfers, keeping my head down as much as I could, there was so much security, and if any them knew what I had done and where I was from, I would be an international fugitive by now, but I just kept reminding myself that I had pulled of the perfect plan. I spoke in a good American accent when needed, I was wearing completely different clothes in case anyone had seen me, I couldn't possibly be placed at the scene and any witnesses that may of seen me would of only been at the shops, or the taxi driver, but none of them knew my name, or even my fake passport name, and they would be looking for an American, not a cockney heading back London.

Two hours after landing in Chicago, I was heading back into the night sky, away from the bright lights below, away from America, away from the whirlwind of the last ninety-six hours, away from a near perfect plan, away from Lars fucking Baron. In nine hours' time, I would be landing in Heathrow, hopefully to restart my life that was taken away from me ten years ago. I took my seat, ordered a beer and sat back in my chair.

What a fucking journey!

Chapter 67
11.30am

I landed in Heathrow 30 minutes earlier than expected, a good tail wind — our pilot informed us. I am not sure if I slept, but I certainly don't remember the last nine hours. I was still confused between sleep and reality, after spending so many years stuck somewhere between the two. Dream, days... dreams, sleep and reality all mixed in together in the deep dark days of life on the inside.

I didn't have mobile with me, but I did have a number for a burner phone that James Bromwich had given me five days ago. We'd pre-arranged a window of time on the day of four hours, so I needed to find a phone box as soon as I was back on my way to Brixton. On my instructions, if the phone had not rung by 14:00pm, he would turn it off and bin it as something must have gone wrong. If something had gone wrong, as far as HMP Brixton prison was concerned, I was released five days ago, so nothing could come back on Bromy. The cameras at the gate would have picked me up leaving, and we purposely met somewhere away from sight, my family would have assumed I did not want to come home and ran off somewhere, I just prayed for their sake that I didn't fuck this one up too!

I found a phone box, took the number out of my wallet that had been scribbled on an old piece of paper, hit in the digits on the payphone and within a few seconds it started ringing.

'Hello,' the other voice quickly said, 'Archie?'

'It's me man, you got the clothes still?' I asked.

'Yes, yes still got them mate, you okay?'

'Yep, all good, mate, meet you at the pickup point in an hour?'

'I will be there Archie, its fucking good to hear your voice, bruv,' he said

'It's good to hear you too, Bromy,' I said through my tired voice

I hung up the phone and continued my journey into London.

I met Jimmy at the pickup point, his back door was open, and he had laid his seats down and put some covers in there, so I was well out of view, I had a quick look around and there were no witnesses to what could have looked like a kidnapping. I jumped in and found the bag with the clothes in that I was wearing where I left HMP Brixton prison five days ago. I even managed to get changed and to get my American clothes into the bag, which would be dumped later somewhere.

Bromy had to act as normal as possible, and he had told me five days ago that I may be in the boot of his motor for some time, as he had planned to have dinner at his girlfriend's house before his shift. I would have to just sit tight back there for as long as it took, which was fine by me, he had put some food back there, and I was tired as fuck so I would just get some sleep if needed. I'm not sure how long I was back there as I must have dozed off, but sometime later I was startled into life as the people carries engine fired up and the car started the short journey to Brixton Nick. As we pulled down the road and took a left turn, he asked if I was ok to just bang twice, to which I gave a quick two bangs on the back seat, the car radio came on. After the short journey the car slowed down, I could hear speaking outside, the voices sounded friendly and familiar to each other, as if they knew each other, the security guards at the entrance of the prison I assumed. Bromy had assured me it would be fine getting through the gates.

We drove on, slowly, for what seemed like an eternity, but was probably only a minute or so, my heart was racing, I was about to break into prison for fucks sake. This was the most critical part of the plan, if we got caught here God knows what would have happened to the both of us. This bit was all down to him, he didn't tell me the plan, but he assured me he knew what to do, and I trusted this man with my life, I mean, who wouldn't after what he had done for me, proper fucking geezer!

As the car slowed to a stop, I heard Bromy's voice, the engine was still ticking over, there was only one voice, he was on the phone. I couldn't clearly hear what was being said, his low voice was muffled through the car, but I did hear the last line of the conversation as the car's engine cut out,

'Yep, we will be there in 2 minutes, grab the door,' I heard him say, he must have someone else helping, perhaps he couldn't have pulled this off alone, I trusted him so I didn't mind.

I didn't know what time it was, but I assume it was late afternoon or early evening by now, Bromy was on the night shift, and I knew the twelve-hour shift for the screws started at 7pm, which was also the time I was set to be released. I wondered how long that was from now? Jesus, we're my family and Holly here yet? They have no idea that I am currently laying in the back of the boot of a screw's car in the prison staff carpark. For the first time in a long time, I managed a little grin to myself, if only Ronny could see me now, he'd laugh his nut off.

The boot popped open, it was dark outside so my eyes adjusted quickly, 'Quick mate, jump out, there is no one around and there are no cameras this end of the car park' Jimmy said in a hurried voice.

There was a 5Ft wall at the end of the carpark, the outside world, my freedom was beyond that wall, I would soon be heading out there, back home, oh fuck I was going home, the realisation dawned on me I WAS FUCKING GOING HOME. I nearly exploded with excitement, but I knew I wasn't done just yet, a little bit further on this messed up crazy journey and I would be there.

'Put this hat on and follow me, quickly,' he said as he passed me a dark navy baseball cap.

We marched across the car park, took a left turn down a narrow alley way where they kept the wheelie bins and towards a fire escape door at the end of the alley, what was behind the door I wondered? Just as we got there the door flung opened, 'Quick lads, in you come,' a familiar face said, I don't think he was a screw, but I had seen him around the prison before.

'Nice one man,' Bromy said to his accomplice,

'I fucking owe you both,' I said.

'Shhhh,' they both said together as they ushered me through the open door and down the hall way and into a small office,

'Here's the plan Archie, if this all goes well you will be a free man in just over an hour.'

'OK, OK mate,' I said, 'what do I do?'

'Danny will be back in a few minutes, he will cuff you, he works the desk, so he has done all the fake release paper work for you, the governor has gone home and no one else is set for release, so you won't see anyone who already thinks you are free. Danny has your belongings, he will take you to the release holding room and take your cuffs off, at 19:00pm exactly, he will come collect you and take you through the doors to where your family will be waiting, you will then be a free man, and I never want to see you again, at least not in here,' he smiled

'I honestly can't find the words to thank you for all your help, not just this but whilst I was in here too. After what I have been through, there are only a few people in the whole world I trust with my life, and Mr Bromwich, you have just been promoted to that exclusive club. I fucking love you bruv, and if you ever EVER need anything you know where I'm at,' I said with a tear in my eye,

'Come here you fucking idiot,' he said as we embraced in the most emotional man-hug I have ever been involved in, I nearly broke down there and then, but I held it together for Bromy.

'Right, you fucker, I need to get to work, behave yourself, Archie Parker.'

'I will man, I promise,' I said as he shook my hand with a good firm handshake. With that, he was gone. I just stared at the door, I didn't really know what else to do, I couldn't sit down I was way too anxious for that, I paced around the room until Jimmy's mate, Danny, came back in.

'I have no idea what you two dick heads have been up to, and I don't really give a fuck but I owed Bromy a favour from a past lifetime, and now I have repaid my dept, stick your hands out,' Danny said as he cuffed me,

'Thank you,' I whispered, he didn't answer, he just led me out of the room, we turned a right, went through some double doors and into the first room on the right,

'This is the release room, it's 18.10pm, you have 50 minutes until I want you the fuck out of here, there are some magazines down there and a coffee machine, help yourself,' Danny said as he took my cuffs off and left the room sharpish.

50 minutes, that was it, 50 minutes, I wondered how many 50 minutes had passed in the last ten years? I started to work it out, there is 1 x 50 minutes in every hour, there are twenty-four hours in a day, so.... Nah fuck that... So I picked up a magazine and tried to read it, FHM, January issue, I found myself flicking through the pictures, I couldn't really give a fuck about the bullshit stories, but the half-naked woman were something to concentrate on, Jesus, the last time I had touch a naked woman was ten years ago, would I still know what to do, could I still satisfy Holly? Fuck, there are so many things on the outside to worry about that on the inside you didn't need to. I started to panic a little, so I dropped the magazine and started pacing around the room, there was a camera in here, I wondered if someone was watching me? Fuck it, I don't care.

There was a clock on the wall that told me it was now 18.34, twenty-six minutes to go.

Fuck I was tired; I hadn't slept properly since the first night in Memphis, which I assume was about 120 hours ago. I would sleep like a baby tonight that for sure. I made a coffee and tried to sit down, this would waste some time.

I sat drinking my coffee, looking at the clock every minute or so, it seemed to go in slow motion. I had my head in my hands trying to comprehend what has just happened, not many people brake back into prison five days after being released, but I had just managed to do it, another little chuckle to myself. The door opened, I looked up at the clock, it was 18.59pm.

'Come on Archie, its home time mate,' Danny said as he beckoned me towards the door.

I took one big deep breath and walked slowly towards him, we turned right and through another set of double doors, straight in front of us were some more doors, before we reached the second set of doors Danny pulled my arm and said,

'Through those doors is your freedom mate, just think before you act as I never want to see you again,' Danny said as he winked at me,

'Oh, don't you worry man, I'm done with this shit.'

And with that he opened the door, the world around me seemed to go in slow motion, again. The first face I saw was my mother, my poor mum had been through so much over the years. Just behind her was my old man, fuck I owe him big time, then I saw my sister, God, I'd missed her funny little face, and then just over my old man's shoulder, I could see Holls, she had stuck around and waited for me for all these years, not many girls would of done that, what a true wonderful person she is, they all are. They were about 5 yards in-front of me, I had waited a lifetime for these small steps, steps to freedom, steps to be reunited with my loved ones again. My mum leaped at me, shortly followed by the old man, my sister and Holly joined in. I broke. I couldn't contain my emotions, the last ten years of pain and suffering came crashing out of me. The police in Koh Phangan, Bang Kwang, being locked up, the disappointment, the let down to everyone I know, Kannika, Mason Stone, Lars Baron, it all caught up with me and I just fell into their arms,

'I'm so, so, so, sorry everyone,' I wept like a baby,

'Don't you worry about all that now, son, let's get you home where you belong,' my dad said as he picked me up. We stood in a group hug for a moment or two, then as one we left the building. Holly linked her arm through mine, as she had done so many times before this nightmare started, she looked at me, smiled, and said…

'I love you, Archie Parker.'

Epilogue 1

It took me nearly a year to pluck up the courage to contact Mr and Mrs Stone. The question I could not answer was, will it really matter if he was guilty or not? If his parents thought he was guilty, perhaps they could deal with it better by growing to hate their son for committing such terrible crimes? I was not a parent, so I just didn't know what to think, or what a parent would think. If it turns out he was not guilty, and he died in such horrible conditions 'thousands of miles away from home, all alone, how would they deal with that? I am not sure I could. But I had made a promise to Mason Stone, my friend, he wanted his parents to know that he was innocent, so in the end I decided to honour my promise to my friend.

So far, I hadn't looked into the story in the American media, surely this was big news back in Mason's homeland? I mean how many good young American kids go to Thailand, meet a girl, rape and murder her and then be sentenced to death? As it turns out, it had been major news.

I hit the words Mason Stone Thailand into a search engine and straight away his face appeared on my screen. It was a picture of Mason before he left his beloved homeland. He looked every inch an innocent young man, his hair was smart, he was wearing a plain white shirt, he looked dressed up for a party, I had never seen him look like his, proper handsome geezer I thought as tears started to stream down my face. I had only ever seen the young broken man he had become in Bang

Kwang. I clicked on the link under his image and the headline read 'LONG ISLAND KILLER RAMPAGE IN PARADISE.'

Oh my god, the whole of his own native country hated him! I scrolled down a little, and for the first time I saw a picture of Kannika, she was as beautiful as Mason had described her, she looked so innocent, she had her whole life ahead of her. The paper article went on to explain how the police had been reported to screaming in the early hours coming from a beach hut on Koh Samui beach, where they caught Mr Stone red handed attacking the young Thai girl, but it was too late, the police could not save her, her head injuries were so severe, she had a cracked skull and was pronounced dead at the scene. It went on to say that Mr Stone had showed no compassion or remorse for his crimes, that he admitted to it straight away and never gave an explanation as to why he done it.

Jesus fucking Christ, I couldn't read any more, but I had to do something about this. I couldn't try and clear his name with the American public, the fucker who actually committed these crimes was also one of their own, and they couldn't look for him as the cunt was dead. But I could send Mason's letter to his family, along with a short letter of my own explaining what had happened to their sweet little boy.

Two weeks before I was released from Bang Kwang, I dug up the little package that Mason had given to me and made me promise to one day deliver to his family, and I sent it to my house in the UK. I didn't want to risk having it on me whilst being released. If I had lost it, or if it had been found and destroyed, I would have never forgiven myself. I sent it home along with another letter to my folks saying that if for whatever reason I don't make it home, then please send this package on to the address inside.

The letter that Mason gave me had his family home address on, I didn't want to just send it to this address as I had no idea if his family still lived there, they may of packed up and fucked off somewhere after what happened, but after a little research online, I was pretty happy they still live in the same address.

Maybe one day in years to come I will visit Huntingdon, Long Island, New York, and go see where my friend, my brother, Mason Stone grew up. But for now, I will send the letters from a post box very far away from my house and try to carry on rebuilding my broken life.

Mr and Mrs Stone.

You don't know me and you have probably never heard of me, in fact it doesn't really matter who I am, what matters is I knew your son, Mason, whilst in prison in Thailand, and I am writing to you to settle any thoughts you may have, that your son is guilty of the terrible crime to his girlfriend, he was not guilty, and this I know for sure.

I first met Mason a couple of months after he arrived in Bang Kwang prison. At first, I wasn't too sure about him, after all he was at the time Thailand's public Enemy Number 1. I assumed he was guilty, why else would he be here? But I got to know Mason very well over a couple of month period, and although it took a while for him to open up to me, he finally did and what he told me shocked me to my core.

I won't go into details as it would be too hard for you to read, but what I will tell you is that Mason met young Kannika whilst staying at a hotel when she was working the bar one night. They instantly hit it off and over the next couple of weeks they became very close and fell completely in love with each other.

To prove that I am no fake and that this letter is hundred percent real; Mason told me that he rang home and spoke to his father one morning telling of his new found love and asked his father for some man-to-man advice, and his father just simply told him to be himself, and if a lady can't love you for who you really are then she won't really love you at all.

As I said, I got to know Mason very well and he spoke about his deep love and sadness for his family, he loved and missed you guys with all of his heart, and he really was the nicest young man I ever have the pleasure of meeting, it was just a shame that we met in such a terrible situation. He was not the animal the press had made him out to be.

I also have a letter for you that Mason wrote, and I promised my friend that I would one day deliver it to you. I am so sorry it has taken so long to reach you, but his letter will be with you in a few days' time. I didn't want to send it to you without my letter first, as I didn't want you to think it was some sick joke.

I hope this letter has helped in some way, if even just a little. I know nothing will ever bring your little boy back, but knowing of his innocence may relieve the pain somewhat...

All my best

A friend of Mason

Epilogue 2

Dear Mum, Dad, Annabelle and Yann

My dearest Family, I hope this letter one day reaches you and can bring you some, if not much, peace. If this has reached you, I have probably already moved onto the next life.

If you are reading this letter that means my good friend from the UK has now been released from Bang Kwang prison in Thailand and is now home with his family where he belongs. He made a silly mistake one night, and he paid deeply for it, but he was the most amazing man I ever had the pleasure of meeting. Because of him and the love he showed me, he gave me hope, hope that one day I could get my message to my family and put your minds at rest about the terrible crimes I was committed of.

The authorities here will not let me send any letters, and they will also not let me receive any as I am, in their eyes, a category A prisoner.

I hope that in your heart of hearts you know I am innocent of what they say I did to my lovely Kannika. I loved her, albeit for a very short time, with all of my heart, and I would never ever have hurt her in any way but unfortunately the evidence against me was too great.

I know what has happened here must have disgraced the family name, and for that I beg of your forgiveness. For now, I wish you all farewell and one day, one day in time, we will all be reunited in heaven together, and we can sail the MAY-STONE in our forever eternal happiness.

I am so sorry.

All my love.

Your son.

Mason xxxx

Printed in Great Britain
by Amazon